What Dreams May Come

What Dreams May Come

A NOVEL
by Richard Matheson

TRANSFORMATIONAL BOOK CIRCLE
Studio City, California

Copyright © 1978 by Richard Matheson

Published by: Transformational Book Circle
12711 Ventura Blvd., Suite 330 Studio City, CA 91604
866-288-4469 (customer service) • 866-300-4386 (orders)
www.transformationalbookcircle.com • info@transformationalbookcircle.com

ISBN 10:1-56861-231-1

08 07 06 05 4321
1st Printing, February 2006

With grateful love, to my wife for adding the
sweet measure of her soul to my existence

To the Reader

An introduction to a novel is almost without exception unnecessary. This is my tenth published novel and the thought of writing introductions to any of the preceding nine never even occurred to me.

For this novel, however, I feel that a brief prologue is called for. Because its subject is survival after death, it is essential that you realize, before reading the story, that only one aspect of it is fictional: the characters and their relationships.

With few exceptions, every other detail is derived exclusively from research. For that reason, I have added, at the conclusion of the novel, a list of the books used for this research. As you will see, they are many and diverse. Yet, despite their wide variation with regard to authors and times and places of publication, there is a persistent, unavoidable uniformity to their content.

You would, of course, have to read them all to prove this to yourself. I urge you to do so. You will find it an enlightening and extraordinary experience.

RICHARD MATHESON
Calabasas, California
August, 1977

"For in that sleep of death what dreams may come,
When we have shuffled off this mortal coil,
Must give us pause."
-Hamlet, Act III, Sc.1

Contents

THIS MORTAL COIL

Introduction

The manuscript you are about to read came into my possession in the following way.

On the evening of February 17, 1976, our doorbell rang and my wife answered it. Several moments later, she returned to the bedroom where we were watching television and said that some woman wanted to see me.

I got up and walked to the front hall. The door was open and I saw a tall woman in her fifties standing on the porch. She was well dressed and holding a large, bulky envelope in her hands.

"Are you Robert Nielsen?" she asked.

I told her that I was and she held out the envelope. "This is for you then," she said.

I looked at it suspiciously and inquired what it was. "A communication from your brother," she replied.

My suspicions increased. "What do you mean?" I asked.

"Your brother Chris has dictated this manuscript to me," she said.

Her words angered me. "I don't know who you are," I told her, "but if you possesse the least knowledge about my brother, you'd know that he died more than a year ago."

The woman sighed. "I know that, Mr. Nielsen," she said, tiredly. "I'm a psychic. Your brother has communicated this material to me from-"

She stopped as I began to close the door, then quickly added, "Mr. Nielsen, please."

There was a sound of such genuine urgency in her voice that I looked at her in surprise.

"I have just undergone six exhausting months transcribing this manuscript," she told me. "I didn't choose to do it. I have my own affairs to deal with but your brother would not let me be until I wrote down every word of his communication and promised faithfully to bring it to you." Her voice took on a desperate tone. "Now you have got to take it and give me peace. "

With that, she thrust the envelope into my hands, turned and hurried down the path to the sidewalk. As I watched, she got into her car and drove off quickly.

I have never seen or heard from her again. I do not even know her name.

* * * *

I have read the manuscript three times now and wish I knew what to make of it.

I am not a religious man but, like anyone, would certainly like to believe that death is more than oblivion. Still, I find It difficult, if not impossible, to accept the story at face value. I keep thinking it is nothing more than that: a story.

True, the facts are there. Facts about my brother and his family which this woman could not possibly have known, unless one goes on the premise that she spent months of laborious-and expensive-research in uncovering them before writing the manuscript. In that case, what is the point of it? What could she have gained from such a course?

The questions, in my mind, about this book are manifold. I will not enumerate them but permit the reader to form his own. Of only one thing I am certain. If the manuscript is true, all of us had better examine our lives. Carefully.

ROBERT NIELSEN
Islip, New York
January, 1978

Sleep of Death

Chapter One

A Blur of Rushing Images

"Begin at the beginning" is the phrase. I cannot do that. I begin at the end–the conclusion of my life on earth. I present it to you as it happened–and what happened afterward.

A note about the text. You have read my writing, Robert. This account may seem unlike it. The reason–I am limited by my transcriber. My thoughts must travel through her mind. I cannot surmount that. All the grains will not pass through the filter. Understand if I appear to over-simplify. Especially at first.

Both of us are doing the best we can.

* * * *

Thank God I was alone that night. Usually, Ian went to the movies with me. Twice a week–because of my work, you know.

That night he didn't go. He was appearing in a school play. Once again–thank God.

I went to a theatre near a shopping center. Cannot get the name through. A big one, which had been divided into two. Ask Ian for the name.

It was after eleven when I left the theatre. I got in my car and drove toward the golf course. The tiny one–for children. Cannot get the word through. All right. Spell it. Slowly now. M-i-n ... i-a ... t-u ... r-e. Good. We have it. There was traffic on the–street? No, wider. Av ... e-nue?

Not exact but good enough. I thought there was an opening and pulled out. Had to stop, a car was speeding toward me. There was room for it to move around me but it didn't. Hit my left front fender, sent me spinning.

I was shaken but had on my belt. Not belt. H-a-r-n-ess. I would not have been too badly injured. But a van came up and hit the right rear fender of my car, knocking me across the middle line. A truck was coming in the opposite direction. Hit my car straight on. I heard a grinding crash, the shattering of glass. I hit my head and blackness swept across me. For an instant, I believed I saw myself unconscious, bleeding. Then came darkness.

* * * *

I was conscious again. The pain was dreadful. I could hear my breathing, an awful sound. Slow and shallow with sporadic, liquid sighs. My feet were icy cold. I remember that.

Gradually, I sensed a room around me. People too, I think. Something kept me from being sure. Sidayshin. No, re-do. Spell slowly. S-e-d-a-t ... sedation.

I began to hear a whispering voice. I couldn't make out the words. Briefly, I could see a form nearby. My eyes were closed but I saw it. I couldn't tell if the form was male or female but I knew that it was speaking to me. When I couldn't hear the words, it went away.

Another pain began, this one in my mind, increasing steadily. I seemed to tune it in as though it were a radio station. It was not my pain but Ann's. She was crying, frightened. Because I was hurt. She was afraid for me. I felt her anguish. She was suffering terribly. I tried to will away the shadows but I couldn't. Tried in vain to speak her name. Don't cry, I thought. I'll be all right. Don't be afraid. I love you, Ann. Where are you?

That instant, I was home. It was Sunday evening. All of us were in the family room, talking and laughing. Ann was next to me, Ian beside her. Richard next to Ian, Marie on the other end of the sofa. I had my arm around Ann, she was cuddled against me. She was warm and I kissed her cheek. We smiled at each other. It was Sunday evening, peaceful and idyllic, all of us together.

I felt myself begin to rise from darkness. I was lying on a bed. The pain was back again, all through me. I had never known such pain before. I knew that I was slipping. Yes, the word is slipping.

Now I heard a ghastly sound. A rattling in my throat. I prayed that Ann and the children were not around to hear it. It would terrify them. I asked God not to let them hear that horrible noise, protect them from that horrible noise.

The thought came to my mind then: Chris, you're dying. I strained to draw in breath but fluids in my windpipe kept the air from passing through. I felt thick and sluggish, trapped in density.

There was someone by the bed. That form again. "Don't fight it, Chris," it told me. I grew angry at the words. Whoever it was, they wanted me to die. I fought against that. I would not be taken. Ann! I called to her in thought. Hold on to me! Don't let me go!

Still I slipped. My body is too badly hurt, I thought in sudden dread. I felt the weakness of it. Then a strange sensation. Tickling. Odd, I know. Ridiculous. But that was it. All over me.

Another change. It was not a bed I lay on but a cradle. I could feel it rocking back and forth, back and forth. Slowly, I began to understand. I wasn't in a cradle and the bed was still. My body was rocking back and forth. There were tiny, crackling noises deep inside me. Sounds you hear when pulling off a bandage slowly. Less pain now. The pain was fading.

Afraid, I fought to re-establish pain. In seconds, it was back, worse than ever. Agonized, I clung to it. It meant I was alive. I would not be taken. Ann! My mind cried out, pleading. Hold on to me!

It was no use. I could feel life draining from me, heard the sounds again, much louder now; the tearing of a hundred tiny threads. I had no sense of taste or smell. Sensation left my toes, my feet. Numbness started up my legs. I struggled to recapture feeling but I couldn't. Something cold was drifting through my stomach, through my chest. It stopped and gathered icily around my heart. I felt my heart thump slowly, slowly, like a funeral procession drum.

I knew, abruptly, what was happening in the next room. I could see an aged woman lying there, gray strands of hair across her pillow. Yellow skin and hands like bird claws; cancer of the stomach. Someone sat beside her, speaking softly. Daughter. I don't want to see this, I decided.

Instantly, I left that room and was in mine again. The pain was almost gone now. I could not restore it no matter how I tried. I heard a humming sound-yes, humming. Still, the threads kept tearing. I felt each severed thread end curling in.

The cold "something" moved again. It moved until it centered in my head. Everything else was numb. Please! I called for help. No voice; my tongue lay paralyzed. I felt my being drawing inward, totally collected in my head. Mimbins were compressed-no, try again. M-e-m-b-ranes. Yes. Pushed out and toward the center all at once.

I began to move out through an opening in my head.

There was a buzzing noise, a ringing, something rushing very fast like a stream through a narrow gorge. I felt myself begin to rise. I was a bubble, bobbing up and down. I thought I saw a tunnel up above me, dark and endless. I turned over and looked down and was stunned to see my body lying on the bed. Bandaged and immobile. Fed through plastic tubes. I was connected to it by a cord which glistened with a silver light. Thin, it joined my body at the top of my head. The silver cord, I thought; my God, the silver cord. I knew that it was all that kept my body living.

Revulsion came now as I saw my legs and arms begin to twitch. Breath had almost ceased. There was a look of agony on my face. Again, I fought-to go back down and join my body. No, I won't go! I could hear my mind cry out. Ann, help me! Please! We have to be together!

I forced myself down and stared at my face. The lips were purple, there was dew-like sweat across the skin. I saw the neck veins start to swell. The muscles of my body had begun to twitch. I tried with all my will to get back in. Ann! I thought. Please calf me back so I can stay with you!

A miracle occurred. Life filled my body, healthy color suffusing the skin, a look of peace across my face. I thanked God. Ann and the children wouldn't have to see me as I'd been. I thought that I was coming back, you see.

Not so. I saw my body in a sack of many colors, drawn up by the silver cord. I felt a dropping sensation, heard a snapping noise-as though a giant rubber band had broken-felt myself begin to rise.

A flashback then. Yes, that's correct. A flashback; just as in the movies but much faster. You've read the phrase and heard it many times: "His whole life flashed before him."

Robert, it's true. So fast I couldn't follow it-and in reverse—the days before the accident, back through the children's lives, my marriage to Ann, my writing career. Colleges, World War Two, high school, grammar school, my childhood and my infancy. 1974-1927, every second of those years. Each movement, thought, emotion; every spoken word. I saw it all. A blur of rushing images.

I sat up on the bed abruptly, laughing. It had only been a dream! I felt alert, all senses magnified. Incredible, I thought, how real a dream can be.

But something was wrong with my vision. Everything was blurred as I looked around. I couldn't see beyond ten feet.

The room was familiar; the walls, the stucco ceiling.

Fifteen feet by twelve. The drapes were beige with brown and orange stripes. I saw a color television set hung near the ceiling. To my left, a chair-orange-red upholstery like leather, arms of stainless steel. The carpeting was the same orange-red.

Now I knew why things looked blurred. The room was filled with smoke. There was no odor though; I found that odd. Not smoke; I suddenly changed my mind. The accident. My eyes were damaged. I was not dismayed. The relief of knowing I was still alive transcended such concern.

First things first, I thought. I had to find Ann and tell her I was all right, end her suffering. I dropped my legs across the right side of the mattress and stood. The bedside table was made of metal, painted beige, a top as in our kitchen. Spell. F-o-r-m-i-c-a. I saw an alcove with a sink. The faucets looked like golf-club heads, you know? There was a mirror hung above the sink. My vision was so blurred I couldn't see my reflection.

I started moving closer to the sink, then had to stop. A nurse was coming in. She walked directly toward me and I stepped aside. She didn't even look at me but gasped and hurried toward the bed. I turned. A man was tying on it, slackjawed, skin a pasty gray. He was heavily bandaged, an array of plastic tubes attached to him.

I turned back in surprise as the nurse ran from the room.

I couldn't hear what she was shouting.

I moved in closer on the man and saw that he was probably dead. How come someone else was in my bed though? What kind of hospital would put two patients in the same bed?

Strange. I leaned in close to look at him. His face was just like mine. I shook my head. That was impossible. I looked down at his left hand. He wore a wedding band exactly like the one I wore. How could that be?

I began to feel an aching coldness in my stomach. I tried to draw the sheet back from his body but I couldn't. Somehow, I had lost the sense of touch. I kept on trying until I saw my fingers going through the sheet, then pulled my hand back, sickened. No, it isn't me, I told myself. How could it be when I was still alive? My body even hurt. Proof positive of life.

I whirled as a pair of doctors rushed into the room, stepping back to let them at the body.

One of them began to blow his breath into the man's mouth. The other had a highp-spell. H-y-p-o-dermic; yes. I watched him shove the needle end into the man's flesh. Then a nurse came running in, pushing some machine on wheels. One of the doctors pressed the ends of two thick metal rods against the man's bare chest and he twitched. Now I knew that there was no relationship between the man and me for I felt nothing.

Their efforts were in vain. The man was dead. Too bad, I thought. His family would be grieved. Which made me think of Ann and the children. I had to find and reassure them. Especially Ann; I knew how terrified she was. My poor, sweet Ann.

I turned and walked toward the doorway. On my right was a bathroom. Glancing in, I saw a toilet, light switch and a button with a red bulb next to it, the word Emergency printed beneath the bulb.

I walked into the hall and recognized it. Yes, of course.

The card in my wallet said to take me there in case of accident. The Motion Picture Hospital in Woodland Hills.

I stopped and tried to work things out. There'd been an accident, they'd brought me here. Why wasn't I in bed then? But I had been in bed. The same one the dead man was in. The man who looked like me. There had to be an explanation for all this. I couldn't find it though. I couldn't think with clarity.

The answer finally came. I wasn't sure it was correct-but there was nothing else. I had to accept it; for the moment anyway.

I was under anesthetic, they were operating on me.

Everything was happening inside my mind. That had to be the answer. Nothing else made sense.

Now what? I thought. Despite the distress of what was taking place, I had to smile. If everything was happening in my mind, then, being conscious of it, couldn't I control it?

Right, I thought. I'd do exactly what I chose. And what I chose to do was find my Ann.

As I decided that, I saw another doctor running down the hall toward me. Deliberately, I tried to stop him as he hurried past but my outstretched hand passed through his shoulder. Never mind, I told myself. In essence, I was dreaming. Any foolish thing could happen in a dream.

I started walking down the hall. I passed a room and saw a green card with white lettering: NO SMOKING-OXYGEN IN USE. Unusual dream, I thought, I'd never been able to read in dreams; words always ran together when I tried. This was completely legible despite the general blurring which continued.

It's not exactly a dream, of course, I told myself, seeking to explain it. Being under anesthesia isn't like being asleep. I nodded in agreement with the explanation, kept on walking. Ann would be in the waiting room. I set my mind on reaching her and comforting her. I felt her suffering as though it were my own.

I passed the nurses' station and heard them talking. I made no attempt to speak to them. All of this was in my mind. I had to go along with that; accept the rules. All right, it's not a dream persay but it was easier to think of it as one. A dream then; under anesthesia.

Wait, I thought, stopping. Dream or not, I can't walk around in my patient's gown. I glanced down at myself, startled to see the clothes I was wearing when the accident occurred. Where's the blood? I wondered. I recalled an instant vision of myself unconscious in the wreckage. Blood had been spraying.

I felt a sense of eggs-no! Sorry for the impatience. E-x-ul-t-a-t-i-o-n. Why? Because I'd reasoned something out despite the dullness of my mind. I couldn't possibly be that man in the bed. He was in a patient's gown, bandaged, fed by tubes. I was dressed, unbandaged, mobile. Total difference.

A man in street clothes was approaching me. I expected him to pass me. Instead, to my surprise, he put his hand on my shoulder and stopped me. I could feel the pressure of each separate finger on my flesh.

"Do you know what's happened yet?" he asked. "Happened?"

"Yes." He nodded. "You've died."

I looked at him in disgust. "That's absurd," I said.

"It's true."

"If I were dead, I wouldn't have a brain," I told him, "I couldn't talk to you."

"It doesn't work that way," he persisted.

"The man in that room is dead, not me." I said, "I'm under anesthesia, being operated on. In essence, I'm dreaming." I was pleased by my analysis.

"No, Chris," he said.

I felt a chill. How did he know my name? I peered at him closely. Did I know him? Was that why he'd appeared in my dream?

No; not at all. I felt distaste for him. Anyway, I thought (the idea made me smile despite my irritation) this was my dream and he had no claim to it. "Go find your own dream," I said, gratified by the cleverness of my dismissal.

"If you don't believe me, Chris," he told me, "look in the waiting room. Your wife and children are there. They haven't been told yet that you've died."

"Wait a minute, wait a minute." I pointed my finger at him, jabbing at the air. "You're the one who told me not to fight it, aren't you?"

He started to reply but I was so incensed by that I wouldn't let him speak. "I'm tired of you and tired of this stupid place," I said, "I'm going home."

Something pulled me from him instantaneously. It was as though my body was encased in metal with a distant magnet drawing me to itself. I hurtled through the air so fast I couldn't see or hear a thing.

It ended as abruptly as it started. I was standing in fog. I looked around but saw nothing in any direction. I began to walk, moving slowly through the mist. Now and then; I thought I caught a fleeting glimpse of people. When I tried to see them clearly, though, they faded off. I almost called to one, then chose not to. I was master of this dream. I wouldn't let it dominate me.

I attempted to distract myself by making believe I was back in London. Remember how I traveled there in 1957 to write a film? It had been November and I'd walked in fogs like this more than once-"pea soup" is a good description. This was even thicker, though; like being underwater. It even felt wet.

Finally, through the fog, I saw our house. That sight relieved me in two ways. One, the very look of it. Two, the way I'd gotten there so quickly. That could only happen in a dream.

Suddenly, an inspiration came to me. I've told you how my body hurt. Even though it was a dream, I still felt pain. Accordingly, I told myself that, since the pain was dream eng-e-n-dered, it wasn't necessary that I feel it. Robert, with the thought, the pain was gone. Which caused another sense of pleasure and relief. What more vivid proof could one require that this was dream and not reality?

I remembered, then, how I had sat up on the hospital bed, laughing, because it had all been a dream. That's exactly what it was. Period.

I was in the entry hall without transition. Dream, I thought and nodded, satisfied. I looked around, my vision still blurred. Wait, I thought. I'd been able to dispel the pain, why not the vision?

Nothing happened. Everything beyond ten feet was still obscured by what appeared to be a pall of smoke.

I whirled at the clicking noise of claws across the kitchen floor. Ginger was running into the front hall; you recall, our German Shepherd. She saw me and began her rocking, bouncing run of joy. I spoke her name, delighted by the sight of her. I bent to stroke her head and saw my hand sink deep into her skull. She recoiled with a yelp and scuttled back in terror, bumping hard against the kitchen door jamb, ears pressed tight to her head, hair erected on her back.

"Ginger," I said. I fought away a sense of dread. "Come here." She's acting foolishly, I told myself. I moved after her and saw her slipping frantically on the kitchen floor, trying to run away. "Ginger!" I cried. I wanted to be irritated with her but she looked so frightened that I couldn't be. She ran across the family room and lunged out through the flap of the dog door.

I was going to follow her, then decided not to. I would not be victimized by this dream no matter how insane it got. I turned and called Ann's name.

No answer to my call. I looked around the kitchen, seeing that the coffee maker was on, its pair of red bulbs burning. The glass pot on the heater plate was almost empty. I managed a smile. She's done it again, I thought. In no time, the house would be per-p-e-r-me-at-ed with a reek of burning coffee. I reached out to pull the plug, forgetting. My hand went through the wire and I stiffened, then forced back amusement. You can't do anything right in dreams, I reminded myself.

I searched the house. Our bedroom and the bathroom.

Ian's and Marie's rooms, their connecting bathroom. Richard's room. I ignored the blurring of my vision. That was unimportant, I decided.

What I found myself unable to ignore was an increasing lethargy I felt. Dream or not, my body felt like stone. I went back inside our bedroom and sat on my side of the bed. I felt a twinge of uneasiness because it didn't shift beneath me; it's a water bed. Forget it, a dream's a dream, I told myself. They're insane, that's all.

I looked at my clock-radio, leaning close to see the hands and numbers. It was six fifty-three. I looked out through the glass door. It wasn't dark outside. Misty but not dark. Yet how could it be morning if the house was empty? At this time, they should all be in their beds.

"Never mind," I said, struggling to get it all together in my mind. You're being operated on. You're dreaming this. Ann and the children are at the hospital waiting for-

A new confusion struck me. Was I really in the hospital?

Or had that been part of the dream too? Was I actually asleep on this bed, dreaming everything? Maybe the accident had never occurred. There were so many possibilities, each one affecting the next. If only I could think more clearly. But my mind felt numb. As though I'd been drinking or taken sedation.

I lay down on the bed and closed my eyes. It was the only thing to do; I knew that much. Presently, I'd wake up with the truth: a dream in the hospital while under anesthesia or a dream in my bed while asleep. I hoped it was the latter. Because, in that case, I'd wake up to find Ann lying by my side and could tell her what a crazy dream I'd had. Hold her lovely warmth in my arms and kiss her tenderly and laugh as I told her how bizarre it is to dream of dreaming.

Chapter Two

This Black, Unending Nightmare

I was exhausted but I couldn't rest, my sleep broken by Ann's crying. I tried to rise, to comfort her. Instead, I hovered in a limbo between darkness and light. Don't cry, I heard myself murmur. I'll wake up soon and be with you. Just let me sleep a while. Please don't cry; it's all right, sweetheart. I'll take care of you.

Finally, I was forced to open my eyes. I wasn't lying down but standing in a mist. I started walking slowly toward the sound of her crying. I was tired, Robert, groggy. But I couldn't let her cry. I had to find out what was wrong and end it so she would-n't cry like that. I couldn't bear to hear her cry like that.

I moved into a church I'd never seen before. All the pews were filled with people. Their forms were gray, I couldn't see their features. I walked down the middle aisle, trying to understand why I was there. What church was this? And why was the sound of Ann's crying coming from here?

I saw her sitting in the front pew, dressed in black, Richard on her right, Marie and Ian to her left. Next to Richard, I could see Louise and her husband. All of them were dressed in black. They were easier to see than the other people in the church yet even they looked faded, ghostlike. I could still hear the sobbing even though Ann was silent. It's in her mind, it came to me; and our minds are so close I hear it. I hurried toward her to stop it.

I stopped in front of her. "I'm here," I said.

She looked ahead as though I hadn't spoken; as though I weren't there at all. None of them looked toward me. Were they embarrassed by my presence and pretending not to see? I glanced down at myself. Perhaps it was my outfit. Hadn't I been wearing it a long time now? It seemed as though I had although I wasn't sure.

I looked back up. "All right," I said. I had difficulty speaking; my tongue felt thick. "All right," I repeated slowly. "I'm not dressed correctly. And I'm late. That doesn't mean ... " My voice trailed off because Ann kept looking straight ahead. I might have been invisible. "Ann, please," I said.

She didn't move or blink. I reached out to touch her shoulder.

She twitched sharply, looking up, her face gone blank. "What's wrong?" I asked. The crying in her mind abruptly surfaced and she jerked her left hand up to cover her eyes, trying to repress a sob. I felt a numbing pain inside my head. What's wrong? I thought. "Ann, what's wrong?" I pleaded.

She didn't answer and I looked at Richard. His face was tight, tears running down his cheeks. "Richard, what is going on?" I asked. My words sounded slurred as though I were drunk.

He didn't answer and I looked at Ian. "Will you please tell me?" I asked. I felt a stab of anguish looking at him. He was sobbing quietly, rubbing shaky fingers at his cheeks, trying to brush away the tears that fell from his eyes. What in the name of God? I thought.

Then I knew. Of course. The dream; it still continued. I was in the hospital being operated on-no, I was asleep on my bed and dreaming-whatever! flared my mind. The dream was continuing and now it included my own funeral.

I had to turn away from them; I couldn't stand to watch them crying so. I hate this stupid dream! I thought. When was it going to end?!

It was torment to me to be turned away when, just behind me, I could hear Ann and the children sobbing. I felt a desperate need to turn and comfort them. To what avail though? In my dream, they mourned my death. What good would it do for me to speak if they believed me dead?

I had to think of something else; it was the only answer.

The dream would change, they always did. I walked toward the altar, following the drone of a voice. The minister, I realized. I willed myself to feel amused. That might be fun, I told myself. Even in a dream, how many men receive the chance to listen to their own eulogy?

I saw his blurred, gray outline now, behind the pulpit.

His voice sounded hollow and distant. I hope he's giving me a royal send-off, I thought, bitterly.

"He is," said a voice.

I looked around. That man again; the one I'd seen in the hospital. Odd that, of everyone, he looked most clear to me.

"Haven't found your own dream yet, I see," I told him.

Odd, too, that I could speak to him without effort.

"Chris, try to understand," he said. "This isn't a dream. It's real. You've died."

"Will you get off that?" I began to turn away.

His fingers on my shoulder once again; solid, nearly pinching my flesh. That was odd too.

"Chris, can't you see?" he asked. "Your wife and children dressed in black? A church? A minister delivering your eulogy?"

"A convincing dream," I said.

He shook his head.

"Let go of me," I told him, threateningly. "I don't have to listen to this."

His grip was strong; I couldn't break it. "Come with me," he said. He led me to the platform where I saw a casket resting on supports. "Your body is in there," he told me.

"Really?" I said. My tone was cold. The casket lid was shut. How could he know I was in there?

"You can see inside it if you try," he answered. Unexpectedly, I felt myself begin to shake. I could look in the casket if I tried. Suddenly, I knew that.

"But I won't," I told him. I twisted from his grip and turned away. "This is a dream," I said, glancing across my shoulder. "Maybe you can't understand that but-"

"If it's a dream," he interrupted, "why don't you try to wake up?"

I whirled to face him. "All right, that's exactly what I'll do," I said. "Thank you for a very good suggestion."

I closed my eyes. All right, you heard the man, I told myself. Wake up. He's told you what to do. Now do it.

I heard Ann's sobbing getting louder. "Don't," I said. I couldn't bear the sound of it. I tried to back off but it followed me. I clenched my teeth. This is a dream and you are going to wake up from it right now, I told myself. Any second now I'd jolt awake, perspiring, trembling. Ann would speak my name in startled sympathy, then hold me in her arms, caress me, tell-

The sobbing kept on getting louder, louder. I pressed both hands against my ears to shut it out. "Wake up," I said. I repeated it with fierce determination. "Wake-up!"

My effort was rewarded by a sudden silence. I had done it! With a rush of joy, I opened my eyes.

I was standing in the front hall of our house. I didn't understand that.

Then I saw the mist again, my vision blurred. And I began to make out forms of people in the living room. Gray and faded, they stood or sat in small groups, murmuring words I couldn't hear.

I walked into the living room, past a knot of people; none of them were clear enough for me to recognize. Still the dream, I thought. I clung to that.

I walked by Louise and Bob. They didn't look at me.

Don't try to talk to them, I thought. Accept the dream. Move on. I walked into the bar room, moving toward the family room.

Richard was behind the bar, making drinks. I felt a twinge of resentment. Drinking at a time like this? I rejected the thought immediately. A time like what? I challenged my mind. This was no special time. It was merely a depressing party in a bleak, depressing dream.

Moving, I caught glimpses. Ann's older brother Bill, his wife Patricia. Her father and stepmother, her younger brother Phil, his wife Andrea. I tried to smile. Well, I told myself, when you dream you really do it up right, no detail overlooked; Ann's entire family, down from San Francisco no less. Where was my family though? I wondered. Surely I could dream them here as well. Did it matter, in a dream, that they were three thousand miles away?

That was when a new thought came to me. Was it possible that I had lost my sanity? Perhaps the accident had damaged my brain. There was a thought! I clutched at it. Brain damage; weird, distorted images. Not just a simple operation going on but something complex. Even as I moved unseen among these wraiths, scalpels might be probing at my brain, surgeons working to restore its function.

It didn't help. Despite the logic of it, I began to feel a sense of resentment. All these people totally ignoring me. I stopped in front of someone; faceless, nameless. "Damn it, even in a dream, people talk to you," I said. I tried to grab him by the arms. My fingers moved into his flesh as though it were water. I looked around and saw the family-room table. Moving there, I tried to pick up someone's glass to hurl it against the wall. It was like trying to grip at air. Anger mounted suddenly. I shouted at them. "Damn it, this is my dream! Listen to me!"

My laughter was involuntary, strained. Listen to yourself, I thought. You're acting as though this is really happening. Get things straight, Nielsen. This is a dream.

I left them all behind, starting down the back hall. Ann's Uncle John was standing in front of me, looking at some photographs on the wall. I walked right through him, feeling nothing. Forget it, I ordered myself. It doesn't matter.

Our bedroom door was closed. I walked through it. "This is insane," I muttered. Even in dreams, I'd never walked through doors before.

My aggravation vanished as I moved to the bed and looked at Ann. She was lying on her left side, staring toward the glass door. She still had on the black dress I had seen her wearing in the church but her shoes were off. Her eyes were red from crying.

Ian sat beside her, holding her hand. Tears ran slowly down his cheeks. I felt a rush of love for him. He's such a sweet and gentle boy, Robert. I reached forward to stroke his hair.

He looked around and, for a moment, which seemed to stop my heart, I thought he was looking at me, seeing me.

"Ian," I murmured.

He looked back at Ann. "Mom?" he said. She didn't respond.

He spoke again and her eyes moved slowly to his face.

"I know it sounds insane," he said, "but ... I feel as if Dad is with us."

I looked at Ann quickly. She was staring at Ian, her expression unchanged.

"I mean right here," he told her. "Wow."

Her smile was one of straining tenderness. "I know you want to help," she said.

"I really feel it, Mom."

She couldn't go on, a great sob racking her. "Oh, God," she whispered, "Chris ... " Tears filled her eyes.

I dropped beside the bed and tried to touch her face.

"Ann, don't-" I started. Breaking off, I twisted from her with a groan. To see my fingers sink into her flesh...

"Ian, I'm afraid," Ann said.

I turned back quickly to her. The last time I'd seen such a look on her face was on a night when Ian had been six and disappeared for three hours; a look of helpless, incapacitated dread. "Ann, I'm here," I said, "I'm here! Death isn't what you think!"

Terror caught me unaware. I didn't mean that! cried my mind. I couldn't take it back though. The admission had been made.

I fought against it, straining to repress it by concentrating on Ann and Ian. But the question came unbidden and I couldn't stop it. What if that man had told the truth? What if this wasn't a dream?

I struggled to retreat. Impossible; the way was blocked. I countered with rage. So what if I had thought it? What if I'd considered it? There was no proof of it beyond that brief consideration.

Better. I felt vengeful justification. I began to touch and prod my body. This is death? I challenged scornfully. Flesh and bone? Ridiculous! It might not be a dream-that much I could allow. But it was certainly not death.

The conflict seemed to drain me suddenly. Once more, my body felt like stone. Again? I thought.

Never mind. I thrust it from my mind. I lay down on my side on the bed and looked at Ann. It was unnerving to lie beside her, face to face, her staring through me like a window. Close your eyes, I thought. I did. Escape through sleep, I told myself. The evidence isn't in by any means. This could still be a dream. But God, dear God in heaven, if it was, I hated everything about it. Please, I begged whatever powers might attend me. Release me from this black, unending nightmare. To know I still exist!

Hovering, suspended, rising inches, then descending in a silent, engulfing void. Was this the feeling of prebirth; floating in liquid gloom?

No, there'd be no sound of crying in the womb. No sense of grief oppressing me. I murmured in my sleep, wanting to rest, needing to rest, but wanting, too, to wake for Ann's sake. "Honey, it's all right." I must have spoken those words a hundred times before waking.

My eyes dragged open, the lids feeling weighted.

She was lying by my side, asleep. I sighed and smiled at her with love. The dream had ended, we were together again. I gazed at her face, sweetly childlike in repose. A tired child, a child who'd wept herself to sleep. My precious Ann. I reached out to touch her face, my hand like iron.

My fingers disappeared inside her head.

She woke up with a start, her gaze alarmed. "Chris?" she said. Again, that momentary leap of hope. Shattered when it quickly grew apparent that she wasn't looking at me but through me. Tears began to well in her eyes. She drew up her legs and clutched her pillow tightly in her arms, pressing her face against it, body shaking with sobs.

"Oh, God, no sweetheart, please don't cry." I was crying too. I would have given up my soul if only she'd been able to see me for a minute, hear my voice, receive my comfort and my love.

I knew she couldn't though. And knew, as well, the nightmare hadn't ended. I turned from her and closed my eyes, desperate to escape in sleep again, let the darkness pull me far from her. Her weeping tore my heart. Please take me away from this, I pleaded. If I can't comfort her, take me away!

I felt my mind begin a downward slide, descending into blackness.

Now it was a dream. It had to be. My life was unreeling before me, a succession of living pictures. Something about it struck me. Hadn't I experienced this before, more briefly, more confusingly?

This was not confusing in the least. I might have been a viewer in an auditorium, watching a film entitled My Life, every episode from start to finish. No, amend that. Finish to start; the film began with the collision-was it real then-and evolved back toward my birth, each detail magnified.

I won't go into all those details, Robert. It's not the story I want to tell-it would take too long. Each man's life is a tome of episodes. Consider all the moments of your life enumerated one by one with full description. A twenty-volume encyclopedia of events; at the very least.

Let me discuss it in brief then, this display of scenes. It was more than a "flash before my eyes." I was more than just a viewer; that became apparent very soon. I relived each moment with acute perception, experiencing and understanding simultaneously. The phenomenon was vivid, Robert, each emotion infinitely multiplied by level upon level of awareness. The essence of it all-this is the important part-was the knowledge that my thoughts had been real. Not just the things I said and did. What went on in my mind as well, positive or negative.

Each memory was brought to life before me and within me. I could not avoid them. Neither could I rationalize, explain away. I could only re-experience with total cognizance, unprotected by pretense. Self-delusion was impossible, truth exposed in blinding light. Nothing as I thought it had been. Nothing as I hoped it had been. Only as it had been.

Failures plagued me. Things I had omitted or ignored, neglected. What I should have given and hadn't-to my friends, my relatives, to Mom and Dad, to you and Eleanor, my children, mostly Ann. I felt the biting pang of every unfulfillment. Not only personal but in my work as well-my failures as a writer. The host of scripts I'd written which did no one any good and, many, harm. I could condone them once. Now, in this stark unmasking of my life, condoning was impossible, self-justifying was impossible. An infinitude of lacks reduced to one fundamental challenge: What I might have done and how irrevocably I fell short of almost every mark.

Not that it was unjust; not that the scales were forced out of balance. Where there had been good, it showed as clearly. Kindnesses, accomplishments; all those were present too.

The trouble was I couldn't get through it. Like the tug of a building rope pulled from a distance, I was drawn from observation by Ann's sorrow. Honey, let me see. I think I spoke those words, I may have only thought them.

I became aware of lying by her side again, my eyelids heavy as I tried to raise them. The sounds she made in sleep were like a knife blade turning in my heart. Please, I thought. I have to see, to know; evaluate. The word seemed vital to me suddenly.

Evaluate.

I drifted down again; to the isolation of my visions. I had left the theatre momentarily; the picture on the screen had frozen. Now it started up again, absorbing me. I was inside it once again, reliving days long gone.

Now I saw how much time I had spent in gratifying sense; again, I will not give you details. Not only did I re-discover every sense experience of my life, I had to live each unfulfilled desire as well-as though they'd been fulfilled. I saw that what transpires in the mind is just as real as any flesh and blood occurrence. What had only been imagination in life now became tangible, each fantasy a full reality. I lived them all-while, at the same time, standing to the side, a witness to their, often, intimate squalor. A witness cursed with total objectivity.

Still always the balance, Robert; I emphasize the balance.

The scales of justice: darkness paralleled by light, cruelty by compassion, lust by love. And always, unremittingly, that inmost summons: What have you done with your lift?

An added mercy was the knowledge that this deep, internal review was witnessed only by myself. It was a private re-enactment, a judgment rendered by my own conscience. Moreover, I felt sure that somehow, every act and thought re-lived was being printed on my consciousness indelibly for future reference. Why this was so, I had no notion. I only knew it was.

Then something strange began to happen. I was in a cottage somewhere, looking at an old man lying on a bed. Two people sat nearby, a white-haired woman and a middle-aged man. Their dress was foreign to me and the woman's accent sounded strange as she spoke to say, "I think he's gone."

"Chris!"

Ann's tortured crying of my name ripped me from sleep. I looked around to find myself in swirling fog, lying on the ground. Standing slowly, every muscle aching, I tried to walk but couldn't. I was on the bottom of a murky lake whose currents swelled against me.

Inanely, I felt hungry. No, that's not the proper word. In need of sustenance. No, more than that. In need of something to add to myself, to help me re-assemble. That was it. I was incomplete; part of me was gone. I tried to think but found it beyond my capacity. Thoughts trickled in my brain like glue. Let go, was all I could think. Let go.

I saw a pale white column of light take form in front of me, a figure inside it. "You wish my help?" it asked. My mind was not perceptive enough to tell if it was male or female.

I tried to speak, then, from a distance, heard Ann call my name again and looked around.

"You could be here for a long time," said the figure.

"Take my hand."

I looked back at it. "Do I know you?" I asked. I could hardly speak, my voice sounding lifeless.

"That's not important now," the figure said. "Just take my hand."

I stared at it with vacant eyes. Ann called my name again, and I shook my head. The figure was trying to take me from her. I wouldn't let it do that. "Get away," I said. "I'm going to my wife."

I was alone in fog once more. "Ann?" I called. I felt cold and fearful. "Ann, where are you?" My voice was dead. "I can't see you."

Something began to draw me through the mist. Something else attempted to restrain me but I willed it off; it wasn't Ann, I knew that, and I had to be with Ann. She was all that mattered to me.

The fog began to thin and I found myself able to advance. There was something familiar about the landscape in front of me: broad, green lawns with rows of metal plaques flush with the surface, bouquets of flowers here and there, some dead, some dying, some fresh. I had been here before.

I walked toward a distant figure sitting on the grass.

Where had I seen this place? I wondered, trying hard to recollect. At last, like a bubble forced up through a sea of ooze, memory rose. Vaughn. Somebody's son. We'd known him. He was buried here. How long ago? the question came. I couldn't answer it. Time seemed an enigma beyond solution.

I saw, now, that the figure was Ann and moved toward her as quickly as I could, my feelings a blend of joy and sorrow; I didn't know why.

Reaching her, I spoke her name. She made no sign that she had seen or heard me and, for some inexplicable reason, I now found myself unsurprised by that. I sat beside her on the grass and put my arm around her. I felt nothing and she did not respond in any way, staring at the ground. I tried to understand what was happening but there was no way I could. "Ann, I love you," I murmured. It was all my mind could summon. "I'll always love you, Ann." Despair began to blanket me. I gazed at the ground where she was looking. There were flowers and a metal plaque.

Christopher Nielsen, 1927-1974. I stared at the plaque, too shocked to react. Vaguely, I recalled some man addressing me, trying to convince me that I'd died. Had it been a dream? Was this a dream? I shook my head. For some reason I could not fathom, the concept that this was, a dream was unacceptable. Which meant that I was dead.

Dead.

How could such a shattering revelation leave me so incredibly apathetic? I should have been screaming with terror. Instead, I could only stare at the plaque, at my name, at the year of my birth and the year of my death.

Slowly, an obsession started gathering in my mind. I was down there? Me? My body? Then I possessed the power to prove it all beyond a doubt. I could travel down there, see my corpse. Memory flickered. You can see inside it if you try. Where had I heard those words? I could see inside what?

Knowledge came. I could descend and look inside the casket. I could see myself and prove that I was dead. I felt my body easing forward, downward.

"Mom?"

I looked around in startlement. Richard was approaching with a thin, young man with dark hair. "Mom, this is Perry," he said. "He's the one I told you about."

I stared incredulously at the young man. He was looking at me.

"Your father is here, Richard," he said, calmly. "Sitting near the plaque with his name on it."

I struggled to my feet. "You can see me?" I asked. I was stunned by his words, his gaze directly on me.

"He's saying something I can't make out," Perry said.

I looked at Ann, anxiety returning. I could communicate with her; let her know I still existed.

She was staring at the young man, her expression stricken.

"Ann, believe him," I said. "Believe him."

"He's speaking again," Perry told her. "To you now, Mrs. Nielsen."

Ann shuddered and looked at Richard, speaking his name imploringly.

"Mom-" Richard looked uncomfortable and adamant at once. " if Perry says that Dad is here, I believe him. I've told you how he..."

"Ann, I am here!" I cried.

"I know how you feel, Mrs. Nielsen," Perry interrupted Richard, "but take my word for it. I see him right beside you. He's wearing a dark blue shirt with short sleeves, blue checkered slacks and Wallaby shoes. He's tall and blond with a husky build. He has green eyes and he's looking at you anxiously. I'm sure he wants you to believe he's really here."

"Ann, please," I said. I looked at Perry again. "Hear me," I entreated him. "You've got to hear me."

"He's speaking again," Perry said. "I think he's saying near me or something."

I groaned and looked at Ann again. She was trying not to cry but couldn't help herself. Her teeth were set on edge, her breathing forced and broken. "Please don't do this," she murmured.

"Mom, he's trying to help," Richard told her.

"Don't do this." Ann struggled to her feet and walked away. "Ann, don't go," I pleaded.

Richard started after her but Perry held him back. "Let her get used to the idea," he said.

Richard looked around uneasily. "He's here?" he asked.

"My father?"

I didn't know what to do. I wanted to be with Ann. Yet how could I leave the only person who could see me?

Perry had placed his hands on Richard's shoulders and turned him until he faced me. "He's in front of you," he said. "About four feet away."

"Oh, God." Richard's voice was thin and shaking. "Richard," I said. I stepped forward and tried to grasp his arms.

"He's right in front of you now, trying to hold your arms," Perry told him.

Richard's face was pale. "Why can't I see him then?" he demanded.

"You may be able to if you can talk your mother into a sitting."

Despite the excitement Perry's words created in me, I could stay with him no longer; I had to be with Ann. His voice faded quickly behind me as I started after her. "He's moving after your mother," he said. "He must want to-"

I could hear no more. Anxiously, I followed Ann, trying to overtake her. Whatever a sitting was-a seance?-Ann had to consent to it. I'd never believed in things like that, never even thought of them. I thought about them now. Perry had seen me, actually seen me. The thought that, with his help, Ann and the children might also see me, perhaps even hear me filled me with elation. There'd be no grief then!

I groaned with sudden dismay. A mist was gathering again, obscuring my view of Ann. I tried to run but my movements grew increasingly labored. I have to reach her! I thought. "Ann, wait!" I called. "Don't leave me!"

You have to move on, it seemed as though I heard a voice say in my mind. I wouldn't listen to it, kept on moving, slower, slower, once more on the bottom of that murky lake. Awareness started failing. Please! I thought. There must be some way Ann can see me and be comforted to know I still exist!

Chapter Three

My Presence is Invalid

I was walking up the hill to our house. On each side of the driveway, pepper trees were stirring in the wind. I tried to smell them but I couldn't. Overhead, the sky was overcast. It's going to rain, I thought. I wondered why I was there.

The front door was no more solid to me than air as I went inside. I knew, then, why I'd come.

Ann, Richard and Perry were sitting in the living room.

Ian must be in school, I thought, Marie in Pasadena at the Academy.

Ginger was lying at Ann's feet. As I stepped into the living room, she lifted her head abruptly and stared at me, ears drawn back. No sound this time. Perry, who was sitting on the sofa next to Richard, turned and looked at me. "He's back," he said.

Ann and Richard looked automatically in my direction but I knew they couldn't see me. "Does he look the same?" Richard asked anxiously.

"Just as he did in the cemetery," Perry answered. "He's wearing the outfit he had on the night of the accident, isn't he?"

Richard nodded. "Yes." He looked at Ann; my gaze was fixed on her. "Mom?" he said. "Will you...?"

She cut him off. "No, Richard," she said quietly but firmly.

"But Dad was dressed like that the night of the accident," Richard insisted. "How could Perry know that if he...?"

"We know it, Richard," Ann interrupted again.

"I'm not getting it from you, Mrs. Nielsen, take my word for it," Perry told her. "Your husband is standing right over there. Look at your dog. She sees him."

Ann looked at Ginger and shivered. "I don't know that," she murmured.

I had to make her see. "Ginger?" I said. Always, when I'd spoken her name, her tail would thump at the floor. Now she only cringed, eyes fixed on me.

I started across the room toward her. "Ginger, come on," I said. "You know me."

"He's walking toward you, Mrs. Nielsen," Perry said. "Would you please...?" she started, then broke off, startled, as Ginger lurched to her feet and ran from the room.

"She's afraid of him," Perry explained. "She doesn't understand what's happening, you see."

"Mom?" Richard said when she remained silent. How well I knew that stubborn silence. I felt compelled to smile despite her lack of inclination to believe in my presence.

"He's smiling at you," Perry said. "He seems to understand your inability to believe he's here."

Ann's expression grew strained again. "I'm sure it's obvious to you that I'd like to believe it," she said. "I just can't-" Breaking off, she drew in breath with effort. "You . . . really see him?" she asked.

"Yes, Ann, yes, he does," I said.

"He just said 'Yes, Ann, Yes,' " Perry told her. "I can see him; just as I described him in the cemetery. Naturally, he doesn't look as solid as we do. But he's very real. I'm not getting information from your mind. I can't even do that."

Ann pressed the palm of her left hand to her eyes. "I wish I could believe," she said, miserably.

"Try, Mom," Richard said. "Ann, please?" I said.

"I know it's hard to accept," Perry said. "I've lived with it all my life so I take it for granted. I could see disincarnates when I was a baby."

I looked at him with sudden distaste. Disincarnates? The word made me sound like a freak.

"I'm sorry," Perry said to me, smiling.

"What happened?" Richard asked and Ann lowered her hand to look at Perry curiously.

"He looked at me with a frown," Perry said, still smiling. "I must have said something he didn't like."

Richard looked at Ann again. "Mom, what do you say?" he asked.

She sighed. "I just don't know."

"What harm can it do?"

"What harm?" She gazed at him, incredulous. "To let myself hope that your father still exists? You know what he meant to me."

"Mrs. Nielsen," Perry started.

"I don't believe in survival after death," Ann interrupted him. "I believe that, when we die, we die and that's the end of it. Now you want me to-"

"Mrs. Nielsen, you're wrong," Perry said. He was supporting my presence yet I felt offended by his self-assertive tone. "Your husband is standing right in front of you. How could that be if he hasn't survived?"

"I don't see him," Ann responded. "And I can't believe it just because you say he's here."

"Mom, Perry's been tested at UCLA," Richard said. "He's been authenticated any number of times."

"Richard, we're not talking about college tests. We're talking about Dad! The man we loved!"

"All the more reason-!" Richard said.

"No." She shook her head. "I just can't let myself believe it. If I did, then found it wasn't true, I'd die myself. It would kill me."

Oh, no, I thought in sudden distress. Once more, that draining exhaustion had come upon me. Whether it was caused by the effort of wanting so badly for Ann to believe or by her continuing sorrow, I had no idea. I only knew I had to rest again. Things were starting to blur before my eyes.

"Mom, just try?" Richard asked her. "Aren't you even willing to try? Perry says we might see Dad if we-"

"Ann, I have to lie down for awhile," I said. I knew she couldn't hear me but I said it anyway.

"He's speaking to you, Mrs. Nielsen," Perry told her. "Now he's leaning over you."

I tried to kiss her hair.

"Did you feel that?" Perry asked.

"No, " she said, tensely.

"He just kissed your hair," he told her.

Her breath caught and she started crying softly. Richard jumped up, moving to her quickly. Sitting on the arm of her chair, he pulled her against himself. "It's all right,

Mom," he murmured. He looked at Perry critically. "Did you have to say that?" he asked.

Perry shrugged. "I told you what he did, that's all, I'm sorry."

The exhaustion was increasing rapidly now. I wanted to remain, to stand in front of Perry, let him read my lips. I didn't have the strength though. Once again, that stone-like feeling overwhelmed my body and I turned away from them. I had to rest.

"Do you want to know what he's doing now?" Perry asked. His tone was peeved.

"What?" Richard was stroking Ann's hair, looking upset. "He's walking into your bar room. Starting to fade. He must be losing strength."

"Can you call him back?" Richard asked.

I could hear no more. I don't know how I made it to our bedroom; the transition was unclear. I only remember that, as I lay down, I thought: Why do I keep getting exhausted when I have no physical body?

* * * *

I opened my eyes. It was dark and still. Something pulled at me, compelling me to stand.

The difference in the way I felt was instantly apparent.

Before, I'd felt weighted. Now I felt as light as down. I almost seemed to float across the room and through the door.

Perry's voice was speaking in the living room. I wondered what he was saying as I drifted down the back hall. Had Ann consented to the sitting yet? I hoped she had. All I wanted was to know that she was comforted.

I moved across the family room and into the bar room. Suddenly, my steps had frozen and I stared in horror toward the living room.

At myself.

My mind could not react. I was struck dumb by the sight.

I knew that I was standing where I was.

Yet I was standing in the living room as well. Dressed in identical clothes. My face, my body. Me, without a doubt.

But how could that be?

I wasn't in that body, I realized then. I only observed it.

Staring, I moved closer. The figure of myself looked corpselike. There was no expression on its face. It might have been a figure of me in a wax museum. Except that it was moving slowly like a winding down automaton.

I tore my gaze from it and looked around the living room.

Ann was there, Richard, Ian and Marie; Perry, talking to the figure. Was it visible to all of them? I wondered, sickened. It was such a hideous sight.

"Where are you?" Perry was asking.

I looked at the cadaverous form. Its lips stirred feebly.

When it spoke, its voice was not my own but a hollow, lifeless muttering as it said, "Beyond."

Perry told my family. He addressed the figure once again.

"Can you describe where you are?"

The figure didn't speak. It shifted on its feet, eyes blinking sluggishly. At last it spoke. "Cold," it said.

"He says it's cold," Perry told them.

"You said we'd be able to see him," Marie said in a tight voice.

I looked at Ann. She was on the sofa, sitting between Ian and Marie, her body looking collapsed. Her face was white and mask-like, she was staring at her hands.

"Please make yourself visible to everyone," Perry said to the figure. Even now, his tone was arbitrary.

The figure shook its head. It answered, "No."

I don't know how I knew it, but I did. The figure wasn't speaking of its own accord. It merely parroted what Perry's mind was feeding it. It wasn't me in any way. It was a puppet he'd constructed with the power of his will.

I moved to Perry angrily and stood in front of him, blocking off his view of the figure. "Stop this," I told him.

"Why can't you manifest yourself?" he asked.

I stared at him. He couldn't see me anymore. He was looking through me, at my wax-like effigy. Just as Ann had looked through me.

I reached out and tried to grab his shoulder. "What have you done?" I demanded.

He had no awareness of my presence. He kept speaking to the figure as I turned to Ann. She was bending forward now, shaking, both palms pressed across her lower face, eyes haunted, staring sightlessly. Oh, God, I thought in anguish. Now she'll never know. The figure had responded with its witless voice. I looked at it, revolted by the sight.

"Are you happy where you are?" Perry asked.

The figure answered, "Happy."

"Have you a message for your wife?" Perry asked. "Be happy," mumbled the figure.

"He says be happy," Perry said to Ann.

With a gagging sound, she struggled to her feet and ran from the room. "Mom!" Ian hurried after her. "Don't break the circle!" Perry cried.

Marie stood up, incensed. "Break the circle? You... ass!"

She ran after Ian.

I looked at the figure standing in our living room like a faded mannequin. Its eyes were those of a catatonic. "Damn you," I muttered. I walked to it suddenly.

To my astonished loathing, I could feel its flesh as I grabbed for it. It was dead and cold.

Revulsion seized me as it grabbed my arms, its icy fingers clutching at me. I cried out, harrowed, and began to struggle with it. I was wrestling with my own corpse, Robert, my dead face inches from me, my dead eyes staring at me. "Get away!" I shouted. "Away," it repeated dully. "Damn you!" I screamed. It muttered, "Damn you." Horrified, my stomach wrenched by nausea, I jerked free of its numbing touch.

"Look out, he's falling!" Perry cried. Suddenly, he fell back on the cushion of the chair he sat on. "He's gone," he murmured.

It was. As I'd pulled free, the figure had started toppling toward me, then, before my eyes, dissolved in midair.

"Something pushed him," Perry said.

"For Christ's sake, Perry." Richard's voice was trembling. "Could I have a drink of water?" Perry asked.

"You said we'd see him," Richard said.

"A drink of water, Richard?" Perry asked.

I looked at him closely as Richard stood and moved toward the kitchen. What was wrong with him? How could he have been so right, then so completely wrong?

I turned toward the kitchen, hearing the gurgle of the Sparklett's bottle being tapped. Why had Richard become involved with Perry in the first place? I wondered. I knew he'd only meant to help but now things were worse than ever.

Turning back, I sat beside Perry. "Listen," I said. He didn't move, hunched over, looking ill. I reached out and touched his arm but he didn't react.

"Perry, what's the matter with you?" I demanded. He stirred uncomfortably. An idea struck me and I repeated the question in my mind.

He frowned. "Get away from me," he muttered. "It's over."

"Over?" If I could have throttled him, I would have.

"What about my wife? Is it over for her?" Remembering, I repeated my words in thought.

"It's over," he said through clenching teeth. "That's it."

I started to think a further message but, the instant I began, I stopped. He had shut himself off, enclosing his awareness in a carapace of will.

I looked around as Richard returned and handed Perry a glass of water. Perry drank it in a long, continuous swallow, then sighed. "I'm sorry," he said. "I don't know what happened."

Richard gazed at him bleakly. "What about my mother?" he asked.

"We can try again," Perry told him.

Richard stopped him with an angry sound. "She'll never try again," he said. "No matter what you tell her now, she won't believe you."

I rose and walked away from them. I had to leave abruptly, that was clear to me. There was nothing more I could do. The thought came overwhelmingly:

From this moment on, my presence is invalid.

There IS more.

I tried to move away from the house, to go on; somewhere, anywhere. Yet, even though the heaviness was gone, even though I felt immeasurably stronger, I was still unable to break free. There was no way I could leave: Ann's despair held me in a vise. I had to stay.

In the instant of my thinking that, I found myself inside the house again. The living room was empty. Time had passed. I couldn't tell how long though; chronology was beyond my grasp.

I walked into the family room. Ginger was lying on the sofa in front of the fireplace. I sat beside her. She didn't even stir. I tried to stroke her head in vain. She slept on. Heavily. The contact had been broken and I didn't know how.

Standing with a defeated sigh, I walked to our bedroom.

The door was open and I went inside.

Ann was lying on the bed, Richard sitting next to her. "Mom, why won't you, at least, allow for the possibility that it might have been Dad?" he was asking her. "Perry swears he was there."

"Let's not talk about it anymore," she said. I saw that she'd been crying again, her eyes red, the flesh around them swollen.

"Is it so impossible?" Richard asked.

"I don't believe it, Richard," she told him. "That's all there is to it."

Seeing the look on his face, she added, "Perry may have certain powers; I'm not denying that. But he hasn't convinced me that there's anything after death. I know there isn't, Richard. I know your father's gone and we have to-"

She couldn't finish, her voice breaking off with a sob.

"Please let's not talk about it anymore," she murmured.

"I'm sorry, Mom." Richard lowered his head. "I was only trying to help."

She took his right hand and held it; kissed it gently, pressed it to her cheek. "I know that," she murmured. "It was very dear of you but... " Her voice trailed off and she closed her eyes. "He's dead, Richard," she said after a few moments. "Gone. There's nothing we can do about it."

"Ann, I'm here!" I cried. I looked around in wretched anger. Was there nothing I could do to let her know? I tried in vain to pick up objects from the bureau. I stared at a small box, trying to concentrate my will on moving it. After a long while, it hitched once, but, by then, I felt exhausted by the effort.

"Dear God." I left the room in sorrow, starting down the hall, then, on impulse, turned back toward Ian's room. His door was closed. No big deal, as Richard likes to say. I went through it in an instant and the loathesome realization struck me: I'm a ghost.

Ian sat at his desk, doing homework, his expression glum.

"Can you hear me, Ian?" I asked. "We've always been close, you and I."

He continued with his homework. I tried to stroke his hair; in vain, of course. I groaned with frustration. What was I to do? Yet I couldn't force myself away either. Ann's grief held me.

I was trapped.

I turned away from Ian and left his room. Several yards along the hall, I walked through the closed door of Marie's room. Now I felt repulsive to myself. Passing through doors seemed like a distasteful party trick to me.

Marie was sitting at her desk, writing a letter. I moved there and stood looking at her. She's such a lovely girl, Robert, tall and blonde and graceful. Talented too; a beautiful singing voice and definite presence on a stage. She'd been working very hard at the Academy of Dramatic Arts, intent on a theatrical career. I'd always had confidence in her future. It's a difficult profession but she's persistent. I'd always planned to make some contacts in the business for her after she was finished with her training. Now I'd never be able to do that. It was one more regret.

After a while, I looked at what she was writing.

We never saw a lot of one another. I mean just the two of us, especially in the last few years. My fault, not his. He tried to get us together-for a day, an evening. He and Ian spent days together, playing golf, going to ballgames, movies. He and Richard spent time together, eating out and talking for hours, getting to know each other. Richard wants to write too and Dad was always helpful and supportive to him.

I only went out with him a few times. Always to something I wanted-a play, a film, a concert. We'd have dinner beforehand and talk. It was always enjoyable but there was never enough of it, I see now.

Still, I always felt close to him. He always took good care of me, was always tolerant and understanding. He took my teasing with good grace and had a wonderful sense of humor. I know he loved me. Sometimes, he'd put his arms around me and tell me directly, tell me that he had great faith in my future. I sent him notes and told him he was the "Best Daddy" in the world and I loved him, but I wish I'd told him in person more.

If only I could see him now. Tell him: Daddy, thank you for all-

She stopped and rubbed her eyes as tears dripped on the letter. "I'm going to ruin it," she mumbled.

"Oh, Marie." I put my hand on her head. If only I could feel it, I thought. If only she could feel my touch and know my love for her.

She began to write again.

Sorry, had to stop to wipe my eyes. I may have to do that several times before I finish this letter.

I'm thinking about Mom now. Dad meant so much to her; she meant so much to him. They had a wonderful relationship, Wendy. I don't think I ever really spoke of it to you before. They were completely devoted to each other. Except for us children, they seemed to have need for no one but each other. Not that they didn't see people. People liked them and wanted to see them, you know that; they were great friends with your Mom and Dad. But togetherness meant more to them than anything.

It's funny. I've talked to lots of kids and almost all of them have trouble visualizing-even conceiving of-their parents making love. I suppose that feeling is universal.

I never had trouble visualizing Mom and Dad. Often, we'd see them standing together-in the kitchen, the family room, their bedroom, anywhere-holding each other closely, not speaking, like a pair of young lovers. Sometimes, they'd stand like that in the pool even. And, always when they sat together-whatever it was for, talking, watching television, anything-Mom would lean against Dad, he'd put his arm around her and her head would lie on his shoulder. They made such a sweet couple, Wendy. They-sorry, tears again.

Later. Another delay to dry my eyes. Anyway, it was easy to think of them making love. It seemed completely right. I remember all the times-after I became old enough to be conscious of it, of course-I'd hear their bedroom door shut quietly and hear the discreet click of the lock. I don't know about Louise or Richard or Ian but it always made me smile.

Not that they never fought. They were real people, vulnerable and both had tempers. Dad helped Mom to let hers out, especially after her breakdown-and, oh, Wendy, all the years he supported her through that! He helped her to release her anger instead of keeping it bottled up: told her, if nothing else, to scream at the top of her lungs when she was driving along in her car. She did and once Katie got so frightened she almost had a heart attack; she was on the back seat and Mom had forgotten she was there when she screamed.

Even though they fought, their fighting never turned them against each other. It always ended with them embracing and kissing, smiling, laughing. They were like children sometimes, Wendy. There were times when I felt like the mother.

You know something else? I've never mentioned this to anyone before. I know Dad loved us and Mom loves us. But there was always this "something" between them, this special rapport we could never touch. Something precious. Something beyond words.

Not that we suffered from it. We were never "left out" or anything.

They never deprived us of anything, always gave us love and support in everything we tried or wanted.

Still, there was this strange element in their relationship, which kept them a unit of two during all those years when the family was a unit of three to six. Maybe it doesn't make sense but it's true. I can't explain it. I only hope I have the same thing in my marriage. Whatever it is, I hope you have it in yours.

Proof of what I say is that I started this letter talking about Dad but ended up talking about Mom and Dad. Because it's impossible for me to talk about him without talking about her as well. They go together. That's the trouble. I just can't visualize her without him. It's as though something complete has been separated and neither half is right now. As though-

I started as I realized something.

For about a quarter of a page of her letter, I'd been picking up her words before she wrote them.

The idea came abruptly.

Marie, I thought. Write what I tell you. Write these words. Ann, this is Chris. I still exist.

I fixed my gaze on her and kept repeating the words. Ann, this is Chris. I still exist. Again and again, directing them to Marie's mind as she wrote. Write them down, I told her. I repeated the words I wanted her to write. Write them down. I repeated the words. Write them down. Repeated the words. Write. Repeated. Write, repeated. A dozen times, then more and more. Write: Ann this is Chris. I still exist.

I became so absorbed in what I was doing that I jumped when Marie gasped suddenly and jerked her hand from the desk. As she stared at the paper in stunned silence, I looked down at it.

She'd written on the paper: *Annths is Chris-istill...*

"Show it to Mom," I told her excitedly. I concentrated on the words. Show it to Mom, Marie. Right now. Quickly, repeatedly.

Marie got up and moved toward the hall, the paper in her hand. "That's it, that's it," I said. That's it, I thought.

She went into the hall and turned toward the doorway of our bedroom. There, she stopped. Following eagerly, I stopped too. What was she waiting for?

She looked in at Ann and Richard. Ann still had his hand against her cheek. Her eyes were closed, she looked asleep.

"Take it in," I told Marie. I grimaced at the sound of my voice. Take it in, I told her mentally. Show it to Mom, to Richard.

Marie stood motionless, gazing at Richard and Ann, her expression uncertain. "Marie come on," I told her, tensed again. Marie, take it to them, I thought. Let them see.

She turned away. "Marie!" I cried. I caught myself. Take it in! I cried with my mind. She hesitated, then turned back toward our bedroom. That's it, take it in to her, I thought. Take it in, Marie. Now.

She remained immobile.

Marie, I pleaded mentally, for God's sake, take it to your mother.

Abruptly, she turned toward her room and strode there quickly, passing through me. I whirled and ran after her. "What are you doing?" I cried. "Don't you hear-?"

My voice failed as she crumpled the sheet of paper and dropped it into her wastebasket. "Marie!" I said. I stared at her, appalled. Why had she done that?

I knew though, Robert; it was not a difficult thing to understand. She thought it was her own subconscious surfacing. She didn't want Ann to suffer any more than she had. It was done out of love. But it dashed my last hope of conveying my survival to Ann.

A wave of paralyzing grief swept over me. Dear God, this has to be a dream! I thought, reverting suddenly. It can't be real!

I blinked. Below my feet, I saw the plaque: Christopher Nielsen, 1927-1974. How had I gotten there? Have you ever "come to" in your car and wondered how you'd driven so far without remembering a moment of it? I had the same sensation then. Except that I didn't know what I was doing there.

Soon enough, it came to me. My mind had cried: It can't be real! That same mind still knew that there was a way of finding out for certain. I'd started doing it once before, it came back to me; then had been restrained by something. I would not be restrained now. There was only one way to know if this were dream or reality. I began descending into the ground. It presented no more hindrance to me than the doors. I sank into blackness. One way to be sure, I kept thinking. I saw the casket lying just below. How could I see in the dark? I wondered. I let that go. Only one thing mattered; finding out. I moved inside the casket.

My scream of horror seemed to echo and re-echo in the confines of the grave. I stared in petrified revulsion at my body. It had started to decay. My face was tight and mask-like, frozen in a hideous grimace. The skin was rotting, Robert. I saw mag-no, let that go. No point in sickening you as I was sickened.

I closed my eyes and, screaming still, drove myself away from there. Coldness swirled around me, clinging wetness. Opening my eyes, I looked around. The fog again, that gray, eddying mist I could not escape.

I started to run. It had to end somewhere. The more I ran the thicker it got. I turned and started running in the opposite direction but it didn't help. The fog continued getting more dense no matter which way I ran. I could see no more than inches ahead. I started sobbing. I might wander in this mist forever! Suddenly, I cried out: "Help me! Please!"

A figure approached from the murk; that man again. I felt as though I knew him even though his face was unfamiliar. I ran to him and clutched at his arm. "Where am I?" I asked.

"In a place of your own devising," he replied.

"I don't understand you!"

"Your mind has brought you here," he said. "Your mind is keeping you here."

"Do I have to stay here?"

"Not at all," he told me. "You can break the binding any time."

"How?"

"By concentrating on what's beyond this place."

I began to ask another question when I felt Ann's sorrow pulling at me once again. I couldn't leave her alone. I couldn't.

"You're slipping back," the man said, warningly.

"I can't just leave her," I told him.

"You have to, Chris," he said. "You either move on or stay the way you are."

"I can't just leave her," I repeated.

I blinked and looked around. The man was gone. So quickly that I had to think he'd been a figment of my mind.

I sank down on the cold, damp ground, inert and miserable. Poor Ann, I thought. She'd have to start a new life now. All our plans were ruined. The places we were going to visit, the exciting projects we had planned. To write a play together, combining her intense memories of the past and her insight with my abilities. To buy a piece of woods somewhere where she could photograph the wild life while I wrote about it. To buy a motor home and take a year to drive around the country, seeing every detail of it. To travel, finally, to the places we had always talked about but never seen. To be together, enjoying life and each other's company.

All ended now. She was alone; I'd failed her. I should have lived. It was my own fault I'd been killed. I'd been stupid and careless. Now she was alone. I didn't deserve her love. I'd wasted many moments in life we could have spent together. Now I'd thrown away the remainder of our time.

I'd betrayed her.

The more I thought about it, the more despondent I became. Why wasn't she right in her belief? I thought bitterly. Better that death was an end, a cessation. Anything was preferable to this. I felt devoid of hope, hollowed by despair. There was no meaning to survival. Why go on like this? It was futile and pointless.

I don't know how long I sat like that and thought like that. It seemed an eternity, Robert-just me, abandoned in chilling, mucilaginous fog, sunk in abject sorrow. Only after a long, long time did I begin to alter what I thought. Only after a long, long time, recall what the man had told me: that I could leave this place by concentrating on what was beyond it. What was beyond it though?

Does it matter? I thought. Whatever it was, it couldn't be worse than this.

All right, try then, I told myself.

I closed my eyes and tried to visualize a better place. A place with sunlight, warmth, with grass and trees. A place like the ones we used to take our cam per to all those years.

I finally settled, in my mind, on a glade of redwood trees in northern California where the six of us-Ann, Louise, Richard, Marie, Ian and I-had stood one August afternoon at twilight, none of us speaking, listening to the vast, enveloping silence of nature.

I seemed to feel my body pulsing; forward, upward. I opened my eyes in startlement. Had I imagined it?

I closed my eyes and tried again, re-visualizing that immense, still glade.

I felt my body pulsing once more. It was true. Some incredible pressure-gentle, yet insistent-was behind me, pushing, bearing. I felt my breath grow larger, larger, achingly large. I concentrated harder and the move accelerated. I was rushing forward, rushing upward. The sensation was alarming but exhilarating too. I didn't want to lose it now. For the first time since the accident, I felt a glimmer of peace within myself. And the beginning of a knowledge; an astonishing insight.

There is more.

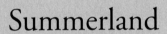

Summerland

Chapter Four

Continutaion at Another Level

I opened my eyes and looked up. Overhead, I saw green foliage and, through it, blue sky. There was no sign of mist; the air was clear. I took a breath of it. It had a cool, invigorating smell. I felt a gentle breeze against my face.

Sitting up, I looked around. I'd been lying on a patch of grass. The trunk of the tree I sat beneath was close by. I reached out and felt its bark. And something more-a kind of energy flowing from it.

I reached down and touched the grass. It looked immaculately cared for. I pushed aside a clump of it and examined the soil. Its color was complementary to the shade of the grass. There were no weeds of any kind.

Pulling out a blade of grass, I held it against my cheek. I could feel a minuscule flow of energy from it as well. I sniffed its delicate fragrance, then put it in my mouth and chewed as I used to do when I was a boy. I never tasted grass like that when I was a boy.

I noticed, then, there were no shadows on the ground. I sat beneath a tree yet not in shade.

I didn't understand that and looked for the sun.

There wasn't any, Robert. There was light without a sun.

I looked around in confusion. As my eyes grew more accustomed to the light, I saw further into the countryside. I had never seen such scenery: a stunning vista of green-clad meadows, flowers and trees. Ann would love this, I thought.

I remembered then. Ann was still alive. And I? I stood and pressed both palms against the solid tree trunk. Stamped on solid ground with my shoe. I was dead; there could be no question about it any longer. Yet here I was, possessed of a body that felt the same and looked the same, was even dressed the same. Standing on this very real ground in this most tangible of landscapes.

This is death? I thought.

I looked at my hands; the details of their lines and ridges, all the varied folds of skin. I examined the palms. I studied a book on palmistry once; for fun, to be able to do it at parties. I'd studied my palms and knew them well.

They were still the same. The life line was as long as ever; I remembered showing it to Ann and telling her not to worry, I was going to be around a long time. We could laugh about that now if only we were together.

I turned my hands over and noticed that their skin and nails were pink. There was blood inside me. I had to shake myself to make certain I wasn't dreaming. I held my right hand over my nose and mouth and felt breath pulsing warmly from my lungs. I pressed two fingers to my chest until I found the right spot.

Heartbeat, Robert. Just as always.

I looked around abruptly at a flash of movement. An exquisite, silver-plumaged bird had landed on the tree. It seemed completely unafraid of me, perching close by. This place is magic, I thought. I felt dazed. If this is a dream I told myself, I hope I never wake from it.

I started as I saw an animal running toward me; a dog, I realized. For several moments, it didn't register. Then, suddenly, it all rushed over me. "Katie!" I cried. She ran toward me as fast as she could, making those frantic little whimpers of joy I hadn't heard in years. "Katie," I whispered. I fell to my knees, tears starting in my eyes. "Old Kate."

Abruptly, she was with me, bouncing with excitement, licking my hands. I put my arms around her. "Kate, old Kate." I could barely speak. She wriggled against me, whimpering with happiness. "Katie, is it really you?" I murmured.

I took a closer look. The last time I had seen her was in an open cage at the vet's; sedated, lying on her left side, eyes staring sightlessly, limbs twitching with convulsions they could not control. Ann and I had gone to see her when the doctor had called. We'd stood beside the cage a while, stroking her, feeling stunned and helpless. Katie had been our good companion almost sixteen years.

Now she was the Katie I remembered from the years when Ian was growing up-vibrant, full of energy, eyes bright, with that funny mouth that, open, made her look as though she were laughing. I hugged her with delight, thinking how happy Ann would be to see her, how happy the children would be, especially Ian. The afternoon she'd died, he'd been at school. That evening, I had found him sitting on his bed, cheeks wet with tears. They'd grown up together and he hadn't even had a chance to say goodbye to her.

"If only he could see you now," I said, hugging her, overjoyed by our reunion. "Katie, Katie." I stroked her head and body, scratched her wonderful floppy ears. And felt a rush of gratitude toward whatever power had brought her to me.

Now I knew this was a lovely place.

* * * *

It's hard to say how long we stayed there, visiting. Katie lay beside me, warm head on my lap, occasionally stretching, sighing with contentment. I kept stroking her head, unable to get over the pleasure of seeing her. Wishing again and again that Ann were there.

It was only after a long time that I noticed the house.

I wondered how I could have missed it; it was only a hundred yards away. The sort of house Ann and I had always planned to build some day: timber and stone with enormous windows and a huge deck overlooking the countryside.

I felt immediately drawn to it; I didn't know why.

Standing, I began to move toward it, Katie jumping up to walk beside me. The house stood in a clearing ringed by beautiful trees-pines, maples and birches. There were no outside walls or fences.

To my surprise, I noticed that there was no door at the entrance either and that what I'd taken for windows were only openings. I noticed, too, the lack of pipes and wires, fuse boxes, gutters and television aerials, the form of the house harmonious with its surroundings. Frank Lloyd Wright would have approved, the thought occurred. I smiled, amused. "He might actually have designed it, Katie," I said. She looked at me and, for a fleeting moment, I got the impression that she understood me.

We walked into a garden near the house. In its center stood a fountain made of what appeared to be white stone. I approached it and dipped my hands into crystal water. It was cool and, like the tree trunk and grass blade, emitted a soothing flow of energy. I took a sip of it. I'd never tasted water so refreshing. "Want some, Kate?" I asked, looking at her.

She made no move but I received another impression: that water was no longer needed by her. Turning back to the fountain, I raised some water in the cupped palms of my hands and washed it over my face. Incredibly, the drops ran off my hands and face as though I'd been waterproofed.

Amazed by each new facet of this place, I walked, with Katie, to a bank of flowers and leaned over to smell them. The subtlety of their odor was enchanting. Too, their colors were as varied as the colors in a rainbow though more iridescent. I cupped my palms around a golden flower edged with yellow and felt a tingling of that energy running up my arms. I put my hands around one flower after another. Each gave off a stream of delicate force. To my added amazement, I began to realize that they were, also, generating soft, harmonious sounds.

"Chris!"

I turned quickly. A nimbus of light was entering the garden. I glanced at Katie as she started wagging her tail, then looked back at the light. My eyes adjusted and it began to fade. Approaching me was the man I'd seen-how many times? I couldn't recall. I'd never noticed his clothes before; a white, short-sleeved shirt, white slacks and sandals. He walked up to me, smiling, arms outstretched. "I felt your nearness to my home and came immediately," he said. "You made it, Chris."

He embraced me warmly, then drew back, still smiling. I looked at him.

"Are you ... Albert?" I asked.

"That's right." He nodded.

It was our cousin Robert-we always called him Buddy.

He looked marvelous; as I recalled him appearing when I was fourteen. Amend that. He looked far more vigorous.

"You look so young," I said. "No more than twenty-five."

"The optimum age," he replied. I didn't understand that. As he leaned over to stroke Katie's head and say hello to her-I wondered how he knew her-I stared at something I haven't mentioned about him. Surrounding his entire form was a shimmering blue radiation shot through with white, sparkling lights.

"Hello, Katie, glad to see him, are you?" he asked. He stroked her head again, then straightened up with a smile. "You're wondering about my aura," he said.

I started, smiling. "Yes."

"Everybody has them," he told me. "Even Katie." He pointed at her. "Haven't you noticed?"

I looked at Katie in surprise. I hadn't noticed-though, now that Albert had mentioned it, it was obvious. Not as vivid as his but perfectly clear.

"They identify us," Albert said.

I looked down at myself. "Where's mine?" I asked.

"No one sees his own," he said. "It would be inhibiting." I didn't understand that either but had another question more demanding at the moment. "Why didn't I recognize you after I died?" I asked.

"You were confused," he answered. "Half awake, half sleeping; in a kind of twilight state."

"It was you in the hospital who told me not to fight it, wasn't it?"

He nodded. "You were fighting too hard to hear me though," he said. "Struggling for life. You remember a vague form standing by your bed? You saw it even though your eyes were closed."

"That was you?"

"I was trying to break through," he told me. "Make your transition less painful."

"I guess I didn't help you much."

"You couldn't help yourself." He patted my back. "It was too traumatic for you. A pity it wasn't easier though. Usually, people are met immediately afterward."

"Why wasn't I?"

"There was no way of getting to you," he said. "You were so intent on reaching your wife."

"I felt I had to," I told him. "She was so frightened."

He nodded. "It was very loving of you but it trapped you in the borderland."

"That was horrible."

"I know it was." He gripped my shoulder reassuringly. "It could have been far worse though. You might have lingered there for months or years-centuries even. It's not uncommon. If you hadn't called for help-"

"You mean, until I called for help, there was nothing you could do?"

"I tried but you kept rejecting me," he said. "It was only when the vibration of your call came through that I could hope to convince you."

It struck me then; I don't know why it took so long. I looked around in awe. "Then ... this is heaven?"

"Heaven. Homeland. Harvest. Summerland," he said. "Take your choice."

I felt foolish for asking but had to know. "Is it a-country? A state?"

He smiled. "A state of mind."

I looked at the sky. "No angels," I said, conscious of only half joking.

Albert laughed. "Can you conceive of anything more cumbersome than wings attached to shoulder blades?" he asked.

"Then there are no such things?" Again, I felt naive for asking but was too curious to repress the question.

"There are if one believes in them," he said, confusing me again. "As I said this is a state of mind. What does that motto on the wall of your office say? That which you believe becomes your world."

I was startled. "You know about that?" I asked. He nodded.

"How?"

"I'll explain it all in time," he said. "For now I only want to make the point that what you think does become your world. You thought it only applied to earth but it applies here even more since death is a refocusing of consciousness from physical reality to mental-a tuning into higher fields of vibration."

I had an idea what he meant but wasn't sure. I guess it showed in my expression for he smiled and asked, "Was that obscure? Put it this way then. Does a man's existence change in any way when he removes his overcoat? Neither does it change when death removes the overcoat of his body. He's still the same person. No wiser. No happier. No better off. Exactly the same.

"Death is merely continuation at another level."

Chapter Five

Into Albert's Home

The idea only struck me then. I can't conceive why it took so long except, perhaps, that there had been so many new amazing things to adjust to that my mind simply hadn't found time for it until that moment.

"My father." I said, "Your parents. Our uncles and aunts. Are they all here?"

" 'Here' is a big place, Chris," he answered with a smile. "If you mean did they all survive, of course."

"Where are they?"

"I'd have to check," he told me. "The only ones I know about for sure are my mother and Uncle Sven."

I felt a glow of pleasure at the mention of Uncle's name.

The image of him sprang to mind: his bald, shiny head, his bright eyes twinkling behind horn rim glasses, his cheery expression and voice, his unfailing sense of humor. "Where is he?" I asked. "What does he do?"

"He works with music," Albert said.

"Of course." I had to smile again. "He always loved music. Can I see him?"

"Certainly." Albert returned my smile. "I'll arrange it as soon as you've become more acclimated."

"And your mother too," I said. "I never knew her very well but I'd certainly like to see her again."

"I'll arrange it," Albert said.

"What did you mean about having to check?" I asked.

"Don't families stay together?"

"Not necessarily," he told me. "Earth ties have less meaning here. Relationships of thought, not blood, are what count."

That sense of awe again. "I have to tell Ann about this," I said. "Let her know where I am-that everything's all right. I want that more than anything."

"There's really no way, Chris," Albert said. "You can't get through."

"But I almost did." I told him how I'd gotten Marie to write my message.

"The two of you must have a great affinity," he said. "Did she show it to your wife?"

"No," I shook my head. "But I could try again."

"You're beyond that now," he said.

"But I have to let her know."

He put a hand on my shoulder. "She'll be with you soon enough," he told me gently.

I had no idea what else to say. The thought that there was no way left to let Ann know I was all right was terribly depressing. "What about someone like Perry?" I asked, remembering suddenly. I told Albert about him.

"Remember that you and he were on the same level then," Albert said. "He wouldn't be aware of you now."

Seeing my expression, Albert put an arm around my shoulder. "She'll be here, Chris," he said. "I guarantee it." He smiled. "I can understand your feeling. She's a lovely person."

"You know about her?" I asked, surprised.

"About her, your children, Katie, your office, everything" he said. "I've been with you for more than twenty years. Earth time, that is."

"Been with me?"

"People on earth are never alone," he explained. "There's always someone as a guide for each individual."

"You mean you were my guardian angel?" The phrase sounded trite but I could think of no other.

"Guide is a better word," Albert said. "Guardian angel is a concept derived by ancient man. He sensed the truth about guides but misinterpreted their identity because of his religious beliefs."

"Ann has one too?" I asked.

"Of course."

"Then can't her guide let her know about me?"

"If she were open to it, yes, easily," he answered and I knew there was no answer there. She was insulated by her skepticism.

Another thought; this one brought about by the discovery that Albert had been near me for decades: a sense of shame as I realized that he'd been witness to many less than admirable acts on my part.

"You were all right, Chris," he said.

"Are you reading my mind?" I asked.

"Something like that," he answered. "Don't feel too badly about your life. Your flaws have been duplicated in the lives of millions of men and women who are, basically, good."

"My flaws were mostly to do with Ann," I said. "I always loved her but, too often, failed her."

"Mostly when you were young," he told me. "The young are too involved with themselves to really understand their mates. The making of a career alone is enough to subvert the capacity to understand. It was the same way in my life. I never got a chance to marry because I came across too young. But I failed to properly understand my mother, my father, my sisters. What's the phrase from that play? 'It goes with the territory, Chris.' "

It occurred to me that he had died before that play was written. I made no mention of it though, still concerned about Ann. "There's really no way at all I can get through to her?" I asked.

"Perhaps something will develop in time," he said. "At the moment her disbelief is an impassable barrier." He removed his arm from my shoulder and patted my back reassuringly. "She will be with you though," he said. "Count on it."

"She won't have to go through what I did, will she?" I asked, uneasily.

"It isn't likely," he answered. "The circumstances are bound to be different." He smiled. "And we'll keep an eye on her."

I nodded. "All right." I wasn't actually reassured by his words but forced my thoughts away from the problem for then. Looking around, I told him that he must be quite a gardener.

He smiled. "There are gardeners, of course," he said. "But not for tending gardens. They require no tending."

"None?" I was amazed again.

"There's no lack of moisture," he told me. "No extremes of heat or cold, no storms or winds, snow or sleet. No random growth."

"Doesn't the grass even have to be mowed?" I asked, remembering our lawns in Hidden Hills and how often Richard, then Ian had to mow them.

"It never grows beyond this height," Albert said.

"You say there are no storms," I went on, making myself concentrate on other things besides my concern for Ann. "No snow or sleet. What about people who like snow? This wouldn't be heaven to them. What about the colors of autumn? I love them. So does Ann."

"And there are places were you can see them," he said. "We have all the seasons in their own locations."

I asked about the flow of energy I'd felt from the tree trunk, grass blade, flowers and water.

"Everything here emits a beneficial energy," he answered. The sight of Kate sitting contentedly beside me made me smile and kneel to pet her again. "Has she been here with you?" I asked.

Albert nodded, smiling.

I was about to say something about how much Ann missed her but held it back. Katie had been her inseparable companion. She adored Ann.

"But you haven't seen my home yet," Albert said.

I stood and, as we strolled toward the house, I commented on its lack of windows and door.

"There's no need for them," he said. "No one would intrude though everyone is welcome."

"Does everyone live in houses like this?"

"They live as they did on earth," he answered. "Or as they wished they had lived. I never had a home like this, as you know. I always dreamed about it though."

"Ann and I did too."

"Then you'll have one like it."

"Will we build it?" I asked.

"Not with tools," he said. "I built this house with my life." He gestured toward it. "Not that it was like this when I first arrived," he said. "Like the rooms of my mind, the rooms of the house were not all that attractive. Some were dark and messy and the air in them was heavy. And, in this garden, mixed among the flowers and bushes were weeds I'd grown in life.

"It took a while to reconstruct," he said, smiling at the memory. "I had to revise the image of it-the image of myself, that is-detail by detail. A section of wall here, a floor there, a doorway, a furnishing."

"How did you do it?" I asked. "With mind," he said.

"Does everyone have a house waiting for them when they arrive?"

"No, most build their houses afterward," he said. "With help, of course."

"Help?"

"There are building circles," he told me. "Groups of people skilled in construction."

"By using their minds?"

"Always with mind," he said. "All things start in thought."

I stopped and looked up at the house which loomed above us. "It's so ... earthlike," I said.

He nodded, smiling. "We're not so distant from our memories of earth that we desire anything too novel in the way of dwelling places." He made a welcoming gesture. "But come inside, Chris."

We walked into Albert's home.

Chapter Six

Thoughts Are Very Real

My first impression, as I entered, was one of absolute reality. The room was immense, beamed and paneled, furnished with impeccable taste-and filled with light.

"We don't have to worry about 'catching' the morning or afternoon sun," Albert told me. "All rooms get the same amount of light at all times."

I looked around the room. No fireplace, I thought. The room seemed made for one.

"I could have one if I wished," Albert said as though I'd voiced the thought. "Some people do."

I had to smile at the ease with which he read my mind.

We'd have a fireplace, I thought. Like the pair of fieldstone fireplaces we had in our home. For atmosphere mostly; they provided little heat. But Ann and I liked nothing better than to lie in front of a crackling fire, listening to music.

I moved to a superbly crafted table and examined it. "Did you make this?" I asked, impressed.

"Oh, no," he said. "Only an expert could create such a beautiful piece."

Without thinking, I ran a finger over its surface, then tried to hide the movement. Albert laughed. "You won't find any dust here," he said, "since there's no disintegration."

"Ann would certainly like that," I told him. She always liked our house to be immaculate and California being what it is, she always had to do a lot of dusting to keep the furniture polished.

Standing on the table was a vase of flowers-brilliant shades of red, orange, purple and yellow. I'd never seen such flowers. Albert smiled at them. "They weren't here before," he said. "Someone left them as a gift."

"Won't they die now that they've been picked?" I asked. "No, they'll stay fresh until I lose interest in them," Albert said. "Then they'll vanish." He smiled at my expression.

"For that matter, the entire house would, eventually, vanish if I lost interest in it and left."

"Where would it go?" I asked. "Into the matrix."

"Matrix?"

"Back to its source to be reused," he explained. "Nothing is lost here, everything recycled."

"If mind creates it and loss of interest can un-create it," I said, "does it have any reality of its own?"

"Oh, yes," he said. "It's just that its reality is always subject to mind."

I was going to ask more but it all seemed too confusing and I let it go as I followed Albert through his house. Every room was large, bright and airy with massive window openings, which overlooked the luxuriant scenery.

"I don't see any other houses," I told him.

"They're out there," Albert said. "It's just that we have lots of room here."

I was going to comment on the absence of a kitchen and bathrooms when the reason became obvious. Clearly, the bodies we possessed did not require food. And, since there was neither dirt nor disposal, bathrooms would be superfluous.

The room I liked best was Albert's study. Each wall had a floor-to-ceiling bookcase packed with finely bound volumes and there were large chairs, tables and a sofa on the polished wood floor.

To my surprise, I saw a line of bound scripts on one of the shelves and recognized the titles as my own. My reaction came in layers-surprise first, as I've said, then pleasure at seeing them in Albert's home, then disappointment that I'd never had my own scripts bound while I was on earth.

My last reaction was one of shame as I realized how many of the scripts dealt with subjects either violent or horrific.

"I'm sorry," Albert said. "I didn't mean to disturb you."

"It's not your fault," I told him. "I'm the one who wrote them."

"You'll have lots of time to write other things now," he reassured me. Kindness, I know, kept him from saying "better" things.

He gestured toward the sofa and I sank down on it as he sat on one of the chairs. Katie sat beside my right leg and I stroked her head as Albert and I continued talking.

"You called this place Harvest," I said. "Why?"

"Because the seeds a man plants in life create the harvest he reaps here," he answered. "Actually, the most authentic name-if one wants to be a purist-is the third sphere."

"Why?"

"It's somewhat complicated," Albert said. "Why don't we wait until you've rested first?"

Odd, I thought. How could he know that I was starting to feel weary? I'd only become aware of it that very moment. "How can that be?" I asked, knowing he would understand the question.

"You've been through a traumatic experience," he told me. "And rest between periods of activity is nature's way; here as on earth."

"You get tired too?" I asked in surprise.

"Well, perhaps not tired," Albert said. "You'll soon find that there's little actual fatigue here. To refresh oneself, however, there are periods of mental rest." He gestured toward the sofa. "Why don't you lie down?" he told me.

I did and looked up at the beamed ceiling, then, after several moments, at my hands. I made a soft, incredulous sound. "They look so real," I said.

"They are," he replied. "Your body may not have fiber but it isn't vapor either. It's simply finer grained than the body you left behind. It still has a heart and lungs to breathe air with and purify your blood. Hair still grows on your head, you still have teeth and finger- and toenails."

I felt my eyelids getting heavy. "Do nails stop growing at the right length like the grass?" I asked.

Albert laughed. "I'll have to check that out," he said.

"What about my clothes?" I asked. My eyes closed momentarily, then opened again.

"They're as real as your body," Albert told me. "Everybody-except certain natives, of course-has, in their mind, the conviction that clothes are indispensable. The conviction garbs them after death."

I closed my eyes again. "It's hard to comprehend it all," I said.

"You still think it's a dream?" he asked.

I opened my eyes and looked at him. "You know about that too?"

He smiled.

I looked around the room. "No, I can hardly believe that," I said. I looked at him sleepily. "What would you do if I did though?"

"There are ways," he said. "Close your eyes while we talk." He smiled as I hesitated. "Don't worry, you'll wake up again. And Katie will stay with you, won't you Kate?"

I looked at her. She wagged her tail, then lay down with a sigh beside the sofa. Albert rose to put a pillow underneath my head. "There," he said. "Close your eyes now."

I did. I actually yawned. "What ways?" I murmured. "Well-" I heard him sit back on his chair. "I might ask you to recall some relative who died, then show the relative to you. I might bring, to your recollection, the details of what happened just before your passing. In an extreme case, I might take you back to earth and show you your environment without you."

Despite the mounting grogginess I felt, I re-opened my eyes to look at him. "You said I couldn't go back," I said.

"You couldn't, alone."

"Then-"

"We could only go as observers, Chris," he said. "Which would only plunge you back into that terrible frustration. You couldn't help your wife, only watch her distress again."

I sighed unhappily. "Will she be all right, Albert?" I asked. "I'm so worried about her."

"I know you are," he said, "but it's out of your hands now, you can see that. Close your eyes."

I closed them again and, for an instant, thought I saw her lovely face in front of me: those childlike features, her dark brown eyes.

"When I met her, all I could see were those eyes," I thought aloud. "They seemed enormous to me."

"You met her on a beach, didn't you?" he asked.

"In Santa Monica, 1949," I said. "I'd come to California from Brooklyn. I was working at Douglas Aircraft from four to midnight. After I finished writing every morning, I went to the beach for an hour or two.

"I can still see the bathing suit she wore that day. It was pale blue, one piece. I watched her but didn't know how to speak to her; I'd never done that sort of thing before.

Finally, I resorted to the age-old 'Have you got the time?' "

I smiled, remembering her reaction.

"She fooled me by pointing to a building in Santa Monica with a clock on it. So I had to think of something else."

I stirred restlessly. "Albert, is there nothing I can do to help her?" I asked.

"Send her loving thoughts," he told me.

"That's all?"

"That's quite a lot, Chris," he said. "Thoughts are very real."

Chapter Seven

Look Where You Are

"Amen to that," I said. "I've seen my own in action." I must have looked grim when I said it for Albert's expression became one of sympathy. "It's a painful thing to learn, I know," he said, "that every thought we have takes on a form we must, eventually, confront."

"You went through the same thing?"

He nodded. "Everyone does."

"Your life flashed before you?" I asked. "From the end to the beginning?"

"Not as rapidly as yours did because I died of a lingering illness," he answered. "And yours was not as quick as that of, say, a drowning man. His removal from life would be so rapid that his subconscious memory would flood out its contents in a few seconds-every impression in his mind released almost simultaneously."

"What about the second time it happened?" I asked.

"The first time wasn't bad; I just observed. The second time, I relived each moment."

"Only in your mind," he said. "You didn't actually relive them."

"It seemed as though I did."

"Yes, it seems very real," he agreed. "And painful."

"More so than it did originally," he said, "because you had no physical body to dull the pain of your re-experienced life. It's a time when men and women come to know what they truly are. A time of purging."

I'd been looking at the ceiling as he spoke. At his final words, I turned to face him in surprise. "Is that what the Catholics mean by purgatory?"

"In essence." He nodded. "A period during which each soul is cleansed by a self-imposed recognition of past deeds and mis-deeds."

"Self imposed," I repeated. "There really is no outside judgment then?"

"What condemnation could possibly be more harsh than one's own when self-pretense is no longer possible?" he asked.

I turned my face away from him and looked out at the countryside. Its beauty seemed to make the memories of my shortcomings all the more acute; especially those concerning Ann. "Is anyone ever happy with what they re-experience?" I asked.

"I doubt it," he said. "No matter who they are, I'm sure they all find fault in themselves."

I reached down and began to stroke Katie's head. If it hadn't been for my memories, it would have been a lovely moment: the beautiful house, the exquisite landscape, Albert sitting across from me, Katie's warm head under my fingers.

There were the memories though.

"If only I'd done more for Ann," I said. "For my children, my family, my friends."

"That's true of almost everyone Chris," he said. "We all could have done more."

"And now it's too late."

"It isn't quite that bad," he said. "Part of what you're feeling IS a sense of incompletion because you didn't get to appraise your life as fully as you should have."

I looked at him again. "I'm not sure I understand that," I said.

"Your wife's grief and your concern for her kept you from it," he said. His smile was understanding. "Take comfort from what you're feeling, Chris. It means you really are concerned about her welfare. If you weren't, you wouldn't feel as you do."

"I wish I could do something about it," I told him.

Albert stood. "We'll talk about it later," he said. "Sleep now-and, until you know what you want to do, plan on staying here with me. There's plenty of room and you're more than welcome."

I thanked him as he came over and squeezed my shoulder.

"I'm going now," he said. "Katie will keep you company. Think of me when you wake and I'll be here."

Without another word, he turned and walked from the study. I stared at the doorway he'd gone through. Albert, I thought. Cousin Buddy. Dead since 1940. Heart attack. Living in this house. I couldn't seem to get it through my head that all of it was real.

I looked at Katie lying on the floor beside the sofa. "Kate, old Kate," I said. Her tail thumped twice. I remembered the blinding tears that afternoon we'd left her at the vet's. Now here she was alive looking at me once more with that bright expression.

I sighed and looked around the room. It, too, looked completely real. I smiled, recalling the French Provincial room in Kubrick's *2001*. Was I being held captive by some alien being? I had to chuckle at the thought.

I noticed then there was no mirror in the room and realized that I had not seen a mirror in the entire house. Shades of Dracula, I thought, amused again. Vampires here? I had to chuckle again. How did one locate the separation line between imagination and reality?

For instance, was I imagining it or was the light in the room really becoming more subdued?

* * * *

Ann and I were in Sequoia National Forest. Hand in hand, we moved beneath the giant redwood trees. I could feel her fingers linked with mine, hear the crunching of our shoes across the carpet of dry needles on the ground, smell the warm, aromatic odor of the tree bark. We didn't speak. We walked side by side, surrounded by the beauty of nature, taking a stroll before dinner.

We'd walked about twenty minutes before we reached a fallen tree and sat on it. Ann released a weary sigh. I put an arm around her and she leaned against me. "Tired?" I asked.

"A little." She smiled. "I'll be fine."

It had been a strenuous if pleasant experience for us.

We'd pulled a rental trailer up the steep hill to Sequoia, our Rambler wagon overheating twice. We'd set up a tent with six cots inside, stored all our supplies in a wooden chest so the bears couldn't get them. We had a Coleman lantern but not a stove so had to maintain a fire under the grate provided by the campground. Most difficult, we had to heat washing water once each day for Ian's diapers; he was only one and a half at the time. The camp looked like a laundry, diapers and baby clothes hanging on lines in all directions.

"We'd better not leave them too long," Ann said after we'd rested a while. The woman in the campsite next to us had offered to keep an eye on the children but we didn't want to over-do the imposition since Louise, the oldest, was only 9, Richard 61/2, Marie not quite 4, and even our "watch dog," Katie, less than a year old.

"We'll go back soon," I said. I kissed her slightly damp temple and squeezed her. "Just rest a few more minutes." I smiled at her. "It's pretty here, isn't it?"

"Beautiful." She nodded. "I sleep here better than at home."

"I know you do." Ann's nervous breakdown had come two years earlier; she'd been in analysis a year and a half now. This was the first major trip we'd made since her breakdown; at the insistence of her analyst.

"How's your stomach doing?" I asked.

"Oh, it's-better." She answered unconvincingly. She'd had stomach problems ever since I'd met her; how incredibly unaware I'd been not to realize it meant something serious. Since her breakdown, the condition had improved but still disturbed her. As her analyst had told her: the deeper buried the distress, the further into the body it went. The digestive system was about as far as it could go to hide.

"Maybe we can buy a camper one of these days," I said; she'd suggested it that morning. "It would make preparing meals a lot easier. Make the whole experience easier."

"I know, but they're so expensive," she said. "And I'm costing so much already."

"I should start making more now that I'm writing for television," I told her.

She squeezed my hand. "I know you will." She lifted the hand to her lips and kissed it. "The tent is fine," she said. "I don't mind it at all."

She sighed and looked up at the redwood foliage high above, bars of sunlight slanting through it. "I could stay here forever," she murmured.

"You could be a forest ranger," I said.

"I wanted to be one," she told me. "When I was a little girl."

"Did you? " The idea made me smile. Ranger Ann.

"It seemed like a wonderful way to escape," she said.

Poor love. I held her tightly against myself. She'd had so much to escape from too.

"Well." She stood. "We'd better mosey on back, Chief."

"Right." I nodded, standing. "The path curves around. We don't have to go back the same way."

"Good." She smiled and took my hand. "Here we go then."

We started to walk again. "Are you glad you came?" she asked.

"Yeah; it's beautiful here," I said. I'd been dubious about taking four young children camping; but then I'd never gone camping as a child so I had nothing to judge by. "I think it's working out great," I said. I didn't know it then but Ann's desire to camp—notwithstanding her anxiety about trying anything new at a time of such mental stress was to open up a world of lovely experience not only for me but for the children as well.

Continuing on, we reached a spot where the path divided.

At the head of the right path was a sign that warned hikers not to go that way.

Ann looked at me with her "wicked little girl" expression.

"Let's go that way," she said, drawing me toward the path on the right.

"But it says not to go that way," I told her. Playing the game.

"C'mon," she urged.

"You want a dying redwood tree to land on our heads?" I asked.

"We'll run if one starts to fall," she said.

"Oh ... " I clucked and shook my head. "Miz Annie, you is-bad," I said, doing my Hattie McDaniel from *Gone With The Wind*.

"Uh-huh." She nodded in agreement, pulling me toward the right hand path.

"You're a poor excuse for a forest ranger," I told her.

Moments later, we reached a rock slope which declined to the edge of a cliff some fifteen yards away. "See?" I told her, trying not to smile.

"Okay, we'll go back now," she said. She repressed a smile. "At least we know why we weren't supposed to come here."

I gazed at her with mock severity. "You're always taking me where I'm not supposed to go," I said.

She nodded in pleased agreement. "That's my job; to bring adventure into your life."

We started across the top of the slope, heading back toward the other path. The surface of the rock was slick with a layer of dry needles so we walked in single file, me behind.

Ann had only gone a few yards when she lost her footing and fell on her left side. I started toward her and slipped myself, tried to get up but couldn't. I began to laugh.

"Chris. "

Her urgent tone made me look toward her quickly. She was starting to slide down the decline, each movement she made to stop herself making her slide further.

"Don't move," I said. My heart was pounding suddenly.

"Spread your arms and legs out wide."

"Chris ... " Her voice trembled as she tried to do what I said and slipped even further. "Oh, my God," she murmured, frightenedly.

"Don't move at all," I told her.

She did as I said and her backward slide was almost checked. I struggled clumsily to my feet. I couldn't reach her with my hand. And if I tried to crawl where she was, both of us would slide toward the edge.

I slipped and fell to one knee, hissing at the pain. Then, carefully, I crawled to the top of the slope, speaking as I Went. "Don't move now, just don't move," I said. "It's going to be all right. Don't be afraid now."

Suddenly, it all came back. This had already happened. I felt a rush of intense relief. I'd find a fallen branch, extend it down to her and pull her to safety. I'd hold her in my arms and kiss her and she'd be-

"Chris!"

Her cry made me whirl. Aghast, I watched her sliding toward the edge. Forgetting everything in panic, I dived down the slope, skidding toward her, looking at her dread-whitened face as she slid backward. "Chris, save me," she pleaded. "Save me. Please. Chris!"

I cried out in horror as she disappeared across the edge and vanished from sight. Her shriek was terrible. "Ann!" I screamed.

I jolted awake, my heartbeat racing; sat up quickly and looked around.

Katie was standing beside the sofa, wagging her tail and looking at me in a way which I could only interpret as concerned. I put my hand on her head. "Okay, okay," I murmured. "A dream. I had a dream."

Somehow, I felt she understood what I was saying.

I put my right palm to my chest and felt the heavy pulsing of my heart. Why had I had that dream? I wondered. And why had it ended so differently from what had really happened? The question harrowed me and I sat up, looking around, then called Albert's name.

I started with surprise as instantly-and, Robert, I mean instantly-he walked into the room. He smiled at my reaction, then, looking closer, saw I was disturbed and asked what was wrong.

I told him about the dream and asked what it meant. "It was probably some symbolic 'leftover,' " he said.

"I hope I don't have any more," I told him, shuddering.

"They'll pass," he reassured me.

Remembering Katie standing by me when I woke, I mentioned it to Albert. "I have the strangest impression that she understands what I say and feel," I said.

"There's understanding there," he replied, bending over to stroke her head. "Isn't there, Katie?"

She wagged her tail, looking into his eyes.

I forced a smile. "When you said think of you and you'd be here, you weren't kidding."

He smiled as he straightened up. "That's how it is here," he told me. "When you want to see someone, you have only to think about them and they're with you. If they wish to be, of course; as I wished to be with you. We always did have a kinship. Even though we were years apart, we were on the same wave length, so to speak."

I blinked in startlement. "Say that again?" I asked.

He did and I'm sure my mouth fell open. "Your lips aren't moving, " I said.

He laughed at my expression.

"How come I didn't notice that before?"

"I wasn't doing it before," he told me. Lips unmoving.

I stared at him, dumbfounded. "How can I hear your voice when you're not talking?" I asked.

"The same way I hear yours."

"My lips aren't moving either?"

"We're conversing with our minds," he answered.

"That's incredible," I said. I thought I said.

"Actually, to speak aloud is rather difficult here," he told me. "But most newcomers don't realize, for quite a while, that they aren't using their voices."

"Incredible," I repeated.

"Yet how efficient," he said. "Language is more a barrier to understanding than an aid. Also, we're able, through thought, to communicate in any language without the need of an interpreter. Moreover, we're not confined to words and sentences. Communication can be enhanced by flashes of pure thought.

"Now," he continued, "I've been wearing this outfit so you wouldn't be taken back by my appearance. If you don't object, I'll return to my natural garb."

I had no idea what he meant. "All right?" he asked.

"Sure," I said. "I don't know what-"

It had to have happened while I blinked. Albert wasn't wearing the white shirt and trousers any longer. Instead, he wore a robe the color of which matched the radiation around him. It was full-length, hanging in graceful folds, a gold sash at its waist. I noted that his feet were bare.

"There," he said. "I feel more comfortable."

I stared at him-a little impolitely, I'm afraid. "Do I have to wear one too?" I asked.

"Not at all," he said. I don't know what my expression was but it obviously amused him. "The choice is yours. Whatever you prefer."

I looked down at myself. It was a little odd, I had to admit, to see the same clothes I'd been wearing the night of the accident. Still, I couldn't see myself in a robe. It seemed a bit too "spiritual" for me.

"And now," Albert said, "perhaps you'd like to take a more extensive look at where you are."

Chapter Eight

Your Problems Lie Herein

An odd thing happened as we left the house. It seemed odd to me at any rate. Albert was unsurprised by it. Even Katie didn't react as I would have expected.

A pearl-gray bird swooped down and landed on Albert's left shoulder, causing me to start.

Albert's words startled me even more. "It's one your wife took care of," he informed me. "I've been holding it for her."

"One my wife took care of?" I asked, glancing at Katie. In life, she'd have launched into a frenzy of barking at the sight. Here, she was completely placid.

Albert explained to me that Ann had come to have a permanent rapport with the injured birds she had nursed back to health. All the birds she'd saved-and there'd been dozens-were here in Summerland, waiting for her. Albert even knew that at one time local children had called Ann The Bird Lady of Hidden Hills.

I could only shake my head. "Incredible," I said.

He smiled. "Oh, you'll see things far more incredible," he told me. He stroked the bird with one finger. "And how are you?" he asked

I had to laugh as the bird fluffed its wings and chirped.

"You're not going to tell me it answered," I said.

"In his own way," Albert told me. "Just as with Katie. Say hello to him."

I felt a little awkward about it but did as he said. The bird hopped instantly onto my right shoulder and it did seem, Robert, as though our minds exchanged something. I don't know how to tell you what that something was except to say that it was charming.

Now the bird flew off and Katie startled me again by barking once, as though saying goodbye to it. Incredible, I thought as we started walking away from the house.

"I noticed you have no mirrors," I said.

"They serve no purpose," he told me.

"Because they're mostly for vanity?" I questioned.

"More than that," he answered. "Those who've marred their appearance in any way by their actions in life aren't forced to witness that marring. If they were, they'd become self-conscious and be unable to concentrate on improving themselves."

I wondered what my own appearance was; knowing that Albert wouldn't tell me if it was unpleasant in any way.

I tried not to think about that as we started up a grassy slope, Katie running on ahead. How trim she looks, I thought with pleasure. Ann would be so happy to see her. They'd spent much time together. Literally, Ann couldn't leave the house without her. We used to laugh at Katie's unfailing awareness of Ann's intention to go out. It seemed, at times, positively psychic.

I put that from my mind too, breathing deeply of the cool, fresh air. The temperature seemed ideal to me.

"Is that why it's called Summerland?" I asked, experimenting to see if Albert knew what I was asking.

He did, replying, "Partially. But, also, because it can reflect each person's concept of perfect happiness."

"If Ann were here with me, it would be perfect," I said, unable to keep her from my thoughts.

"She will be, Chris."

"Is there water here?" I asked, abruptly. "Boats? That's Ann's idea of heaven."

"There are both," he said.

I looked up at the sky. "Does it ever get dark?"

"Not totally," he said. "We do have twilight though."

"Was it my imagination or did the light in your study dim as I was going to sleep?"

"It dimmed," he said. "Corresponding to your need for rest. "

"Isn't it an inconvenience not to have days and nights? How do you schedule yourself?"

"By activities," he answered. "Isn't that, essentially, the way people in life do it? A time to work, a time to eat, a time to relax, a time to sleep? We do the same-except, of course, that we don't have to eat or sleep."

"I hope my need for sleep disappears soon," I said. "I don't relish the idea of more dreams like the one I had."

"The need will go," he said.

I looked around and had to make a sound of incredulity.

"I suppose I'll get used to all this," I said. "It's awfully hard to believe though."

"I can't describe how long it took me to accept it," Albert told me. "Mostly, I couldn't understand how it was possible for me to be admitted to a place I'd always been positive didn't exist."

"You didn't believe in it either," I said. It made me feel better to hear that.

"Very few people do," he replied. "They may give lip service to the notion. They may even want to believe it. But they rarely do."

I stopped and leaned over to remove my shoes and socks. Picking them up, I carried them as we started off again. The grass felt warm and soft beneath my feet.

"You don't have to carry them," Albert said.

"I wouldn't want to litter a place as beautiful as this." He laughed. "You won't," he said. "They'll vanish presently."

"Into the matrix?"

"Right."

I stopped to put down the shoes and socks, then strolled on with Albert; Katie was beside us now, moving easily. Albert noticed my backward glance and smiled. "It takes a while," he said.

Moments later, we reached the summit of the slope and, stopping, looked across the countryside. The closest sight I can compare it to is England-or, perhaps, New England-in the early summer; rich green meadows, thick woods, colorful patches of flowers and sparkling brooks-all domed by a deep blue sky with snowy clouds. No place on earth could compare to this, however.

Standing there, I drew in deep breaths of the air. I felt completely sound, Robert. Not only were the pains from the accident gone but there was no longer a trace of aching in my neck and lower back; you know the problems I had with my spine. "I feel so good," I said.

"You've accepted where you are then," Albert told me.

I didn't understand that and asked what he meant.

"Many people arrive with the physical convictions they possessed at death," he said. "They believe they're sick and continue to be so until they realize they're in a place where sickness can't exist on its own. Only then are they whole. The mind is all; remember that."

"Speaking of which," I told him, "I seem to be able to think better too."

"Because you're not encumbered by a physical brain any longer."

In looking around, I'd caught sight of an orchard of what looked like plum trees. I decided that they couldn't be but they aroused a question in my mind. "You said it isn't necessary, here, to eat," I said. "Does that mean you're never thirsty either?"

"We get our nourishment directly from the atmosphere," he answered. "The light, the air, the colors, the plants."

"We have no stomachs then," I said. "No digestive organs."

"No need for them," he responded. "On earth our bodies eliminated everything from what we ate but the energy of sunlight originally imparted to the food. Here, we ingest that energy directly."

"What about reproductive organs?"

"You still have them because you expect to have them. In time, when you understand their lack of purpose, they'll disappear?"

"That's weird," I said.

He shook his head, a sad smile on his lips. "Consider those whose lives depended on those organs," he said. "Who, even after death, retain the need and use of them because they can't conceive of existence without them. They're never satisfied, of course, never fulfilled; it's only an illusion. But they can't break free of it and it impedes their progress endlessly. That's weird, Chris."

"I can understand that," I conceded. "Still, part of my relationship with Ann was physical."

"And there are people here, who love each other, who have sexual relations," he said, startling me again. "The mind is capable of anything, always remember that. In time, of course, these people usually realize that physical contact isn't as integral here as it was in life.

"For that matter," he continued, "we don't have to use our bodies at all; we only possess them because they're familiar to us. If we chose, we could perform any function with our minds alone."

"No hunger," I said. "No thirst. No fatigue. No pain."

I made a sound of bemusement. "No problems," I concluded.

"I wouldn't say that," Albert told me. "Except for the lack of need for what you've mentioned-and the absence of need to earn a living-everything is still the same. Your problems are unchanged. You still have to solve them."

His words made me think of Ann. It was disturbing to believe that, after all the hardships she'd suffered in life, there'd be no respite for her here. That seemed unjust.

"There's help, here, as well, remember," Albert said, picking up my thought again. "A good deal more perceptive too."

"I just wish I could let her know all this," I told him. "I can't get rid of this sense of apprehension about her."

"You're still picking up her distress," he replied. "You should let go."

"Then I'd lose contact completely," I said.

"It isn't contact," he told me. "Ann isn't aware of it-and it only holds you back. You're here now, Chris. Your problems lie herein."

Chapter Nine

The Power of Mind

I knew he was right and, in spite of continuing anxiety, tried to put it from my mind. "Is walking your only means of transportation here?" I asked to change the subject.

"By no means," Albert said. "Each of us possesses our own personal method of rapid transit."

"What's that?"

"Since there are no space limitations," he answered, "travel can be instantaneous. You saw how I came to you when you called my name. I did it by thinking of my house."

"Does everyone travel that way?" I asked in surprise.

"Those who wish to," he said, "and can conceive of it."

"I don't follow you."

"Everything is mental, Chris," he told me. "Never forget that. Those who believe that transportation is confined to cars and bicycles will travel that way. Those who feel that walking is the only way to get around will walk. There's a vast difference, here, you see, between what people think is necessary and what really is. If you look around enough, you'll find vehicles, greenhouses, stores, factories, et cetera. None of which are needed, yet all of which exist because someone believes they are needed."

"Can you teach me to travel by thought?" I asked.

"Certainly. It's just a matter of imagination. Visualize yourself ten yards ahead of where you are."

"That's all?"

He nodded. "Try it."

I closed my eyes and did. I sensed a feeling of vibration; then, abruptly, felt myself glide forward in a leaning posture. Startled, I opened my eyes and looked around. Albert was about six feet behind me, Katie running to my side, tail wagging.

"What happened?" I asked.

"You stopped yourself," he said. "Try again. You don't have to close your eyes."

"It wasn't instantaneous," I said. "I felt myself moving."

"That's because it's new to you," he told me. "After you get used to it, it will be instantaneous. Try again."

I looked at a spot beneath a birch tree some twenty yards away and visualized myself standing there.

The movement was so rapid, I couldn't follow it. I cried out in surprise as I tumbled to the ground. There was no pain. I looked around to see Katie running toward me, barking.

Albert was beside me before she was; I didn't see how he did it. "You're trying too hard," he said with a laugh.

My smile was sheepish. "Well, at least it didn't hurt," I said.

"It will never hurt," he replied. "Our bodies are impervious to injury."

I got on my knees and patted Katie as she reached me.

"Does it frighten her?" I asked.

"No, no, she knows what's happening."

I stood up, thinking how Ann would enjoy it. Imagining the look on her face the first time she tried it. She always loved new, exciting things; loved to share them with me.

Before my sense of apprehension could return, I chose a hilltop several hundred yards away and visualized myself standing there.

A feeling of vibration again; I should say altering vibration. I blinked and I was there.

No, I wasn't. I looked around in confusion. Albert and Katie were nowhere in sight. What had I done wrong now?

A flash of light appeared in front of me, then Albert's voice said, "You went too far."

I looked around for him. In between the blinking of my eyes, he was in front of me, holding Katie in his arms.

"What was that flash of light?" I asked as he set her down.

"My thought," he said. "They can be transported too."

"Can I send my thoughts to Ann then?" I asked quickly.

"If she were receptive to them, she might get something," he answered. "As it is, sending thoughts to her would be extremely difficult if not impossible."

Again, I willed away the deep uneasiness which thoughts of Ann produced in me. I had to have faith in Albert's words. "Could I travel to England by thought?" I said, asking the first question to occur to me. "I mean England here, of course; I presume there is one."

"There is indeed," he said. "And you could travel there because you did in life, and know what to visualize."

"Where exactly are we?" I asked.

"In a counterpart of the United States," he told me. "One naturally gravitates to the wave length of his own country and people. Not that you couldn't live where you chose. As long as you were comfortable there."

"There's an equivalent, here, to every country on earth then?"

"At this level," Albert answered. "In higher realms, national consciousness ceases to exist."

"Higher realms?" I was confused again.

"My father's house has many mansions, Chris," he said. "For instance, you'll find, in the hereafter, the particular heaven of each theology."

"Which is right then?" I asked, completely baffled now.

"All of them," he said, "and none. Buddhist, Hindu, Moslem, Christian, Jew-each has an after-life experience which reflects his own beliefs. The Viking had his Valhalla, the American Indian his Happy Hunting Ground, the zealot his City of Gold. All are real. Each is a portion of the overall reality.

"You'll even find, here, those who claim that survival is nonsense," he said. "They bang their nonmaterial tables with their nonmaterial fists and sneer at any suggestion of a life beyond matter. It's the ultimate irony of delusion.

"Remember this," he finished. "For everything in life, there's a counterpart in after-life. This includes the most beautiful as well as the ugliest of phenomena."

I felt a chilling sensation as he said that; I didn't know why and, somehow, didn't want to know. Hastily, I changed the subject. "I feel awkward in this outfit now," I said. I spoke impulsively but, having done so, realized that I had spoken the truth.

Albert sounded concerned as he asked, "I haven't made you feel that way, have I?"

"Not at all. I just-" I shrugged. "Well, how do I change?"

"The way you changed locations."

"With imagination; mind?"

He nodded. "Always with mind, Chris. That can't be emphasized enough."

"Right." I closed my eyes and visualized myself wearing a robe like Albert's. Instantly, I felt that "altering" sensation again, this time something like a thousand butterflies fluttering around me for an instant. The description is inexact but I can do no better.

"Is it done?" I asked.

"Look," he told me.

I opened my eyes and looked down.

I had to laugh. I'd often worn a long, velour caftan around the house but it had been nothing like what I wore at that moment. I felt somewhat guilty to be so amused but couldn't help myself.

"It's all right," Albert told me, smiling. "A lot of people laugh the first time they see their robes."

"It's not like yours," I said. Mine was white, without a sash.

"It will alter in time as you do," he told me.

"How is it made?"

"By the imposition of mental imagery on the ideoplastic medium of your aura."

"Come again?"

He chuckled. "Let's just say that, while on earth, clothes may make the man, here the process is definitely reversed. The atmosphere around us is malleable. It, literally, reproduces the image of any sustained thought. It's like a mold waiting for imprints. Except for our bodies, no form is stable unless concentrated thought makes it so."

I could only shake my head again. "Incredible."

"Not really, Chris," he said. "Extremely credible, in fact. On earth, before anything is created materially, it has to be created mentally, doesn't it? When matter is put aside, all creation becomes exclusively mental, that's all. You'll come, in time, to adopt the power of mind."

Chapter Ten

Memory Still Haunts

As we continued on, Katie walking by my side, I began to realize that Albert's robe and sash connoted some advanced condition on his part, mine my "beginner's" status.

He knew my thoughts again. "It all depends on what you make of yourself," he said. "What work you do."

"Work?" I asked.

He chuckled. "Surprised?"

I had no answer. "I guess I never thought about it."

"Most people haven't," he said. "Or, if they have, they've visualized the hereafter as some sort of eternal Sunday. Nothing could be further from the truth. There's more work here than on earth. However-" He held up a finger as I started to speak. "-work that's undertaken freely, for the joy of doing it."

"What kind of work should I do?" I asked.

"That's up to you," he said. "Since there's no need to earn a living, it can be what pleases you most."

"Well, I've always wanted to write something more useful than scripts," I told him. "Do it then."

"I doubt if I'll be able to concentrate until I know that Ann is all right."

"You've got to leave that be, Chris," he said. "It's beyond your reach. Plan on writing."

"What would be the point of it?" I asked. "For instance, if a scientist, here, wrote a book on some revolutionary discovery, what good would it do? No one would need it here."

"They would on earth," he said.

I didn't understand that until he explained that no one on earth develops anything revolutionary alone; all vital knowledge emanates from Summerland-transmitted in such a way that more than one person can receive it.

When I asked him what he meant by "transmitted" he said mental transmission-although scientists here are constantly attempting to devise a system whereby the earth level may be contacted directly.

"You mean like radio?" I asked.

"Something like that."

The concept was so incredible to me that I had to think about it before speaking again.

"So when do I start working?" I finally asked. What I had in mind, of course, was losing myself so completely in some endeavor that time would pass quickly and Ann and I would be together again.

Albert laughed. "Well, give yourself a little time," he said. "You just arrived. You have to learn the ground rules first."

I had to smile and Albert laughed again. "Not the best phrase I could have chosen," he said. He patted me on the shoulder. "I'm glad you're willing to work. Too many people come here only wanting to take things easy. Since there are no needs, this can easily be accomplished. It soon becomes monotonous though. One can even be bored here."

He explained that all kinds of jobs were available with obvious exceptions. There's no need for a Health Department or a Sanitation Department, Fire or Police Department, nor for food or clothing industries, transportation systems, doctors, lawyers, realtors. "Least of all," he added, smiling, "morticians."

"What about people who worked in those professions?"

"They work at something else." His smile faded. "Or some of them continue doing the same thing. Not here, of course."

That chilling sensation again; the hint of "another place."

I didn't want to know about it. Once more, I was conscious of my own effort to change the subject-though equally unconscious of why I felt so strongly about it. "You said you'd explain the third sphere," I told him.

"All right." He nodded. "I'm no expert, mind you, but-" He explained that earth is surrounded by concentric spheres of existence which vary in width and density, Summerland being the third. I asked how many there are altogether and he answered that he wasn't sure but had heard there are seven-the bottom one so rudimental that it actually blends with earth.

"Is that where I was?" I asked. As he nodded, I went on.

"Until I started upward."

"It's a mistake to use the words 'up' and 'down' to describe these spheres," he said. "It's not that simple. Our world is set apart from earth only by a distance of vibration. In actuality, all existence coincides."

"Then Ann is really close by," I said.

"In a sense," he replied.

"Still, is she conscious of the television waves surrounding her?"

"She is if she turns on a receiver."

"But she's not a receiver herself," he said.

I was going to ask if we could help her find a receiver when I remembered the experience with Perry. That was no answer, I decided. I couldn't put her through that again.

I looked around the flowering meadow we were crossing. It reminded me of one I saw in England in 1957; I was working on a script there, you recall. I spent a weekend at the producer's cottage and, on Sunday morning, very early, looked across this lovely meadow from the window of my room. I remembered the intense green silence of it-which brought to recollection all the lovely places I had seen in life, the lovely moments I'd experienced. Was that another reason why I'd fought so hard to keep from dying? I wondered.

"You should have seen me struggle," Albert said, picking up my thought once more; it seemed he could do it at will. "It took me nearly six hours to let go."

"Why?"

"Mostly because I was convinced there was no more to existence," he said.

I recalled that, as I died, I'd become conscious of what was happening in the next room. "Who was that old woman?" I asked, making use, again, of his awareness of my thoughts.

"No one you knew," he answered. "As your physical senses faded, your psychic senses grew acute and you achieved a brief state of clairvoyance."

Memories of the death experience started flooding back to me. I asked him what the tingling sensation had been and he answered that it had been my etheric double disengaging itself from the nerve ends of my physical body. I didn't know what he meant by my etheric double but let it go for then, because of the other questions I wanted to ask.

Those noises like the breaking of threads, for instance. Nerve ends tearing loose, he answered; starting from my feet and working upward to my brain.

The silver cord connecting me to my body as I floated above it? A cable connecting the physical body to the etheric double. An enormous number of nerve ends joined at the base of the brain, interwoven through the matter of the brain. Filaments gathered into an etheric "umbilical" cord attached to the crown of the head.

The sack of colors drawn up by the cord? My etheric double being removed. The origin of the word "body" is the Anglo-Saxon "bodig" meaning abode. Which is what the physical body is, you see, Robert. A transient dwelling for the real self.

"But what happened after my death?"

"You were earthbound," he said. "That state should have ended in approximately three days."

"How long did it last?"

"In earth terms? Hard to say," he answered. "Weeks, at least. Maybe longer."

"It seemed endless," I remembered, shuddering.

"I don't wonder," he told me. "The agony of being earthbound can be indescribable. I'm sure the memory still haunts."

Chapter Eleven

Memories Somehow Shadowed

"Why did everything look so vague?" I asked, "and feel so ... wet; that's the only word I can think of to describe it."

I'd been in the densest part of the earth's aura he told me, an aqueous region which was the source of myths about the waters of Lethe, the River Styx.

Why hadn't I been able to see anything beyond ten feet after I died? Because I'd seen no further than that when I was dying and carried that last impression with me.

Why did I feel sluggish and stupid, unable to think clearly? Because two-thirds of my consciousness had been inoperative, my mind still enveloped by etheric matter which had been part of my physical brain. Accordingly, my responses had been confined to the instinctive and repetitive reactions of that matter. I'd felt dull-witted, miserable, lonely, fearful.

"And exhausted," I said. "I kept wanting to sleep but I couldn't. "

"You were trying to reach your second death," Albert told me.

Once more, I was startled. "Second death?"

Achieved by sleeping and permitting the mind to re-experience its life on earth, he told me. I'd been kept from that sleep by Ann's extreme grief and my desire to comfort her. Instead of purging myself in that "approximately three days" I'd been held captive in a "sleepwalking" state.

The fact is, Robert, that a person newly deceased is in exactly the frame of mind he was at the moment of death, accessible to influences from the earth plane. This condition fades in sleep but, in my case, memories were renewed and kept vivid by my twilight state. This was complicated further by Perry's influence.

"I know Richard only meant to help," I said.

"Of course he did," Albert agreed. "He wanted to convince your wife that you'd survived; an act of love on his part. But, in doing so, he was, without knowing it, instrumental in delaying further your second death."

"I still don't know what you mean by my second death," I told him.

"The shedding of your etheric double," he said. "Leaving the shell of it behind so your spirit-or astral-body could move on."

"Is that what I saw at the seance?" I asked in surprise, "my etheric double?"

"Yes, you'd discarded it by then."

"It was like a corpse," I said, with disgust.

"It was a corpse," he told me. "The corpse of your etheric double."

"But it spoke," I said. "It answered questions."

"Only as a zombie might." he explained. "Its essence was gone. The astral shell as it's called is no more than an aggregate of dying molecules. It has no genuine life or intelligence. The young man didn't know it but it was his own psychic power which animated the shell, his own mind which fed it answers."

"Like a puppet," I said, recalling what I'd thought at the time.

"Exactly," Albert nodded.

"That's why Perry couldn't see me at the seance then."

"You were beyond his psychic sight."

"Poor Ann," I said. The memory was painful. "It was horrible for her."

"And could have done her harm if she'd pursued it," Albert added. "Contact with nonphysical states of being can have a peculiar effect on the living."

"If only she knew all this," I said, unhappily. "If only everyone on earth knew it," he replied.

The attitudes of people toward those who've died is vital, you see, Robert. Since the consciousness of the deceased is so vulnerable to impressions, the emotions of those left behind can have a powerful effect on it. Intense sorrow creates a vibration which actually causes pain to the departed, holding them back from progression. Actually, it's unfortunate that people mourn the dead, prolonging the adjustment to the hereafter. The deceased need time to reach their second death. The funeral ceremony was meant to be a medium of peaceful release, not a ritual of grief.

Did you know, Robert, that, in extreme unction, the seven centers of the body-covering the vital organs-are anointed to assist the dying person to withdraw vitality from those organs in preparation for complete withdrawal through the silver cord? And absolution of the dead was established to make certain that the silver cord is severed and all etheric matter withdrawn from the body.

There are so many things which can be done to make the death process easier. Pressures on certain nerve centers. Certain tones sounded. Certain lights utilized. Certain mantras chanted softly, certain incenses burned. All designed to help the dying person concentrate his senses for departure.

Most importantly, remains should always be cremated three days following death.

I told Albert about my body in the cemetery; of that hideous moment in which I'd seen it.

"She didn't want your body burned," he said, "she loves you so, she wants you down there so she can visit and talk to you. It's understandable-but regrettable since it isn't you at all."

"What does cremation do that burial doesn't?"

Frees the departed from a tie which has a tendency to keep it near the physical body, he answered. Also, in extreme cases, where there's difficulty in breaking the cord even after death, the fire severs it immediately. And, after the astral shell has been discarded rather than it decaying slowly along with the body above which it hovers, cremation disposes of it quickly.

"This tie you mention," I said. "Is that what made me feel compelled to see my body?"

He nodded. "People can't forget their bodies easily. They keep wanting to see the thing they once believed to be themselves. That desire can become an obsession. That's why cremation is important."

I wondered, as he spoke, why I was feeling more and more upset. Why I kept associating everything he said with my troubled thoughts about Ann. What was I afraid of? Albert had reassured me constantly that we would be together again. Why couldn't I accept that?

I thought again about my frightening dream. Albert had called it a "symbolic leftover." That made sense but still it disturbed me. Every thought regarding Ann disturbed me now, even the happy memories, somehow, shadowed.

Chapter Twelve

Losing Ann Again

Unexpectedly, Albert said: "Chris, I have to leave you for awhile. There's some work I must do."

I felt embarrassed. "I'm sorry," I told him. "It never crossed my mind that I was taking up time needed elsewhere. "

"Not at all." He patted my back. "I'll send someone to continue walking with you. And, while you're waiting-you asked about water-take my hand."

I did as he said. "Close your eyes," he told me, picking up Katie.

The instant I did, I felt a sense of rapid motion. It was over so quickly it might have been imagined.

"You can open them now," Albert said.

I did and caught my breath. We were standing on the shore of a magnificent, forest-rimmed lake. I looked in wonder at the huge expanse of it, its surface calm except for tiny wavelets, the water crystal clear, each ripple refracting light into spectrum colors.

"I've never seen a lake so beautiful," I said.

"I thought you'd like it," he said, putting down Katie.

"I'll see you later at my house." He gripped my arm. "Be at peace," he told me.

I blinked and he was gone. Like that. No flash of light, no indication of departure. One instant, he was there, the next, he wasn't. I glanced down at Katie. She didn't seem at all surprised.

I turned to gaze at the lake. "It reminds me of Lake Arrowhead," I said to Katie. "You remember the condominium we had up there?" She wagged her tail. "It was nice but nothing like this." There, browning foliage was always visible among the green, debris marred the shoreline and, at times, a mist of smog hovered above the surface of the lake.

This lake was perfection and the forest and air, perfection.

Ann would love this, I thought.

It disturbed me that, surrounded by such beauty, I should still be conscious of distress regarding her. Why was I unable to let go of it? Albert had told me repeatedly to do so. Why, then, did this anxiety persist?

I sat beside Katie and stroked her head. "What's wrong with me, Kate?" I asked.

We looked into each other's eyes. She did understand; I could doubt it no longer. I almost seemed to sense a wave of understanding sympathy from her.

She lay beside me and I tried to will distress from my mind by thinking of the times we had spent at Lake Arrowhead. Weekends during the year and, for as long as a month at a time during summers, we'd go there with the children. I was doing well in television at the time and, in addition to the condominium, we owned a speedboat, keeping it stored at the North Shore Marina.

Many a summer day was spent on the lake. In the morning, after breakfast, we'd make our lunches, put on bathing suits and drive to the Marina, Katie with us. We'd speed to a favorite cove of ours at the south end of the lake where the children-Richard and Marie, Louise when she and her husband visited-would put on water skis and be towed. Ian was too young at the time so we'd bought him a ski sled which he'd christened Captain Zip. Ann liked to ride it too because she had trouble skiing.

I thought about the sight of Ann lying on that sled, laughing breathlessly as she bounced across the dark, blue waters of the lake. I thought about Ian riding it, grinning with delight, especially when he was able to stand up on it.

For lunch, we'd anchor in the cove and eat our sandwiches and chips and cold soda from the ice chest. The sun would be warm on our backs and I'd take deep, unspoken pleasure watching Ann and our lovely, tanned children as we ate and talked and laughed together.

Happy memories weren't helping. They made me feel more melancholy knowing those times could never be recaptured. I felt an aching loneliness inside me. I missed Ann so; missed the children so. Why hadn't I told them, more often, how I loved them? If only we could share this lovely place. If only Ann and I-

I shook myself impatiently. Here I was in heaven, mind you-heaven!-and still brooding. I'd survived death; all my family would survive it. We would, all of us, be together again. What was the matter with me?

"Come on, Kate," I said, standing quickly. "Let's take a walk." More and more, I was beginning to appreciate what Albert had said about the mind being all.

As we began to hike along the shore, I wondered, momentarily, if Albert had meant for me to stay where he'd brought me so this "someone" could locate me. Then, I realized that whoever the someone was, he'd find me by thinking of me.

There was a beach before us and we started to walk along it. The sand was soft underfoot, no stones or pebbles anywhere in sight.

Stopping, I knelt and picked up a handful of the sand. It was without grit, firm in consistency yet soft to the touch' while undeniably cohesive, it felt like powder. I let some run between my fingers and observed the delicately multicolored granules as they fell. I lifted my hand and looked at them more closely. In form and color, they resembled miniature jewels.

I let the rest fall to the beach and stood. The sand didn't stick to my palm or knee as it would have on earth.

Again, I had to shake my head in wonderment. Sand. A beach. Deep forest encompassing a lake. Blue sky overhead.

"And people doubt there's afterlife," I said to Katie. "I did myself. Incredible."

I was to say and think that last word many times again; and not only with pleasure.

Moving to the edge of the lake, I stared at it closely, watching the delicate purl of surf. The water looked cold. Remembering the chill of Lake Arrowhead, I put my toes in gingerly.

I sighed as I felt the water. It was barely cool, emitting pleasant vibrations of energy. I looked down at Katie. She was standing in the water next to me. I had to smile. She'd never gone in water in her life; she always hated it. Here, she seemed completely content.

I walked into the lake until the level reached my shins; the bottom as smooth as the beach. Leaning over, I put my hand into the water and felt the energy flowing up my arm. "Feels good, huh, Kate?" I said.

She looked at me, wagging her tail and, once more, I felt a surge of happiness seeing her look as she had in her prime.

I straightened up, a palmful of water cupped in my hand.

It shimmered with a delicate glow and I could feel its energy pulsing into my fingertips. As before, when it ran off my skin, it left no dampness.

Wondering if it would do the same with my robe I submerged until the water was up to my waist. Katie didn't follow now but sat on the beach, watching me. I didn't get the impression she was afraid to follow, simply that she chose to wait.

Now I was immersed in energy and kept walking until the water was up to my neck. It felt like a cloak around me, vibrating subtly. I wish I could describe the sensation in more detail. The best I can say is that it was as though an invigorating, low-watt electric charge were soothing every cell in my body.

Leaning back on impulse, I felt my feet and legs buoyed up and lay in the water, rocking gently, looking at the sky. Why was there no sun? I wondered. It didn't disturb me; it was more pleasant to look at the sky without a glare to bother the eyes. I was just curious.

Another curiosity struck me. I couldn't die; I was already dead. No, not dead, that word is the prime misnomer of the human language. What I mean is that I knew I couldn't drown. What would happen if I put my face beneath the water?

Rolling over deliberately, I looked beneath the surface. It didn't hurt my eyes to gaze through the water. Moreover, I could see everything clearly, the bottom immaculate, unmarred by stones or growths. At first, restrained by habit, I held my breath. Then, prevailing on myself, I took a· cautious breath, expecting to gag.

Instead, my nose and mouth were bathed by a delicious coolness. I opened my mouth and the sensation spread to . my throat and chest, invigorating me even further.

Turning onto my back, I closed my eyes and lay in the cool cradle of the water, beginning to think about the times Ann and the children and I had enjoyed our pool together. Every summer-especially on Sundays-we'd enjoy "family days" as Ian used to call them.

We had a slide and Ann and the children loved to come hurtling down it, crashing into the water. I smiled, remembering Ann's hoot of half-scared delight as she shot down the curving decline, holding her nose, her legs and body arcing out into space, landing in the water with an enormous splash, her bright face surfacing.

We had a floating volleyball net and played long games lunging and splashing, laughing, shouting, kidding each other. Then Ann would bring out dishes of fruit and cheese and a pitcher of juice and we'd sit and talk, then, after a while, play volleyball and slide again, dive and swim for hours more. Later in the afternoon, I'd light the charcoal in the barbecue and grill chicken or hamburgers. Those were long and lovely afternoons and I remembered them with joy.

I recalled that Ann had been unable to swim for a long time after we were married. She was afraid of the water but, finally, braved enough swimming lessons to get herself started.

I remembered the time she and I were in the Deauville Club in Santa Monica; we'd been members for a while. It was Sunday afternoon and we were in the basement, in the huge, Olympic-sized pool, Ann practicing.

It had been a terrible month for us. We'd almost gotten a divorce. Something to do with my career, Ann's anxiety not permitting me to travel. I'd lost a sizeable screenwriting assignment in Germany and been more upset than I should have been. Financial insecurity had always been a dread to me; something from our past, Robert-Dad and Mom separating, the depression years. Anyway, I overreacted and Ann overreacted, telling me she wanted me to leave.

We actually went out one night to discuss the details of our separation. It seems incredible to me now. I remember the night vividly: some French restaurant in Sherman Oaks, the two of us sitting and eating dinner, both getting indigestion as we calmly sifted over the particulars of our divorce. Item: would we keep the house in Woodland Hills?

Item: should we separate the children? Item: no, I can't go on. Even as I transmit these words, I feel the crushing nausea of that evening.

We came so close; within a hair's breadth. Or so it seemed. Maybe it had never been that close. It seemed inevitable at the time however. Until the penultimate moment. The moment past the calm discussion, the moment to actually separate, me packing clothes and driving off, leaving Ann behind. Then it collapsed. Literally, it was inconceivable to us; as though, by divorcing, we would voluntarily permit ourselves to be torn in half.

So this day at the Deauville was the first day after we had reconciled.

The pool seemed enormous because, except for us, it was unoccupied. Ann started across the width of it near the deep end. She'd done it several times already and I'd hugged her when she'd made it, congratulating her-no doubt ten times as effusively as I might ordinarily have done because of our reconciliation.

Now she was trying it again.

She was halfway across when she swallowed some water and started to choke and flounder. I was with her and grabbed her quickly. I had flippers attached to my feet and, by kicking hard, was able to keep us both afloat.

I felt her arms go tight around my neck and saw the expression of fear on her face. "It's all right, honey," I said. "I have you." I was glad I had the flippers or I couldn't have supported her.

Now memory went wrong again. I'd felt a bit uneasy at first but basically confident because I knew, somehow, that this had already happened, that I'd helped her to the side of the pool where she'd clung to the coping, frightened and breathless but safe.

This time it was different. I couldn't get her there. She felt too heavy; my legs were unable to move us. She struggled more and more; began to cry. "Don't let me sink, Chris, please."

"I won't, hang on," I said. I pumped my legs as hard as I was able to but couldn't keep us up. We both submerged, then bobbed up again. Ann cried out my name, her voice shrill with panic. We sank again and I saw her terrified face beneath the water, heard her cry out in my mind: Please don't let me die! I knew she couldn't speak the words but heard them clearly nonetheless.

I reached for her but the water was becoming murky now, I couldn't see her clearly anymore. I felt her fingers clutch at mine, then slip away. I clawed at the water but couldn't reach her. My heart began to pound. I tried to see her but the water was dark and cloudy Ann! I thought. I thrashed around in desperate anguish, feeling for her. I was there. That was the horror of it. I was really in that water, helpless and incapable, losing Ann again.

Chapter Thirteen

An End to Despair

"Hello!" I raised my head abruptly, shaken from the dream. On shore, I saw a nimbus of light by Katie. Standing, I gazed at it until it faded and I saw a young woman standing there, wearing a pale blue robe.

I don't know why I said it. Something about the way she stood, the color and shortness of her hair; the fact that Katie seemed so pleased to see her.

"Ann?" I asked.

She was silent for moments, then replied, "Leona."

My eyes saw then. Of course it wasn't Ann. How could it be? I wondered, momentarily, whether Albert had sent this woman because she might remind me of Ann. I couldn't believe he'd do that and decided that the thought was unjust. Anyway, she didn't look like Ann, I saw now. The dream had made me see her as I'd hoped, not as she was.

I looked down at myself as I walked onto the beach. The water was flowing from my robe. It was dry before I reached the woman.

Straightening up from stroking Katie's head, she extended her hand. "Albert sent me," she said. Her smile was very sweet, her aura a steady blue, almost the color of her robe.

I gripped her hand. "I'm pleased to meet you, Leona," I said. "I guess you know my name."

She nodded. "You thought I was your wife," she said. "She was in my thoughts when you came," I explained.

"A pleasant memory," I'm sure.

"It was when it began," I answered. "It soon became unpleasant though." I shivered. "Terrifying really."

"Oh, I'm sorry." She took hold of my hands. "There's nothing to be terrified of," she assured me. "Your wife will join you before you know it."

I felt a flow of energy from her, similar to that of the water. Of course the people would have it too, I realized. I must not have noticed when Albert took my hand-or else both hands had to be held for the flow to function.

"Thank you," I said as she released her grip. I had to try and think more positively. I'd been told by two different people now that Ann and I would be together again. Surely, I could accept it.

I forced a smile. "Katie was happy to see you," I said.

"Oh, yes, we're good friends," Leona replied.

I gestured toward the lake. "Quite an experience being in the water," I said.

"Isn't it?" As she spoke, I wondered, suddenly, where she'd come from and how long she'd been in Summerland.

"Michigan," she told me. "Nineteen fifty-one. A fire."

I smiled. "This reading of minds will take some getting used to," I said.

"It isn't really mind reading," she responded. "We all have mental privacy, but certain thoughts are more accessible." She gestured toward the countryside. "Would you like to walk some more?" she asked.

"Please. "

As we started from the lake, I looked back. "It would be nice to have a home overlooking it," I said.

"I'm sure you will then."

"My wife would love it too."

"You can have it ready for her when she comes," she suggested.

"Yes." The idea was pleasing to me. Something definite to do while waiting for Ann: the preparation of our new home. That plus working on a book of some kind would make the time pass quickly. I felt a rush of delight. "Are there oceans here as well?" I asked.

She nodded. "Fresh water. Calm and tideless. No storms or heavy seas."

"And boats?"

"Absolutely."

Another rush of pleased anticipation. I'd have a sailboat waiting for Ann too. And maybe she'd prefer a home on the ocean. How pleased it would make her to find our dream house waiting for her on the coast, a sailboat· for her pleasure.

I drew in deeply of the fresh, sweet air and felt immeasurably better. Her drowning had only been a dream-a distorted leftover from an unpleasant incident now long past.

It was time to begin concentrating on my new existence. "Where did Albert go?" I asked.

"He works to help those in the lower realms," Leona said. "There's always much to do."

The phrase "lower realms" evoked a sense of uneasiness again. The "other" places Albert had spoken of; the "ugly" places-they were as real, apparently, as Summerland. And Albert actually went to them.

What did they look like?

"I wonder why he didn't mention it," I said, trying not to let myself feel anxious again.

"He knew you needed an uncomplicated introduction to this world," Leona said. "He would have told you in time."

"Am I imposing on him to stay in his home?" I asked. "Should I get my own?"

"I don't know whether that's possible yet," she answered.

"But don't feel in the least uncomfortable about staying with Albert. I know he's delighted about your being there."

I nodded, wondering what she meant about it not being possible yet for me to have my own home.

"We have to earn the right," she answered my unspoken question. "It happens to almost all of us. It took me a long while to achieve my own home."

I realized, by what she'd said, how kind Albert had been in not telling me that, at the moment, I had no choice but to remain with him. Never mind, I thought. That didn't bother me. I'd never been averse to earning my way.

"Albert must be quite advanced," I said.

"He is," she replied. "I'm sure you noticed his robe and aura."

All right, I told myself. Ask questions; start learning. "I'm curious about the aura," I said. "Can you tell me something about it? For instance, does it exist in life?"

For those who can see it, she told me. It signifies the presence of the etheric double and the spirit body. The etheric double exists within the physical body until death and the spirit body exists within the etheric double until the second death, each possessing its own silver cord. The cord connecting the physical body to the etheric double is the thickest, that connecting the etheric double to the spirit body about an inch in diameter. A third cord thin as spiders web connects the spirit body to-well, she wasn't sure, Robert.

"Pure spirit, I imagine," she said. "And, incidentally, the reason I know about the aura is that it's part of my field of study here."

"You don't suppose Albert just might have had the idea I'd be asking such a question, do you?" I asked.

Her returned smile was my answer.

She continued, telling me that the aura of the etheric double extends an inch or two beyond the limits of the physical body, the aura of the spirit body up to several feet beyond the limits of the etheric double, taking on more luminosity the further it is from the dimming effect of the body.

She told me that auras all look different, the range of colors unlimited. People unable to think of anything beyond material sensation have auras which are red to brown, the lower their concepts the darker the colors. The auras of unhappy souls emit a deep, depressing green. A lavendar radiation means that the person is acquiring a more spiritual consciousness. Pale yellow indicates that the individual is sad and has a longing for lost earth life.

"No doubt that's what mine looks like," I told her.

When she didn't reply, I smiled. "I know," I said. "No mirrors either."

She smiled back.

I am going to be positive, I vowed. Let there be an end to despair.

Chapter Fourteen

To Know Ann's Destiny

"There it is," Leona said. I looked ahead, reacting, with amazement, to the sight. I'd been so intent on her words, I'd failed to notice a city in the distance.

I say a city, Robert, but how different from a city on earth. No dingy haze of smog above it, no smoke or traffic din. Instead, a series of astonishingly lovely buildings of every size, none more than two or three stories high, all standing in clear-aired silence. You've seen the Music Center in downtown Los Angeles. That will give you some faint concept of the clarity of line I saw, the use of space to balance mass, the sense of peaceful uniformity.

It struck me how vividly I was able to see it despite our distance from it. Every detail stood out. A photographer would call it perfection of focus, depth and color.

When I mentioned it to Leona, she told me that we possess what might be called telescopic sight. The description is, again, inadequate, the phenomenon far more complex than mere telescopics. In effect, distance is eliminated as a sight factor. If one looks at a person several hundred yards away, that person is visible to the very color of their eyes-without the image being magnified. Leona explained it by saying that the spirit body can project an energy "feeler" to the object under inspection. In essence, the ability is mental.

"Do you want to go there quickly or shall we continue walking?" Leona asked.

I told her I was enjoying the walk if it didn't take up too much of her time; I didn't want to make the same mistake with her I had with Albert. She replied that she was enjoying a period of rest and was happy to walk with me.

We'd reached a lovely foot bridge which traversed a fast moving brook. As we started across, I stopped and looked at the rushing water. It had the appearance of liquid crystal, every movement scintillating with the colors of the rainbow.

Turning my head, I leaned over, curious. "That sounds like ... music?" I asked, amazed.

"All things give off a kind of music," she told me. "When you've been here a while, you'll hear it everywhere. It's just that the movement of this water is so rapid, the sound is more easily noticeable."

I shook my head in awe as the sounds kept altering in a sort of formless yet harmonic melody. I thought, for a moment, of Mom's favorite piece Die Moldau. Had Smetana sensed that music in the moving waters of the river?

Staring down at the brook, I remembered a stream near Mammoth Lake. We'd parked the camper just above it and, all night, listened to it splashing across rocks and stones; a lovely sound.

"You look sad," Leona said.

I couldn't repress a sigh. "I'm remembering a camping trip we took." I tried to put aside the feeling of depression-I really did-but, once again, was gripped by it.

"I'm sorry," I apologized. "It just seems that, the more beauty I see the worse it gets because I want to share it with my family, mostly my wife."

"You will," she told me.

"I hope so," I murmured.

She looked surprised. "Why did you say that?" she asked. "You know you'll see her again."

"But when?" I asked.

She looked at me for several moments before replying.

"Would you like to know?"

I started sharply. "What?"

"There's an Office of Records in the city," she told me. "Its main job is to keep a register of people newly arrived but they can, also, provide information regarding those yet to come."

"You mean I can find out when Ann is going to join me?" It seemed too marvelous to be true.

"We'll ask," Leona told me.

I drew in trembling breath. "Let's not walk there, please," I said.

"All right." She nodded understandingly and held out her hand. "Albert told me that you've traveled by mind a little but-"

"Yes, please help me," I said, interrupting her in my excitement.

"Wait here, Katie," she said and took my hand.

I closed my eyes. That indescribable sense of movement again. With nothing visual for reference, I was more aware of it mentally than physically; there was no wind, no vertigo, no feeling of pressure.

When I opened my eyes, an instant later, we were in the city, standing on a broad avenue paved-is that the proper word?-with grass. I could see that the city was laid out like Washington-an enormous hub with radiating spokes of thoroughfares, one of which we stood on. On each side of us were buildings- some with steps or pavement leading up to them-a material resembling alabaster, all of delicate pastel shades.

The buildings here are broad, not high-circular, rectangular or square, magnificently designed with simple lines, constructed of what looks like translucent marble. Each is surrounded by sumptuous grounds which include ponds, streams, brooks, waterfalls and small lakes. My immediate and overwhelming-impression was one of space.

I saw a taller building in the center of the city and asked Leona what it was. She told me that it was a place of rest for those whose lives had been terminated by violence or long, debilitating illness; I thought of Albert when she said that. As I gazed at the building, I began to see a blue light shining down on it. Leona told me that it was a beam of healing vibration.

I forgot to mention that, when I opened my eyes, I saw many moving nimbuses of light which, shortly, faded to reveal people going about their business. None seemed in the least surprised by our precipitous appearance but smiled and nodded to us as they passed.

"Why do I see everyone as light first?" I asked.

"There's such powerful energy in the spirit body that its rays overwhelm the sight of those not used to it," she explained. "You'll adjust." She took me by the arm. "The office is this way."

I know it sounds bizarre for me to speak about the heavy beating of my heart. It did beat heavily though. I was about to find out how long I'd have to wait before Ann and I would be together again and the suspense was oppressive. Perhaps it was to avoid such a reaction in me that Albert hadn't told me about the Office of Records. He may have thought it better that I, simply, knew she was to join me and wasn't concerned about the amount of time involved. I recalled that Leona had hesitated before telling me. What I was about to do was probably not encouraged, I decided.

The paving we were on now looked like smooth, white alabaster which, although. It appeared solid, felt springy underfoot. We were entering a large square with thickly foliaged trees of every variety growing on immaculate lawns. In the center of the square, five paths leading to it, was an immense, circular fountain of some dozen jets. If I had not been so anxious, I would have been enchanted by the musical tones emitted by the splashing water.

Leona told me-to distract me? I wonder-that every tone was created by a combination of smaller jets, each a separate note. The entire fountain could be-and was, at times-manipulated so that a complex piece of music could be played as though on an organ console. At the moment, the fountain was sending forth a series of harmonic chords.

Just ahead, now, was the Office of Records, Leona told me. I tried to keep my pace a steady one but kept increasing its speed. I couldn't help it. More than anything else in this incredible new world, I wanted to know Ann's destiny.

Chapter Fifteen

When Ann Was to Join Me

The Office of Records interior was immense and peopled-by Leona's word-with thousands. Notwithstanding, there was little sign of noise and bustle as there would have been on earth.

Nor was there red tape. Within minutes-understanding that I use a term for earth time which is not valid here-I was in a private chamber with a man who had me sit across from him and gaze into his eyes; like everyone I'd met or seen, he was extremely cordial.

"What is your wife's name?" he asked.

I told him and he nodded. "Would you concentrate on her?" he said.

I thought about the way she looked: her short-cut, brunette hair threaded with gray, her large brown eyes, her small, upturned nose, her lips and delicate ears, the perfect balance of her features. "It's nice to be married to a beautiful woman," I used to tell her. She'd smile with pleased appreciation, then, invariably, shake her head and answer, "I'm not beautiful." She believed it too.

I thought about her tall, graceful figure. She took form in my mind as though she stood before me. Ann always moved well. I recalled her movements with pleasure. Recalled her warmth and softness against me when we made love.

I thought about her gentleness-her patience with the children and with me. Her compassion for the suffering animals as well as people. Recalled how carefully and tirelessly she cared for us when we were ill. How carefully she tended ailing dogs and cats and birds. She had a wonderful rapport with them I never saw in anyone else.

I thought about her sense of humor-which she rarely displayed. The children and I always kidded with each other and Ann laughed with us. Her own humor she kept under wraps because she didn't think it existed. "You're the only one who ever laughs at my jokes," she used to say. "That's because you have to though."

I thought about her faith in me through all the years of my attempts to succeed as a writer. Never once did she doubt I'd make it. "I always knew you would," she said to me more than once. Simply; with total conviction.

I thought about her painful background; her stern, often absent Navy father, her erratic, immature and, ultimately, terminally ill mother. Her unhappy childhood, her insecurities, her breakdown and beginning of analysis. The years it took to give her any confidence in herself. The horrible anxieties she suffered on the few occasions when I had to travel any distance at all. Her dread of traveling herself, of losing emotional control in front of strangers. Yet, despite these fears her bravery in-

"All right," the man said quietly.

I focused my eyes on him. He was smiling. "You care for her a great deal," he said.

"Yes, I do." I looked at him anxiously. "How long will it take before you know?"

"A little while," he said. "We have many such requests, especially from newcomers."

"I apologize for pressing you," I said. "I know you must be very busy. But I'm terribly anxious."

"Why don't you and the young lady walk around a bit?" he suggested. "Take a look at the city, then return. We should know by then."

I was disappointed, I admit. I'd thought it would be possible to find out instantaneously; that the information was stored or something.

"Would that it were that simple," he said, picking up my thought. "It requires a rather complex process of thought links however."

I nodded.

"It won't be too long," he reassured me.

I thanked him and he took me back to Leona. I was quiet as we left the building and she told me not to be disheartened.

I made an effort to cheer myself. After all, wasn't I better off now than before? I'd thought I was going to have to wait all those years for Ann's arrival never knowing when she was to arrive. Now, at least, I'd know how long it was to be. It would give me a goal.

I vowed that I wouldn't be dismayed by what I learned.

Ann was only forty-eight. Undoubtedly, she had a good thirty to forty years remaining. Nor would I have wanted it any other way. I'd wait in good cheer however long it took.

"Shall we look around the city until they have your answer?" Leona asked.

"All right," I smiled at her. "I do appreciate your kindness and your company."

"I'm happy to be with you."

I looked at the different buildings as we crossed the square. I was about to ask about them when I accidentally bumped into another man. That's not an apt description really. On earth, I would have collided with him, perhaps painfully. Here, I felt as though I'd struck a cushion of air. Then the man moved past me, smiling and patting me cordially on the shoulder.

I asked Leona what had happened and she told me that my body is surrounded by a field of energy which prevents collision. Only when contact is desired does the field neutralize itself-as when the man patted my shoulder to reassure me.

As we walked around the fountain, I asked Leona how the buildings were made. I was determined not to dwell on that all-important answer coming from the Office of Records.

The buildings, she told me, are designed by people who knew about such things during their lives or who learn about it in Summerland. They create the model image of a building in their minds, which appears from the matrix. They correct the model as needed, then instruct those who were builders on earth-or who learned to be here-and, together, all their minds in unified concentration, they cause the matrix to produce a full-scale impression of the structure. They stop before it's completed, correct to perfection, then proceed until solidification takes place.

"They just concentrate on empty space?" I asked, the notion flabbergasting me.

"It isn't really empty, of course," she said. "They stand in front of the desired site and ask for help from the higher spheres. Soon a beam of light descends from above, another concentrated beam is projected by the builders and designers and, in time, the conception takes on density."

"They look so real," I said.

"They are real," she replied. "And, albeit created by thought, far longer-lasting than those on earth. Here, there's no erosion and materials never decay with age."

I asked her if anyone lived in the city and she answered that those who preferred to live in cities on earth prefer it here as well. Of course, the disadvantages they endured on earth no longer exist: no crowding, no crime, no unbreathable air, no traffic commotion.

Mostly though, she told me, cities are centers for instruction and study: Schools, colleges, universities, art galleries, museums, theatres, concert halls, libraries.

"Are plays written on earth performed in the theatres?" I asked.

"If they're appropriate," she said. "Nothing that's sordid though. Nothing conceived merely to harrow an audience."

"Albert mentioned a line from a play he couldn't have seen on earth," I said.

"He may have seen it here," she told me. "Or on earth. It's possible, when one is advanced enough, to visit earth."

"And its people?"

Leona's smile was understanding. "You'll be able to see her later if you wish," she said. "By then, you may not want to though."

"Not want to?" I couldn't understand how she could say such a thing.

"Not from a lessening of devotion," she explained, "but, because your presence can do no good for her and-well, because descending to that level isn't all that pleasant."

"Why?" I asked.

"Because-" She hesitated for a moment or two before going on. "-one has to lower one's entire system to adjust to it-which can be physically and mentally uncomfortable." She smiled and touched my arm. "Better to avoid it," she said.

I nodded but couldn't believe I'd ever want to avoid it. If in addition to knowing when Ann was due to join me, I could actually see her from time to time, the wait could be endurable.

I was about to ask another question when I noticed that- as Leona had predicted- the nimbuses of light were starting to fade and I could see the people more clearly. I confess- not to my credit-that I felt momentary surprise at seeing other races as well as my own. I realized, then, how rarely I'd seen them in my life-especially at home- and how terribly limiting a view that creates.

"What would a rabid segregationist say?" I asked as we walked by a black man, exchanging smiles with him.

"I doubt if he'd even be in Summerland," Leona said.

"Anyone who couldn't understand that what's important is a man's soul, not the color of his skin, would never be content here."

"All races living in harmony," I said. "It could only happen here."

I was taken back to see a sad smile on her face. "I'm afraid that's true," she agreed.

When we passed a man with one arm, Leona saw my look of startlement as I turned to stare at him.

"How can that be?" I asked. "Isn't this a place of perfection?"

"He's a newcomer too," she explained. "In life, he only had one arm and, since the spirit body responds entirely to mind, it reflects his conviction about the missing arm. Once he understands that he can be whole, the arm will appear."

I said it once again, Robert. I'm sure you would have too.

"Incredible." I looked at the city and its resplendent beauty and felt a burst of happiness. Now I could be newly fascinated by everything around me because, within a short while, I'd know when Ann was to join me.

Chapter Sixteen

No Certainty of Resolution

We were approaching a two-story structure which, like the others, had the texture and translucence of alabaster which Leona told me was the Hall of Literature.

We ascended the broad steps and went inside. Like the Office of Records, there were many people inside but almost total silence. Leona escorted me into a large, high-ceilinged room the walls of which were shelved with books. Spaced throughout the room were large, attractive tables, dozens of people sitting at them, reading.

I realized, abruptly, why it was so quiet, the main source of sound absent since we conversed with our minds. "We can talk and not disturb anyone," I said. "A perfect library."

She smiled. "That's right."

I looked around the room. "What kind of books are these?"

"The histories of every nation on earth," she told me. "As they were though-nothing suppressed."

"That must be an eye-opener," I said, thinking of the near impossibility, on earth, of trying to establish the literal truth of history.

"It is indeed," Leona agreed. "The history books on earth are largely fictional."

We walked around the room and I noticed that, like every object in Summerland, the books, too, emitted a faint yet visible radiation.

"Are there books here that were published on earth?" I asked, remembering my scripts in Albert's home.

Leona nodded. "As well as some that are yet to be published there."

"How does that work?"

"The contents will be impressed on the brains of living persons."

"Will they know they didn't really write the book?"

"That's a rather complicated question," Leona said. "Generally speaking, however, they don't know."

"I'd like to read one of those," I said.

"They're not usually available," she told me. "Those who read them might, in some way, mar them, how I'm not exactly sure. I wanted to read a particular book once, though, and was told that, since everything here is mental, my thoughts might alter the contents of the book."

She took me to another room which was devoted to books on psychic science, the occult, metaphysics. Walking among, the racks, I felt emanations from them more powerful than those in the history room.

She stopped at one of the racks and pulled out a volume, handing it to me. Its vibrations were rather unpleasant. "It's customary to show first visitors this book or one like it," Leona said.

I turned the book to read the title on its spine: *The Fallacy of Afterlife*. Despite the uncomfortable sensation the book imparted, I had to smile. "Ironical to say the least," I said.

As I returned the book to its shelf, I began to feel a sense of anxiety about Ann again. She didn't believe in afterlife, I'd heard her say it. Was it possible that she might, literally: refuse to accept the evidence of her senses?

"I wouldn't be concerned about that," Leona said. "She'll believe in you. The rest will follow."

I won't describe our full tour of the Hall of Literature; it is not really part of my story. Suffice to say, the building and its contents were unendingly impressive. When I commented on the intimidation of all that knowledge to be studied, Leona reminded me that I had unlimited time in which to study it.

As we left the building, I turned to her questioningly. "I don't think they'd be quite ready yet," she said.

"All right," I nodded. Patience, I told myself. A little more time and you'll know.

"Would you like to see one of our art galleries?" Leona asked.

"Fine."

She squeezed my arm. "It'll be very soon now."

We exchanged a smile. "I apologize for being so selfish," I said, "I haven't asked a single question about you."

"There's lots of time for that," she replied. "Your first priority is your wife."

I was about to reply when another surprise occurred. A woman passed us with a strange, drifting kind of movement, looking as though she were in a coma, walking underwater. For several moments, she reminded me of the waxy image of myself I'd seen at the seance and I felt a chill. "Who is she?" I asked.

"She's still alive," Leona said. "Her spirit self is journeying here in sleep. It happens now and then."

"She doesn't know she's here?"

"No. And probably won't remember when she wakes."

I turned to watch the woman move off slowly and mechanically and saw a silver cord attached to the crown of her head, trailing into the air before it faded. "Why don't people remember?" I asked.

"Because the memory is in the spirit mind and the physical brain is unable to tap it," Leona answered. "I've been told that there are people who astral journey here and are entirely conscious of it both during and after but I've never seen one."

I watched the woman moving away and couldn't help thinking: If Ann could do that. Even if she didn't know it was happening, I could see her for a short while, maybe even touch her. The thought filled me with a longing so acute that it was almost physical. Remembering her warmth and softness against me, I could actually feel it in my flesh.

With a pained sound, I turned back to Leona to find her smiling understandingly. I returned the smile with effort. "I'm not good company, I know," I told her.

"Of course you are." She took my hand. "Come on, we'll take a brief look at the gallery, then find out when she'll be with you again."

The building ahead was circular, its marble-like exterior carved with beautiful designs of flowers and foliage.

Its interior was massive, containing what seemed to be an endless, curving gallery, the walls of which were hung with great paintings. Groups of people stood appreciating and examining, many of them teachers with their students.

I recognized a Rembrandt and commented on what a perfect reproduction it was.

Leona smiled. "The one on earth is the reproduction," she told me. "This is the original."

"I don't understand."

The painting in front of me was the one Rembrandt had in mind, she explained; as perfect as his genius could envision it. What he did on earth to reproduce that perfect mental image was subject to the limitations of his brain and body and created with materials subject to decay. This was his unmitigated vision-pure and eternal.

"You mean all artists on earth are only reproducing paintings already in existence here?"

"In existence because they created them," Leona said. "That's what I meant when I said that the question regarding whether a person knows that he or she is receiving creative impressions is rather complicated. Rembrandt's thoughts first created this painting from the matrix, then he reproduced it in physical terms. If we were experts, we'd be able to see how much more perfect this painting is than the one on earth."

Every work of art here is alive. Colors glow with reality. Each painting seems almost-not a good description but the closest I can come-three-dimensional, possessing all the qualities of relief. From a short distance, they look like real scenes rather than flat representations.

"In many ways, I think that the happiest people here are the artists," Leona told me. "Matter here is so subtle yet so readily manipulated. The artist's creativity can be fulfilled without limitation."

I tried hard to maintain an interest in what she was showing and telling me-and it was fascinating. Still, in spite of all her attempts, thoughts of Ann kept creeping back. So much so that, when Leona said, "I think we can find out now," I uttered an uncontrollable sound of relief.

"Can we go there by thought?" I asked.

She smiled and took my hand. This time, I didn't close my eyes and still couldn't follow it. We were in the gallery; I blinked; and the man from the Office of Records was in front of us.

"Your wife is scheduled to cross over at the age of seventy-two," he told me.

Twenty-four years, was my immediate thought. It was such an appallingly long time.

"Remember that time is measured differently in Summerland," he reminded me. "What would seem an eternity on earth can pass very quickly here if you're active."

I thanked him and Leona and I left the Office of Records. I continued walking with her. I made conversation. I smiled and even laughed. But something was wrong. I kept thinking: everything is settled now. In twenty-four years we'll be together again. I'd involve myself in study and activity, prepare a home for us. Exactly what she'd like. On the ocean. With a boat. Everything was settled.

Why, then, was there no assurance? No certainty of resolution?

Chapter Seventeen

This Dismaying Connection

The horrible turning point occurred soon afterward; I cannot express the precise interval. On earth, it might have been a week, perhaps less; I cannot say. I only know the shock came dreadfully soon.

I'd been disappointed that I'd have to wait so long for Ann. Albert told me not to dwell on the waiting aspect of it but the certainty of its occurrence. I tried; I really did. I made an effort to convince myself that my disturbance was unwarranted, that it had no bearing on Ann's situation.

I began to occupy myself with other things.

First of all, our father. I saw him once, Robert. He is in another part of Summerland. Albert took me to see him and I had a talk with him, then left. Does that sound strange to you? I feel it will in light of your relationship with him. I'm sorry if it strikes a discordant note; but blood is not thicker than water here. Rapport is a matter of thoughts, not genes. Simply stated, he died before I got a chance to know him. He and Mom were separated when I was a young child so that there could be no affinity. Accordingly, though I was pleased to see him and he to see me, neither of us felt any compelling urge to further the relationship. He is a fine man though. He had his problems but his dignity is unquestionable.

"Here, we are divided by sympathies rather than miles," Albert said. "You've seen, in personal detail, how powerful my union is with Ann and our children. And I'm certain that, if Mom were to pass over as I "dictate" this journal to you, our relationship would be much closer since it was so in life.

Uncle Eddy and Aunt Vera aren't together. He lives simply, in a lovely spot where he gardens. I always felt that he was not fulfilled in life. Here, he is. Aunt Vera has found the "heaven" she desired and believed she would find-totally religious. She goes to church almost constantly. I saw the edifice. It looks exactly like the church she attended on earth. The ceremony is identical too, Albert informed me. "You see, Chris, we were right," Aunt Vera said to me. And, as long as she believes it, her Summerland will be contained within the boundaries of that conviction. There's nothing wrong with it. She's happy. It's just that she's limited. To repeat: there is more.

One final item. I discovered that Ian had been praying for me without telling anyone. Albert told me that my post-death state would have been far worse except for that. "A prayer for help always eases that experience," were his words.

I return now to my account.

* * * *

It began at Albert's house; a gathering of his friends. I'll say it was evening since there was a kind of twilight in the sky, a soft and restful half-illumination.

I won't attempt to tell you everything they spoke about.

Although they tried to make me part of the conversation most of it was far beyond my understanding. They spoke, at length, about the realms "above" this one. Levels at which the progressing soul becomes at one with God-formless independent of time and substance though still aware of personal identity. Their discussion was intriguing but as far over my head as it was over Katie's.

I thought I was only part of the background. Yet, when I thought-in reaction to the gathering and what they were saying-And all of us are dead, Albert turned to me with a smile. "On the contrary," he said. "All of us are very much alive."

I apologized for the thought.

"No need for that." He lay his hand on my shoulder and gripped it firmly. "I know it's difficult. And consider this. If you, here, can think that, visualize how much more difficult it is for anyone on earth to conceive of afterlife."

I wondered if he were trying to reassure me about Ann's inability to conceive of it.

"It certainly is one of the great pities of the world that virtually no one has any idea what to expect when death comes," Leona remarked.

"If men only felt about death as they do about sleep, all terrors would cease," said a man named Warren. "Men sleep contentedly, assured that they will wake the following morning. They should feel the same about the end of their lives."

"Couldn't something be invented which would allow the human eye to see what occurs at that moment of death?" I asked, trying not to think of Ann.

"Someday it will be invented," a woman named Jennifer told me. "A camera-like device which will photograph the departure of the true self from the body."

"What's needed even more, though," Albert said, "is a 'science of dying'-physical and mental aids to accelerate and ease the separation of bodies." He looked at me. "Those things I mentioned earlier," he reminded me.

"Will people ever have that science?" I asked.

"They should have it already," he answered. "No one should be unprepared for survival. Information regarding it has been available for centuries.

"For example," said another of his friends; a man named Phillip. " 'As to man's survival after so-called death, he sees as before, he hears and speaks as before; smells and tastes; and when touched he feels the touch as before. He also longs, desires, craves, thinks, reflects, loves, wills as before. In a word, when a man passes from one life into the other, it is like passing from one place into another carrying with him all the things he had possessed in himself as a man.' Swedenborg wrote those words in the eighteenth century."

"Wouldn't the problem be solved immediately if direct communication were devised?" I asked. I looked at Albert. "That 'wireless' you spoke of earlier."

"In time, that, too, will happen," Albert said. "Our scientists are at work on it constantly. It's a tremendously difficult problem though."

"It would certainly make our work easier if there were such a wireless," said another of Albert's friends; a man named Arthur.

I looked at him in surprise. It was the first time, since I'd arrived in Summerland, that I'd heard an inflection of bitterness in anyone's voice.

Albert put his hand on Arthur's shoulder. "I know," he said. "I remember how distraught I was when 1 first began our work."

"It seems to grow more difficult all the time," Arthur said.

"So few people, who come across, possess awareness of any kind. All they bring along with them are worthless values. All they desire is a continuation of what they had in life no matter how misguided or degraded." He looked at Albert with a pained expression. "Will those people ever progress?" he asked. "Even with our help?"

As they continued talking, I could feel myself becoming apprehensive once again. What exactly was Albert's work? I wondered. And to what dark places did it take him?

Worst of all, why did I continue to associate this anxiety with Ann? It made no sense to me. She possessed awareness. Her values weren't worthless. She wasn't misguided and she could never be called degraded.

Why, then, was I unable to break this dismaying connection?

Chapter Eighteen

The Return of Nightmare

Albert ended the conversation by announcing that he had a surprise for me. We all departed from his house and, while the others traveled ahead by thought, Albert suggested that he and I walk a while, Katie joining us.

"I could tell that Arthur's words disturbed you," he said. "They shouldn't. The people he referred to have nothing to do with you."

"Why do I keep worrying about Ann then?" I asked.

"You're still concerned about her. It will take some time before that ends. But there's no connection between Ann and what Arthur was talking about."

I nodded, wanting to believe him. "I wish, to God, there were direct communication," I said. "A few words between us and everything would be resolved." I looked at him. "Will it ever happen?" I asked.

"It must, one day," he said. "It is a complex problem though. Not one of distance as I've indicated, but of difference in vibration and belief. At present, only the most advanced psychics on earth can cope with it."

"Why can't everyone on earth handle it?" I asked.

"They could, with proper training," Albert said. "The only ones we know of that can do it, though, are those born with the gift-or who acquire it by accident."

"The gift?"

"An ability to utilize the etheric senses despite their encapsulation in the physical body."

"Can't I find a psychic with that ability?" I asked. "Communicate with him? With her?"

"What if that person wasn't anywhere near your wife?" he said. "More likely, what if you did manage to communicate with such a person, he or she transmitted the message to your wife and she refused to believe it?"

I nodded, sighing. "And the one time I might have communicated," I recalled, "it went so badly that it probably destroyed any possibility of Ann's ever believing."

"That was unfortunate," Albert agreed.

"And he saw me," I said, dismayed by the memory. "He actually read my lips."

"He, also, thought your discarded double was you," Albert reminded me.

"That was hideous," I said.

He put an arm across my shoulders. "Try to have faith, Chris," he told me. "Ann will be with you; it's meant to be. And, in the meantime, perhaps a thought relay might help."

I looked at him curiously.

"Sometimes a group of minds can join forces to contact someone left on earth," he explained. "Not in words," he added quickly, seeing my expression. "In feeling," seeking to impart a sense of comfort and assurance.

"Would you do this?" I asked.

"I'll set it up as soon as possible," he said. "Put your hand on Katie now and take my hand. I did so and, immediately, found myself beside him at the edge of an enormous amphitheatre which was below ground level. It was crowded with people.

"Where are we?" I asked, straightening up from Katie.

"Behind the Hall of Music," he said.

I looked around. It was a stunning spot in the twilight illumination, the descending amphitheatre surrounded by lawns and masses of beautiful flowers with tall trees in the background.

"Is there going to be a concert?" I asked.

"Here's someone to explain it to you," Albert said, smiling. He turned me around.

I knew him in an instant, Robert. There was very little difference in the way he looked. His appearance was one of vigorous health but he hadn't grown younger, looking much as I remembered him. "Uncle!" I cried.

"Hello, Chris!" he greeted me. We embraced each other, then he looked at me. "So you're with us now," he said, smiling.

I nodded, smiling back. Uncle Sven was always my favorite, as you know.

"Katie, my girl," he said, stooping to pet her. She was obviously pleased to see him. He stood up, smiling at me again. "You're surprised at how I look," he said.

I didn't know what to say.

"A natural curiosity," he said. "One can remain at any age one chooses here. I prefer this one. Wouldn't it be silly to have nothing but young people here?" I had to laugh at the quizzical look he gave Albert.

Albert laughed too, then told me he was going to try and arrange for the thought relay.

After he was gone, I explained about Ann and Uncle nodded. "Good, the relay will help," he said. "I've seen it work."

His confident manner made me feel much better. I even managed a smile. "So you're working in music," I said. "I'm not surprised."

"Yes, music was always a great love," he said. He gestured toward the grass. "Let's sit," he said. "You'll like it better here than in the amphitheatre; I won't tell you why, I'll let you be surprised."

We sat and Katie lay beside us. "Is there a lot of music here?" I asked.

"Oh, yes, it plays a large role in Summerland," he answered. "Not only as diversion but as a way by which a person can achieve higher levels."

"What is it you do?" I asked.

"I specialize in the study of the best methods of conveying musical inspiration to those who have a talent for composition on earth," he said. "Our studies are tabulated and transferred to another group who consider the best means of communicating with these talented people. A third group does the actual transmission. Then-but I'll tell you about it later, the concert is about to start." How he knew I couldn't tell since everything was out of sight beneath ground level.

He was right though; it was about to begin. I know you're not a classical music lover, Robert, but it might intrigue you to read that the main composition to be performed was Beethoven's Eleventh Symphony.

I saw quickly why Uncle had suggested that we sit above the level of the amphitheatre. Listening is not the whole experience. No sooner had the orchestra begun to play-an unfamiliar overture by Berlioz-than a flat, circular surface of light rose from it to float level with the topmost seats.

As the music continued this circular sheet of light became more dense, forming a foundation for what followed.

First, four columns of light shot up into the air at equal spaces. These long, tapering pinnacles of luminosity remained poised, then descended slowly to become broader until they resembled four circular towers each topped with a dome.

Now the basic surface of light had thickened and risen slowly to form a dome above the entire amphitheatre. This continued to rise until it was higher than the four columns. There, the immense musical form remained stationary. Soon, the most delicate of colors began diffusing throughout the structure. As the music went on, this coloration altered constantly, one subtle shade blending into the next.

Because I couldn't see the amphitheatre, orchestra or audience, it was as though some kind of magical architecture was taking place in front of me. I learned that all music emits shapes and color but not every composition creates such vivid formations.

The value of any musical thought form depends on the purity of its melodies and harmonics. In essence, the composer is a builder of sound, creating edifices of visible music.

"Does it vanish when the music ends?" I whispered, then realized that, since we spoke by thought, I didn't have to whisper.

"Not immediately," he answered. "Time must be allowed between pieces for the form to dissolve so as not to conflict with the next one."

I was so enchanted by the shimmering architecture that I was scarcely conscious of the music which created it. I recalled that Scriabin had tried combining light and music and wondered if that inspiration had come from Summerland. I also thought how Ann would love this sight.

The beauty of the color reminded me of a sunset she and I had watched together at Sequoia.

This was not the trip we made when Ian was a baby. This' was sixteen years later, our first camping trip without the children. We took a walk our first afternoon in the Dorst Creek campground; a two-mile hike to Muir Grove. The trait was narrow and I walked behind her, thinking more than once how cute she was with her jeans and white sneakers, her red and white jacket tied around her waist, scuffing the dust as she moved, looking around with childlike curiosity, stumbling often because she didn't watch the path. Nearing fifty, Robert, and she seemed younger to me than ever.

I remember sitting, cross-legged, in the grove with her, side by side, our eyes closed, palms upturned, closely ringed by five immense Sequoia trees, the only sound a faint but steady rushing of wind far above us. A thought occurred to me; the first line of a poem; Wind in the high trees is the voice of God.

Ann loved that afternoon as I did. There was something about nature-in particular the stillness of a forest-to which she reacted well; the total silence seeping into one's very flesh. Outside of our home, it was one of the few places she felt entirely free of anxieties.

When we walked back to the campground, it was nearing sunset. We stopped at an enormous, sloping rock face that overlooked a vista of giant stands of redwood trees.

We sat there watching the sunset, talking quietly. First about the landscape and what it must have been like before the first man saw it. Then about how man has taken this magnificence and methodically demolished it.

Gradually, we talked about ourselves; our twenty-six years together.

"Twenty-six," Ann said as though she couldn't quite believe it. "Where did they go, Chris?"

I smiled and put my arm around her. "They were well spent."

Ann nodded. "We've had our times though."

"Who hasn't?" I answered. "It's better now than ever, that's all that matters."

"Yes." She leaned against me. "Twenty-six years," she said. "It doesn't seem possible."

"I'll tell you what it seems like," I told her. "It seems like last week that I spoke to a cute little X-ray technician trainee on the beach in Santa Monica and asked her what time it was and she pointed at a clock."

She laughed. "I wasn't very friendly, was I?"

"Oh, I persevered," I said, squeezing her. "You know, it's odd. It really does seem like last week. Does Louise actually have two children of her own? Is 'baby' Ian on the verge of college? Have we really lived in all those houses, done all those things?"

"We really have, Chief," Ann said. She grunted, amused.

"How many open houses have we gone to at the children's schools, I wonder? All those desks we sat at, hearing what our kids were being taught."

"Or what they were doing wrong." She smiled. "That too."

"All those cookies and coffee in Styrofoam cups," I recalled.

"All those horrible fruit punches."

I laughed. "Well..." I stroked her back. "I think we did a reasonable job of raising them."

"I hope so," she said. "I hope I haven't hurt them."

"Hurt them?"

"With my anxieties, my insecurities. I tried to keep it all from them."

"They're in good shape, Mother," I told her. I rubbed her back slowly, looking at her. "So, I might add, are you."

She looked at me with a tiny smile. "We've never had the camper to ourselves before."

"I hope it doesn't rock too much at night," I said. "We'll be the scandal of the camp-ground."

She made an amused sound. "I hope not too."

I sighed and kissed her temple. The sun kept going down, the sky bright red and orange. "I love you, Ann." I told her.

"And I love you."

We sat in silence for a while before I asked, "Well, what next?"

"You mean right now?"

"No; in years to come."

"Oh, we'll do things," she told me.

Sitting there, we planned the things we'd do. Lovely plans, Robert. We'd come to Sequoia in the autumn to see the changing colors. We'd camp on the river at Lodgepole in the spring, before the crowds began arriving. We'd back pack into the high country, maybe even try cross-country skiing in the winter if our backs held out. We'd ride a raft down a rushing river; rent a houseboat and sail it through the back rivers of New England. We'd travel to the places in the world we'd never seen. There was no end to the things we could do now that the children were grown and we could spend more time together.

* * * *

I woke up suddenly. Ann was crying out my name.

Confused, I looked around in the darkness, trying to remember where I was. I heard her cry my name again, and suddenly, remembered. I was in the camper, in Sequoia. It was the middle of the night and she had taken Ginger outside. I'd woken when she left, then fallen back asleep again.

I was out of the camper in seconds. "Ann?!" I shouted. I ran to the front of the truck and looked toward the meadow. There was a flashlight beam.

I began to smile as I started toward it. This had already happened, I knew. She'd walked into the meadow with Ginger and suddenly her flashlight beam had startled a feeding bear. She'd screamed my name in fright and I'd gone running to her, held her in my arms and comforted her.

But, as I moved toward the flashlight beam. it changed. I felt myself go cold as I heard the growling of a bear, then Ginger snarling. "Chris!" Ann shrieked.

I rushed across the uneven ground. This isn't really happening, I remember thinking. It didn't go this way at all.

Abruptly, I was on them, gasping at the sight: Ginger fighting with the bear, Ann sprawled on the ground, the flashlight fallen. I snatched it up and pointed it at her, crying out in shock. There was blood on her face, skin hanging loose.

Now the bear hit Ginger on the head and, with a yelp of pain, she fell to the ground. The bear turned toward Alln and I jumped in front of it, bellowing to chase it away. It kept coming and I hit it on the head with the flashlight, breaking it. I felt a bludgeoning pain on my left shoulder and was knocked to the ground. I twisted around. The bear was on Ann again, snarling ferociously. "Ann!" I tried to stand but couldn't; my left leg wouldn't hold my weight and I crumpled back to the ground. Ann screamed as the bear began to maul her.

"Oh, my God," I sobbed. As I crawled toward her, my right hand touched a rock and I picked it up. I lunged at the bear and grabbed its fur, began to smash at its head with the rock. I felt blood running warmly on my hands; Ann's blood, mine. I howled in rage and horror as I pounded on the bear's head with the rock. This couldn't be! It had never happened!

"Chris?"

I started violently, refocusing my eyes.

Albert was standing next to me; the music still played. I looked up at his face. His tight expression harrowed me. "What's wrong?" I asked. I stood up quickly.

He looked at me with an expression of such anguish that it seemed as though my heart stopped beating. "What is it?" I asked.

"Ann has passed on."

First, a jolt; as though I'd been struck. Then a feeling of excitement mixed with sorrow. Sorrow for the children, excitement for myself. We'd be together again!

No. The look on Albert's face did not encourage such a feeling and a sense of cold, aching dread engulfed me. "Please, what is it?" I begged.

He put his hand on my shoulder. "Chris, she killed herself," he said. "She's cut herself away from you."

It was the return of nightmare.

This
Mortal Coil

Chapter Nineteen

One Harrowing Possibility

I felt numb as I sat on the grass, listening to Albert. He'd led me from the amphitheatre; we were seated in a quiet glade.

I say that I was listening but I really wasn't. Words and phrases reached my consciousness disjointedly as thoughts of my own opposed the continuity of what he said. Troubled recollections mostly; of the times I'd heard Ann say, "If you died, I'd die too. If you went first, I don't think I could make it."

I knew, then, why I'd felt that sense of constant dread despite the fascinations of my first exposure to Summerland. Somewhere, deep inside, an apprehension had been mounting; an inner knowledge of something terrible about to happen to her.

I knew why I'd had those nightmarish visions of her begging me to save her. Again, in memory, I saw her look of terror as she slid across the cliff edge, sank beneath the churning waters of the pool, fell in bloody shock before the bear's attack. The cliff and pool and bear had all been symbols of my fear for her, not dreams but premonitions. She'd been pleading for my help, asking me to stop her from doing what she'd felt herself about to do.

Albert's voice reached my attention. "Because of her childhood traumas, the children grown, your death-" I stared at him. Had he said something about sleeping pills? His thought broke off and he nodded.

"God. " I put my face in my hands and tried to weep. But I could summon nothing; I was empty.

"The death of someone with whom a person has been long and closely associated leaves a literal vacuum in that person's life," Albert said. "The streams of psychic energy directed toward that lost someone now have no object."

Why was he telling me these things? I wondered.

"That sitting may have played a part as well," he said. "They, sometimes, distort the mental balance."

I looked up at him; not with understanding.

"Despite what your wife said," he continued, "I think she hoped there was an afterlife. I think she placed considerable reliance on that sitting. When it turned out to be, from her standpoint, a delusion, she-" His voice trailed off.

"You said you'd keep an eye on her," I reminded him.

"We did," he said. "There was no way of knowing what she planned to do though."

"Why was I told that she was scheduled to come across at the age of seventy-two?"

"Because she was," he said. "In spite of what was scheduled though, she possessed the will to circumvent that scheduling. That's the problem, don't you see? There's a natural time fixed for each of our deaths but-"

"Then why am I here?" I asked. "Was that accident the natural time for my death?"

"Presumably so," he answered. "Maybe not. At any rate, you weren't responsible for that death. Ann was responsible for hers. And to kill one's self is to violate the law because it deprives that self of working out the needs of its life."

He looked upset now, shaking his head. "If only people would realize," he said. "They think of suicide as a quick route to oblivion, an escape. Far from it, Chris. It merely alters a person from one form to another. Nothing can destroy the spirit. Suicide only precipitates a darker continuation of the same conditions from which escape was sought. A continuation under circumstances so much more painful-"

"Where is she, Albert?" I interrupted.

"I have no idea," he said. "When she killed herself she merely discarded the denser part of her body. What remains is held magnetically by earth-but where on earth could be impossible to discover. The corridor between the physical and astral worlds is, to all intents and purposes, endless."

"How long will she be there?"

He hesitated.

"Albert?"

His sigh was heavy. "Until her natural departure time arrives."

"You mean-?" I stared at him in disbelieving shock. I couldn't restrain my gasp. "Twenty-four years?"

He didn't answer. He didn't have to; I knew the answer myself by then. Nearly a quarter of a century in the "lower realm"-that place I hadn't dared to even think about before because it had evoked such apprehensions in me.

A sudden hope. I clutched at it. "Won't her etheric body die as mine did?"

"Not for twenty-four years," he said. "It will survive as long as she's held in the etheric world."

"It isn't fair," I said. "To punish someone who was out of her mind."

"Chris, it isn't punishment, " he said. "It's law."

"But she had to be out of her mind with grief," I persisted.

He shook his head. "If she had been, she wouldn't be where she is," he answered. "It's as simple as that. No one put her there. That she's there is proof that she made a willful decision."

"I can't believe it," I said. I stood and walked away from him.

Albert rose and followed me. When I stopped to lean against a tree, he stood beside me. "It can't be all that awful where she is," he tried to reassure me. "She always tried to live an honorable life, was a good wife and mother, a decent human being. Her plight certainly isn't that of those who have lived basely. It's just that she's lost her faith and has to stay where she is until her time comes."

"No," I said, determinedly.

He didn't reply. I sensed his confusion and looked at him. He knew, then, what I had in mind and, for the first time since we'd come together, I saw a look of disquiet on his face. "Chris, you can't," he told me.

"Why?"

"Well ... in the first place, I don't believe it can be done," he said. "I've never seen it done, never heard of anyone even attempting it."

A cold dread seized me. "Never?"

"Not at this level," he answered.

I gazed at him helplessly. Then resistance came again, restoring my determination. "Then I'll be the first," I said. He regarded me with deep concern.

"Don't you understand? She's there for a purpose. If you help, you distort that purpose, you-"

"I have to, Albert," I said, desperately. "Don't you understand? I can't just leave her there for twenty-four years. I have to help her."

"Chris-"

"I have to help her," I repeated. I braced myself. "Will' someone try to stop me?"

He avoided the question. "Chris, even if you found her, which is probably impossible, she'd look at your face and not recognize you. Hear your voice and not remember it at all. Your presence would be incomprehensible to her. Not only would she not accept your offers of help, she wouldn't even listen to you."

I asked again. "Will someone try to stop me?"

"That's not the point, Chris," he said. "You have no conception of the dangers in-"

"I-don't-care!" I said. "I want to help her!"

"Chris, there's nothing you can do."

I struggled to control myself. "Albert, isn't there the remotest possibility that my talking to her might make a difference? That she might, in some infinitesimal way, achieve some kind of understanding which might help to make her state a little more endurable?"

He looked at me in silence for what seemed an endless time before replying. "I wish I could say yes," he said, "but I can't."

I felt myself slump. Willfully, I stood erect again. "Well, I have to try," I told him. "I will try, Albert. I don't care how dangerous it is."

"Chris, please don't speak so thoughtlessly about those dangers," he said. Another first. I'd never heard the faintest tinge of criticism in his voice before. I'd heard it now.

We stood in silence, looking at each other. Finally, I spoke.

"Will you help me find her, Albert?" I asked. He began to speak but I cut him off. "Will you help me, Albert? Please?"

Silence again. At last, he replied. "I'll try," he said. "I don't believe it's possible but" He raised a hand to keep me from speaking. "I'll try, Chris," he said.

* * * *

Time with its multiple torments had returned to my existence.

I was waiting outside a building in the city, pacing anxiously. Albert was inside, trying to arrange a mental link with Ann. He'd warned me more than once that I would probably be disappointed. He'd never seen a link successfully made to anyone in the lower realm. Certain people could travel there, Albert among them. They could not locate specific individuals in advance, however, since all those in the lower realm were barred from communication by their own particular insularity.

Only if they asked for help- I had to slump down on a bench as weariness-a sense of inner weight-returned to me as well. I closed my eyes and prayed that Albert would locate her somehow.

My Ann.

As I thought her name, a vision filled my consciousness: night time; she and I sitting in bed together, my arm around her shoulders as we watched television.

She'd fallen asleep again. She always seemed to fall asleep when I held her with her head resting on my chest. I never woke her and did not this time. As always, I sat motionless, the television set forgotten as I gazed at her face. As always, tears welled slowly in my eyes. No matter the threading of gray in her hair, the lines of time on her face. She always had that trusting child's expression in her sleep.

At least when I was holding her.

She was clutching my hand as she often did, her fingers twitching now and then. My hand ached from her grip but I didn't stir. Better that my hand ached than I woke her. So I sat immobile, gazing at her face as she slept, thinking how much I loved this dear, sweet child-woman pressed against me.

"Chris?"

I started, opening my eyes. Albert stood before me. Rising hastily, I looked at him. He shook his head.

At first, I refused to believe. "There has to be a way," I insisted.

"She's cut off," he said. "Not asking for help because she doesn't believe that such a thing exists."

"But-"

"They couldn't find her, Chris," he said. "They tried every possible way. I'm sorry."

Walking to a nearby brook, I sat on its bank and stared into the crystal, moving water.

Albert sat beside me, patting my back. "I'm truly sorry," he said.

"Thank you for trying," I murmured. "I did discover one thing," he told me. I looked at him quickly.

"You feel so strongly about each other because you're soul mates."

I didn't know how to take that, how to react. I'd heard the phrase, of course, but only in the most banal of ways, within the context of trivial ballads and poetry.

"What it means, literally," Albert said, "is that you both possess the same wave length, your auras a vibratory unison."

Reaction failed me still. What good was knowing this if it didn't help Ann?

"That's why you fell in love with her so quickly when you met her on the beach that day," Albert had continued. "Your soul was celebrating a reunion with her."

I could only stare at him. Somehow, the news did not surprise me. I'd never been superstitious in life. Yet I'd always insisted, to Ann, that we hadn't met by accident.

Still, of what value was it to know this?

"That's why you felt so strongly about being with her after your death," Albert said. "Why you never stopped-"

"Then it's why she felt so strongly," I broke in. "She had to kill herself. To join me; achieve that unison again."

"No." Albert shook his head. "She didn't do it to join you. How could she have when she didn't believe that was possible?" He shook his head again. "No, she killed herself to terminate her existence, Chris. As she believes your existence was terminated."

"To terminate her pain, Albert."

"All right, her pain," he said. "It wasn't her decision to make though. Can't you see that?"

"I know she was suffering, that's all I know."

He sighed. "It is the law, Chris, take my word for it. No one has the right-"

"What good is knowing all this if it can't help me find her?" I interrupted, miserably.

"Because," he said, "since you are soul mates, I've been authorized to continue helping you in spite of my reservations."

I gazed at him, confused. "If she can't be found-" I broke off haplessly, a sudden vision jarring me: the two of us, like Flying Dutchmen of the spirit, wandering eternally in search of Ann. Is that what he meant?

"There's one way left," he said. He put a hand on my shoulder. "One harrowing possibility."

Chapter Twenty

Losing Ann Forever

Deja vu can be a ghastly term depending on the moment one relives. And it was with a sense of cold, devouring oppression that I moved through mist toward the building ahead. Release me from this black, unending nightmare. I recalled that plea in my mind.

It was recurring now.

I have been here before, the further thought assailed me. It didn't help that Albert walked beside me this time. Despite his presence, I was isolated with my private fears as I walked into the church.

As before, the pews were filled with people. As before, their forms were gray and faceless. As before, I drifted down the middle aisle, trying to understand why I was there. I didn't know what church it was. I only knew that, this time, I could not hear Ann's weeping because Ann was dead.

They were in the front row, sitting close together. The sight of them made me cry out in despairing recognition. I could see their faces clearly, paled and drawn by sorrow, tears in their eyes and trickling down their cheeks. Emotion brought forgetfulness. Without thinking, I moved to them and tried to put my arms around them. Instantly, I knew they were oblivious to me, staring toward the front of the church. The agony I'd felt at my own funeral returned, doubled now because I knew the funeral was Ann's.

I looked around suddenly, a thought occurring to me. I'd been an observer at my own funeral. Was it conceivable-?

"No, Chris," Albert said. "She isn't here."

I avoided the sight of my children, unable to bear the expressions on their faces, the knowledge that they were alone now.

"This woman was beloved in many ways," I heard a voice intone.

I looked toward the altar and saw the vague form of the minister delivering his eulogy. Who was he? I wondered. I didn't know him. He didn't know Ann. How could he speak of her as though he did? "As wife and mother, friend and companion. Loved by her late husband, Christopher, and by her children, Louise and Marie, Richard and Ian."

I turned away from him in distress. What right did he have to say-?

The thought evaporated as I saw what Albert was doing. He was standing in front of Richard, his right hand on Richard's head as though he were bestowing a wordless benediction on my son.

"What are you doing?" I asked.

He raised his left hand, saying nothing, and I knew he wanted silence. I stared at him. In several moments, he left Richard and moved in front of Marie, placing his hand on her head in the same way. For a moment, the sight of her staring directly at his solid (to me) body without seeing it struck me as bizarre. I wondered, once more, what Albert was doing.

Then I turned away again, too agonized to face the sight of Marie. How had I failed to notice it before? A sense of sick despair enveloped me as I walked to the casket. Thank God it was closed, I thought. At least the children were spared that.

Another thought came suddenly. I remembered Albert telling me, at my funeral, that I could look inside the casket if I tried. Was that, also, true now? The despair grew deeper. No, I thought. I didn't want to see her that way. Her real self was elsewhere. Why look at the shell?

I forced myself to turn from the casket. Closing my eyes, I began, instead, to pray for Ann. Help her to find peace, please help her to be comforted. I found my gaze returning to the children. Once more, the pain of seeing them became intense. Please be done, I thought to Albert. I couldn't bear this any longer. Staring at the stricken faces of my children, helpless to comfort them, unable to reach them in any way.

Albert had his hand on Ian's head. Suddenly, he turned, a quick smile on his lips. "Be thankful for your Ian," he said.

"I'm thankful for them all," I answered, not understanding.

"Of course," he said. "The thing is, though, that Ian's prayer may help us find your wife."

* * * *

We were walking toward the border of Summerland now.

We could have traveled there by thought but-Albert had told me-the stress of leaving so abruptly might have caused me discomfort.

"Understand now," he repeated, "Ian's prayer isn't a direct channel to Ann. It only starts us on the path. Finding her will still be difficult."

"But not impossible," I said.

He nodded. "Not impossible."

Ian's prayer again, I thought, remembering how he'd helped me once before.

"It's as though he knows," Albert said. "Not consciously, perhaps, but somewhere deep inside himself. It's what I was hoping for. When there were no prayers from any of your other children-not because they love their mother any less but because they believe that prayers are hypocritical-I thought our cause was lost-and it would have been whatever your determination. But then I was in contact with your younger son's mind and hope was revived."

"How long will it take to find her?" I asked.

"You must understand," he said. "We may never find her. We're only in possession of a general bearing, not a step-by-step route."

I resisted panic and nodded. "I understand," I said. "Let's hurry though."

Albert stopped. We were walking by a large, attractive looking park with-the sight was anomalous-a tall, iron fence around it. "Chris, come in here with me," Albert said. "I have something to say before we continue."

I wanted to go on as fast as possible, not stop and listen.

But the urgency in his voice permitted no other course so I walked beside him through a gateway to the park, past an ornamental pond. I noticed that it had no fish in it and that the soil around its bank looked somewhat drab.

I noticed, too, at that point, that the shrubbery and plants were limited and, while certainly not ugly, were, in no degree, as verdant as the other growth I'd seen in Summerland. The grass, too, had what looked like bare spots.

Across the park, I saw some people ambling slowly, others seated on benches. None wore robes but, instead, were dressed in fashionable earth clothes. They didn't look very pleasant, their expressions those of false dignity. Those on the benches sat stiffly, faces set. Everyone I looked at had an air of postured nonchalance.

None were speaking.

Chapter Twenty-One

The Mortal Coil

I was about to ask about them when we reached a bench which-oddly, I thought-looked somewhat in need of paint. Albert gestured toward it and asked me to sit.

I did so and he took his place beside me.

"I'm walking you to the edge of Summerland for two reasons," he began. "The first, as I've told you, is to let your system gradually adjust to rather unpleasant alterations in environment. The other is to get you used to walking again as a means of locomotion. Once we depart from Summerland, we'll be subject to the grosser atmosphere of where we'll be and unable to travel by thought."

I looked at him curiously. Is that what he'd stopped to tell me?

"Most of all," he continued, answering my question instantly, "I want to emphasize the profound danger you will be in when we're traveling through the lower realm. You found our visit to your wife's funeral disturbing. It was nothing compared to what you'll soon be experiencing. While we were at the funeral, we maintained a distance from the influences of that level. In the lower realm, we will have to actually take on those influences in order to function. I can protect you to a certain degree but you must be prepared for the onset that will strike you-every dark emotion that you left behind on entering Summerland.

"You must, also, be prepared to see some terrible sights. As I've said, the way to Ann is not distinct. It may take us through some ghastly places. I want you to understand this now. If you feel you can't face them-"

"I don't care what I have to face," I said.

He regarded me in silence, obviously wondering if I had the remotest concept of what he was telling me.

"Very well," he finally said, "assuming that you have the strength to resist what you'll have to face, I warn you, with the greatest emphasis, of the dangers which will threaten you if and when we actually find Ann."

I confess to startlement at that.

"The search for her will involve many frightening dangers," he said, "but these are external dangers. If we find Ann and you try to help her, you'll be subject to internal threat. Returning to a level of primitive development, you'll be strongly influenced by it. Lowering your vibration to that of earth's, you will no longer be able to think clearly but will be subject to the same confusion of thought with which your wife lives constantly. In this weakened state, you will not only risk losing your effort on her behalf, you could very easily be so affected that you'd become as much a prisoner' of that level as she is."

He put his hand on my shoulder and gripped it tightly.

"You would, then, lose everything you've gained," he said, "not only losing Ann but yourself as well."

A current of uneasiness washed over me and I couldn't respond.

"You can return to where you were," Albert said. "Frankly, I'd be much relieved if you did. That way, you'd only have to wait for her for twenty-four years which would quickly pass for you.

"By going on, you may lose her for a much longer time." I closed my eyes, feeling chilled and weak. I mustn't leave her there, I thought. I have to help her. Still, I was afraid and not unrealistically according to what Albert had told me. What if I wasn't strong enough? Wasn't it better to wait those twenty-four years, knowing, for certain, that we'd be together again? Wasn't that infinitely preferable to trying to help her now and possibly running the risk of losing Ann forever?

Chapter Twenty-Two

Inside the Lower Realm

"Gentlemen?" At the sound of the man's voice, I opened my eyes. He stood before the bench, addressing us. "I'm afraid you'll have to leave," he said. "This is a private park."

I stared at him. A private park in Summerland? I began to speak but Albert cut me off. "Of course," he said. "We didn't realize."

"That's quite all right," the man replied. He was middle aged, distinguished looking, dressed with care. "If you'll leave immediately," he told us, "no more need be said."

"Right away," Albert agreed, rising from the bench. I looked at him, not understanding. It seemed unlike him to allow this man to exclude us from a park in Summerland without a word of reaction. I stood and began to speak again but Albert took my arm and whispered, "Never mind."

The man observed us with polite remoteness as we started toward the gateway.

"What is this?" I asked.

"It wouldn't help to challenge him," Albert told me. "He wouldn't understand. These people here are in a strange condition. In life, they never did actual harm to anyone and are causing no harm here-hence the relative graciousness of their surroundings.

"On the other hand, there is no way to pierce their shell of affectation. They live a limited existence which they, nonetheless, believe to be completely appropriate to their class.

"They think they're in a 'smart' location, you see, a spot restricted to those of their social standing. They have no conception of the fact that, in Summerland, there are no sets or cliques. They are living a delusion of group superiority which words cannot affect."

I shook my head as we left the park.

"Grotesque," I said.

"It's nothing compared to what you face if we continue on."

We walked in silence for a while. Somehow, I sensed that we were not continuing toward the edge of Summerland but circling where we were, Albert giving me time to make up my mind.

At last, I did.

"Since the risk is mine, not Ann's," I said, "I want to continue. She can only be helped."

"Except," he reminded me, "in the sense that, if you become imprisoned in the etheric world, your reunion could be delayed-" He stopped and I knew he'd been about to tell me how long our reunion might be delayed. A hundred years? A thousand? Fear took hold of me again. Was I foolish to attempt this? Wasn't twenty-four years preferable to-?

The decision came at that: the thought of Ann alone in God only knew what dreadful place for nearly a quarter of a century. I couldn't let that happen without trying to help.

I wouldn't.

"All right," Albert said, knowing my decision as I made it. "We'll go on then. And I admire your devotion, Chris. You may not realize it yet but what you're about to do is very courageous."

I didn't reply but, as we walked on, realized that, subtly, we had altered our direction and were, once more, moving toward the edge of Summerland. Ahead, I saw a small church. Like the park, it was not unattractive yet lacked that perfection which marked everything I'd seen before in Summerland. Its color was a dingy brown, its brickwork chipped and faded. As we drew closer to it, I began to hear a congregation singing. "Weary of earth and laden with my sins. I gaze at heaven and long to enter in."

I looked at Albert, startled.

"But they're here," I said.

"They don't know it," he replied. "So they spend their time singing dreary hymns and listening to dreary sermons."

I felt a sense of anxiety pervading me again. If it could be like this in Summerland itself, what would it be like when we'd left this realm entirely?

* * * *

Albert stopped.

We faced a stretch of flinty ground with patches of grass that looked dry and wasted.

"We'd better change our clothing now," he said. "Wear shoes."

I was about to ask him why, then knew he wouldn't have suggested it if it weren't a necessity. I concentrated on the change. The fluttering sensation on the surface of my skin seemed slower here, as though it labored. I looked down, seeing, with a start, that, once more, I was wearing the outfit I'd had on the night of the accident.

I turned my gaze to Albert. He was wearing a blue shirt and trousers, a beige jacket.

"The clothes I was wearing when they took me to the hospital," he said.

I felt myself grimace as he spoke. "Is it going to be like this from now on?" I asked. The air felt liquid and granular in my throat.

"We'll have to start adjusting to the changes in environment," he told me. "Visualize yourself as you'd have to be to exist here without discomfort."

I tried and, gradually, began to have the impression of feeling myself thicken. The feeling was subtle, but distinct. The texture of my flesh took on a certain density and now the air was breathable. How different in my lungs though, no longer crystal clear and invigorating. This air was heavy. It supported my existence, nothing more.

I looked around the countryside as we walked on-if countryside is the word for what I saw. No fruitful landscape here; only barren ground, dying grass, stunted, virtually defoliated trees, no sign of water. And no houses which came as little surprise. Who would, willingly, reside here? was my thought.

"You'll see those who-willingly-reside in places which are so appalling that, by comparison, this is a place of beauty," Albert said.

I tried not to shudder. "Are you trying to dissuade me?" I asked.

"Prepare you," he said. "Even so, no matter what I say, you cannot possibly envision what you may be forced to see."

Again, I was about to question him, again decided not to do it. He knew; I didn't. I had better not waste energy contesting anything he told me. I needed my resources for whatever lay ahead.

What lay immediately ahead was a desolate prairie-like expanse. As we walked across it, the turf grew less and less resilient and I noted the beginning of jagged cracks in the ground. There were no breezes now. The air lay still and weighted, getting cooler as we progressed. Or was it retrogressed?

"Am I imagining the light fading again?" I asked.

"No," he answered quietly. His tone of voice seemed to be declining with the look of the terrain, growing more withdrawn as moments passed. "Except it isn't fading to help you rest. It's fading because we're almost to the lower realm-which is, also, called the darker realm."

There was a man ahead. He stood impassive, watching our approach. I thought that he was someone who, for some unknowable reason, chose to live there.

I was wrong.

"This is where the lower realm begins," he told us. "It's no place for the curious."

"I'm here to help someone," I said.

The man looked at Albert who nodded and said, "That's right."

"You aren't entering just to look," the man said warningly.

"No," Albert told him. "We're searching for this man's wife to try and help her."

The man nodded and put his hand on our shoulders. "Go with God then," he said. "And be alert at all times. Be aware."

Albert nodded again and the man removed his hands from our shoulders.

The very second we crossed the border I was uncomfortable, oppressed, filled with an almost overwhelming desire to turn and flee back to that safer place. I had to will myself from retreating.

"Tell me if you want to go back," Albert said. Had he gotten my thought or was it obvious what I'd be thinking at that moment?

"All right," I said.

"No matter when you feel it," he added.

I knew, then, that he couldn't reach my mind anymore. "We have to speak aloud now, don't we?" I said.

"Yes," he answered. It was disconcerting to see his lips move again. Somehow, that sight did more to convince me we were in the lower realm than anything I felt or saw.

What did I see? Almost nothing, Robert. We walked through a colorless vista, the dull sky blending with the ground until it seemed as though we trudged across a gray continuum.

"Is there no scenery here at all?" I asked.

"Nothing permanent," he said. "Whatever you may see-a tree, a bush, a rock-will only be a thought form created by some person on this level. The overall appearance represents the composite mental image of its inhabitants."

"This is their composite mental image?" I asked. Soundless; hueless; lifeless.

"It is," he said.

"And you work here?" I felt stunned that anyone who had the choice would elect to work in this forbidding place.

"This is nothing," was all he said.

I was not mistaken in my observation. His voice was less than it had been in Summerland. Clearly, the inertness of this place affected even speech. What did I sound like I wondered?

"It's getting cold," I noticed then.

"Conceive of warmth around you," Albert said.

I tried, discovering that, gradually, the cold became less harsh.

"Is it better?" Albert asked. I said it was.

"Remember though," he told me, "as we travel further, it will require more and more adaptive concentration on your part to adjust to the effects of the environment. A concentration which will grow harder and harder for you to command."

I looked around, a new uneasiness beginning. "It's getting dark now," I said.

"Conceive of light around you," Albert told me.

Conceive of light? I thought. I tried although I couldn't understand how it could help.

It did however. Bit by bit, the shadows gathering about us started to lighten.

"How does it work?" I asked.

"Light, here, is obtained exclusively by the action of thought on the atmosphere," he told us. "Let there be tight is more than just a phrase. Those who come to this realm in an unprogressed state are quite literally 'in the dark,' their minds not advanced enough to produce the light which would enable them to see."

"Is that why they can't go higher?" I asked, thinking uneasily of Ann. "Because they actually can't see to find their way?"

"That can be part of it," he said. "However, even if they could see with their eyes, their systems would be unable to survive in a higher realm. The air, for instance, would be so rarefied to them that breathing would be painful if not impossible."

I looked around the bleak, unending countryside. "This could be called Winterland," I said, the sight depressing me.

"It could," he agreed. "Except that memories of winter on earth are, often, pleasant ones. Nothing here is pleasant."

"Does your work here ... succeed?" I asked.

He sighed and, glancing at him in the nocturnal light, I saw that his expression was one of melancholy; a look I'd never seen on his face before. "You know, from personal experience, how difficult it is to make people on earth believe in afterlife," he said. "It is far more difficult here. The reception I've usually gotten is that of a naive church worker in the most vile of ghettos, my words greeted with scornful laughter, coarse jokes, verbal abuse of every kind. It isn't hard to understand why so many dwellers in this realm have been here for ages."

I looked at him with such dismay that he looked surprised, then, realizing what he'd said, suddenly repentant. Even he had lost perception here.

"I'm sorry, Chris," he said. "I didn't mean that Ann would be here that long. I've told you how long."

He sighed again. "You see what I meant about the atmosphere of this place affecting one's thinking. Despite what I believe, I've already let it work on my convictions. The larger truth, of course, is that every soul will eventually rise. I've never heard of any spirit being permanently abandoned no matter how evil. And your Ann is far from evil. All I intended to say is that there are misguided souls who have been in this realm for what amounts-to them at any rate-to an eternity."

He said no more and I did not pursue it. I didn't want to think of Ann being held here endlessly-or of myself a prisoner inside the lower realm.

Chapter Twenty-Three

Entry to Dark Thoughts

There was an odor in the air; a smell which I can only describe as one of corruption. Ahead lay what appeared to be a sprawling collection of hovels. I'd say a village but there seemed no arrangement to the shacks and huts. "What is this place?" I asked.

"A gathering place for those of similar nature," Albert said.

"She isn't-" I began to ask, then couldn't finish, the idea too dismaying to voice.

"I don't think so," Albert answered.

I was going to say thank God when it occurred to me that where Ann was might be worse than this. I tried to resist the thought but was unable to dislodge it. I knew it was unjust to her but couldn't help it, the baleful influence of the realm was affecting my mind.

There was no sound ahead as we approached the haphazard jumble of shanties. All I could hear was the scuffing of our shoes on the gray, flinty soil. Off to our right, saw some people moving aimlessly, others standing motionless, all dressed In shabby clothes. Who were they? I wondered. What had they done-or failed to do-that they should be there?

We walked within a few yards of a group of them; several men and women. Even though Albert had said he didn't think that Ann was there, I found myself looking closely at the women. None of the people glanced at us as we passed. "Can't they see us?" I asked.

"We're of no interest to them," Albert said. "They're absorbed by their own concerns."

I saw some people sitting on boulders and it gave me an odd sensation to realize that those boulders were created by their minds. They sat, heads bowed, hands hanging loosely, staring at the ground, immobile in their desolation. I know that, unless they were deaf, they heard us walking by but none gave any sign of noticing our presence.

Again, I found myself looking at the women. Don't, I thought abruptly. She isn't here. But Albert didn't say that, came the sobering response. He said that he didn't know. Was it possible? I thought, looking closer still.

We were so near to several of the people now that I could make out their features despite the gloom.

The sight made me catch my breath.

"Get used to it," Albert said, "you'll see worse."

His tone seemed almost unsympathetic and I glanced at him, wondering uneasily if the place was changing him. If he were unable to resist it, what hope was there for me?

Shivering, I looked back at the people. Ann couldn't be here; she couldn't.

The features of the men and women were exaggerated, like those of acromegalies; not so much the faces of people, but bloated caricatures of them.

In spite of my resolve, I looked intensely at the women.

Was that Ann's malformed face?

I fought it off. No! She wasn't there!

"She isn't here, is she?" I pleaded moments later, not strong enough to retain conviction.

"No," he murmured and I exhaled long and hard.

We passed a young man lying on the ground, his clothing torn and stained by grime. I thought, at first, that he was looking at us, then realized, from the cast of his eyes, that his gaze was on his thoughts, a stare of withdrawn despondency.

I swallowed as I looked at his lost expression and the fetid air felt as though it were trickling down my throat like cold glue.

"Why do they look like this?" I asked, pained by the sight.

"One's appearance retrogrades with one's mind," Albert answered. "The same thing happens on earth, people's faces altering, over a period of time, with their actions and thoughts. This is only a logical-if terrible-extension of that process."

"They all look so grim," I said.

"They are," he replied. "Grim in their preoccupation with themselves."

"Were they-are they-all so bad?" I asked.

He hesitated before answering my question. Finally, he said, "Try to understand, Chris, when I tell you that this is nothing compared to what lies ahead. The people you see here may not be guilty of sins which were, in any way, horrendous. Even a minor transgression takes on darker aspects when one is surrounded by those who have committed similar transgressions. Each person multiplies and amplifies the failures of the others. Misery loves company, is what they say on earth. It should be: Misery, in company, grows ever worse.

"There's no balance here, you see. Everything is negative and this reverse animation feeds upon itself, creating more and more disorder. This is a level of extremes-and extremes of even a lesser nature can create a painful habitat. You see their auras?"

I hadn't noticed in the paucity of light but, as he called them to my attention, I did. All consisted of drab shades of gray and brown; dismal, muddy colors. "These people are all the same then," I said.

"Fundamentally," Albert replied. "Which is one of the curses of this realm. There can be no rapport between the people because they're all alike in essence and can find no companionship, only mirror images of their own shortcomings. "

Abruptly, Albert turned to his right. I looked in that direction and saw the first-relatively-rapid movement I'd observed in this place-the lumbering hobble of a man behind a hut.

"Mark!" Albert shouted.

I looked at him in startlement. He knew the man?

Albert sighed unhappily as the man remained out of sight. "He always runs away from me now," he said.

"You know him?"

"I've been working with him for a long, long time," he answered. "There've been times when I thought I'd almost gotten through, convinced him that he wasn't a prisoner here but had brought himself to such a plight." He shook his head. "He won't believe it though."

"Who is he?" I asked.

"A businessman," he said. "A man who, in life, concerned himself with nothing but the acquisition of wealth. He spent almost no time with his family or friends. Days and nights, for seven days a week, fifty-two weeks a year, he thought only of monetary gain.

"And yet he feels betrayed. He thinks he should be. rewarded for what he did. I worked damned hard, is his constant lament. No matter what I say, he tells me that. As though his total absorption in profit was its own justification. As though he had no responsibility to anyone or anything else. An occasional donation to some charitable cause convinced him of his generosity.

"Remember Marley with his chains?" Albert asked. "The simile is apt. Mark is encumbered with chains too. He just can't see them."

I looked to my left and stopped in sudden alarm as I saw a woman who looked so much like Ann that I was sure it was her and started toward her.

Albert held me back. "It isn't Ann," he said. "But-" I struggled in his grip.

"Don't let your anxiety to find her make you see her where she isn't," he cautioned.

I looked at him in surprise, then started turning back toward the woman. She did look like Ann, I told myself.

I stared at her. There was little actual resemblance. I blinked and looked more closely. I had never suffered from hallucinations in my life. Was it to start now? I kept staring at the woman. She was sitting, huddled, on the ground, covered from head to toe by a network of thin, black threads. She didn't move but stared ahead with lifeless eyes. I take that back. Like the young man, she was staring inwardly, gazing at the darkness of her mind.

"Can't she break those threads?" I asked.

"With the least of effort," Albert answered. "The thing is, she doesn't believe she can and the mind is everything. I'm sure her life on earth must have been one of great, self-pitying frustration. Here, that feeling is exaggerated to the point you see."

"I thought she looked like Ann," I said, confused.

"Remember what that man said," Albert told me. "Be alert at all times."

I looked at the woman as we walked off. She didn't look at all like Ann. Still, she made me wonder. Was Ann in a similar plight, imprisoned in some other place like this? The thought was harrowing.

As we continued through the silent, formless village, past its mute and wretched population, I began to feel so tired that it brought back memories of the weariness I'd felt just after death. Lacking the strength to do otherwise, I found myself beginning to hunch over as I walked, taking on the posture of some of the nearby people.

Albert took hold of my arm and straightened me. "Don't let yourself be drawn in or we'll never reach Ann," he said. "We're just starting out."

I forced myself to walk erectly concentrating on resistance to the weariness. It helped immediately.

"Be aware," Albert repeated what the man had told us.

"I'm sorry," I said. A wave of depression beset me. Albert was right. We were just starting out. If I was vulnerable already, how could I hope to reach-?

"You're hunching over again," Albert warned.

Dear God, I thought. It has happened so quickly, the slightest thought affecting me. I would resist it though, I vowed. I wouldn't let myself succumb to the dark blandishments of this realm.

"A powerful place," I murmured.

"If you let it be," Albert replied.

Speech, I thought. Silence was the enemy; negative reflection. "What are those threads around that woman?" I asked.

"The mind is like a spinning wheel," Albert told me. "In life, it constantly weaves a web which, on the day of our passing, surrounds us for better or worse. In that woman's case, the web became a snare of selfish concerns. She can't-"

I didn't hear the rest of what he said because my gaze was drawn to a group of people crouching and kneeling around something I couldn't see, their backs to us, their hands rapidly conveying something to their mouths. All of them looked bloated.

Hearing the sounds they made-grunting, snarling, rending noises-I asked what they were doing.

"Eating," Albert said. "No, change that. Gluttonizing."

"But if they have no bodies-"

"They can never be satisfied, of course," he said. "They do it all from memory, only believing that they eat. They might, as easily, be drunkards swilling nonexistent liquor."

I diverted my eyes from the sight. Those people, Robert, were like creatures gorging on a kill. I hate this place, I thought.

"Chris, walk erect," Albert said.

I almost groaned. That instant of hatred had been strong enough to bend me forward. More and more, I was beginning to appreciate the import of that man's words: Be aware.

To our left now, I could see a tall, gray structure which resembled a rotting warehouse. Its massive doors were open and, seeing hundreds of people moving about inside, I started in that direction. Maybe Ann-

I was forced to stop as vibrations from the structure hit me so hard that I gasped as though physically struck.

I stared at the figures moving in the cavernous gloom, their clothes hanging loosely on their bodies, their features distended and pale. Each person walked with bowed head, taking no notice of anyone around, pushing others aside without a vestige of reaction if they happened to collide. I don't know how I knew it but their thoughts were open to me, massed on one dark theme: We're here forever and there is no hope for us.

"That isn't true," I said. For Ann's sake, I couldn't let myself believe that.

"It's true as long as they believe it," Albert said.

I turned my head to shut away the sight. This must be hell, I thought; limitless and grim, a place of-

"Chris!"

"Oh, God," I murmured, frightened. I was hunched again, my movements slowing, aging. Would I never be able to resist the baleful influences of this realm? Was there no hope at all that I-?

"Chris!" Albert stopped and forced me upward. Holding my arms tightly, he gazed into my eyes and I felt a flow or something coursing through my body, restoring energy. "You've got to remain alert," he said.

"I'm sorry," I muttered. No, don't be sorry, be strong! I told myself.

I tried to concentrate on resisting as we moved on through the nebulous light, leaving the dingy sprawl of huts behind.

* * * *

This place was not silent.

As we neared it, sounds of anger and contention rose in volume; people quarreling, their voices strident, savagely vindictive.

Soon I saw them.

No one touched another person. Contact was entirely by words; vicious, cruel, assaulting words. A malicious haze hovered just above the people, an intermingling of their murky auras ugly red flashes of fury darting between them.

Albert had warned me that we approached an area where violent spirits crowded together. This section was the least of it, he told me as we walked. The violence here was, at least, confined to verbal abuse.

"Is this a place you've gone to before?" I asked. I had to speak loudly to make myself heard.

"One of them," he answered.

As we circuited the mobs of clashing people, I began to feel their icy thrusts of venom at us. They didn't even know who we were yet they hated us completely.

"Can they harm us?" I asked, uneasily.

"Not if we refuse to accept their wrath," Albert told me. "They're far more likely to do harm to living people who aren't aware of their existence. Fortunately, their mass thought rarely focuses. If, on occasion, it does, stronger mentalities above become aware of it and dissipate the output so it cannot hurt the innocent on earth.

"Of course there are individuals on earth whose nature is receptive to these thoughts; who provide an access to them. These cannot be helped. That's the pitfall of free will. Any man or woman possesses the capacity to give entry to dark thoughts."

Chapter Twenty-Four

The Floor of Hell

The more we walked now, the more repelled and nervous I became. A kind of aching restlessness filled me. I felt cramped and stifled as though the atmosphere were closing in around my body. The air in my lungs tasted vile, unclean, as thick as mucilage.

"Adjust your system again," Albert said.

Once again-I'd done it five times now; or had it been six?-I visualized myself as I would have to be to function under these new conditions. Not function in comfort, God knew; that concept had long since left my system. Survival was all that I could hope for now.

Once more, I felt my body clotting. So much so, now, that I might have been alive on earth again, my flesh congealed and weighted, my bones coagulated into hardness.

"Adjust your mind as well," Albert told me. "This will be the worst you've seen."

I drew a deep breath, grimacing at the taste and odor of the fetid air. "Is this really helping?" I asked.

"If there were any other way to find her, rest assured we'd take it," Albert said.

"Are we any closer to her?"

"Yes," he said, "and no."

I turned to him in irritation. "What does that mean?" I demanded.

His urgent look reminded me to quell my anger. At first I couldn't, then, realizing that I must, I strained to keep myself controlled. "Are we any closer?" I asked.

"We're moving in the right direction," he replied. "I just haven't been able to locate her yet."

He stopped and looked at me. "I'm sorry that I can't explain it any better," he said. "I can say that, yes, it's helping. Please believe me."

I nodded, returning his look.

"Tell me if you want to go back," he said. "Go back?"

"Let me look for her-I want to find her, Albert. Now."

"Chris, you've got to-"

I turned away from him in fury, then looked back as quickly. He was only warning me. My new impatience with him was a sign that the environment was affecting me again.

I started to apologize, then felt myself begin to tense with anger once again. I almost lashed out at him. Then a beam of reason pierced the dark resentment in my mind and I knew, once more, that he was only trying to help. Who was I to argue with a man who had come to this awful place to help others? What in God's name was the matter with me?

My sentiments reversed themselves again. I was disconsolate once more, stricken by my inability to-

"Chris, you're hunching again," Albert said. "Concentrate on something positive."

A burst of alarm. I willed my clouding mind to think of Summerland. Albert was my friend. He was taking me to find Ann, his only motivation, love.

"Better." Albert squeezed my arm. "Hold onto that, whatever it is."

"I'll try," I said. "I'm sorry I slipped again."

"It isn't easy to remember here," he said. "And simple to forget."

Even those words, meant as explanation, like a shadowy magnetism, had a tendency to pull me down. Again, I thought of Summerland, then of Ann and of my love for her. That was better.

I would concentrate on Ann.

The light was getting dimmer as we walked now. Even with my concentration on an area of light around me, the nimbus seemed to shrink as though some outside pressure forced it in. Albert's light was stronger but even his illumination soon became no brighter than that of a dying candle flame. It seemed as though I felt a gathering thickness in the air. We might have been moving along the· bottom of a deep and murky sea. There were no people anywhere in sight, no structures. All I saw ahead were rocks, a line of craggy boulders.

Moments later, we had reached the crater edge.

Leaning forward, I looked down into the blackness of it, then pulled back sharply at a rush of something from below-something toxic and malignant.

"What?" I muttered.

"If there is any place I've been to that deserves the name of Hell, this is it," Albert told me. It was the first time I had ever heard the sound of misgiving in his voice and it made my fear increase. The constant throughout all of this had been his strength. If this place frightened him ...

"We must go down there though," he said. I wasn't sure if he was telling me or steeling himself for the ordeal.

I drew in laboring breath. "Albert, she isn't down there," I said, I pleaded.

"I don't know," he answered. His expression was grave. "I only know we have to go there if we want to find her."

Shuddering, I closed my eyes and tried to remember Summerland. To my dismay, I found myself unable to do it. I strained to conjure up a vision of the lakeshore I had stood on, the exquisite scenery-

The thought was gone. I opened my eyes and stared out at the vast, dark crater.

It was miles in circumference with precipitous walls. All I could make out on its floor-it was like trying to pick out details in a night-shrouded valley-were huge masses of rock as though some cataclysmic landslide had occurred in eons past. I thought I made out openings but wasn't certain. Were there tunnels in the rock? I shuddered again, trying not to let myself imagine what sort of beings might exist in those tunnels.

"We have to go this way?" I asked. I knew the answer in my mind but heard my voice speak nonetheless, my tone one of faltering dread.

"Chris, let's go back," he said. "Let me look on my own."

"No." I braced myself. I loved Ann and would help her.

Nothing in the depths of Hell would keep me from it.

Albert looked at me and I returned his gaze. His appearance had changed. He was as I remembered him on earth. Nothing of perfection could survive in this place and his features bore the cast I recollected from my youth. He'd always looked a little pale, a little ill. He looked that way again-as I was sure I looked.

I could only pray that, underneath his pallor, the resolution of the man I'd met in Summerland was still intact.

* * * *

We were climbing down an angling, rocky fissure. It was far too dim to see clearly but I could feel slime on the surface of the rocks, a jellylike matter which exuded a smell of decay. Once in a while, some small thing crawled across my fingers, startling me. When I twitched my fingers whatever they were darted swiftly into cracks. Teeth clenched, I forced myself to concentrate on Ann. I love her and was here to help her. Nothing else was stronger than that. Nothing.

As we descended gradually, the feeling of-how shall I describe it?-materiality began to crowd the air. It was as though we climbed down through some unseen, grumous fluid. Adjustments came by seconds now. We were part of the environment, our very flesh adapting to it automatically.

The air-could it be called that?-was totally repulsive, dense and sticky, foul of odor. I could feel it ooze around my body, crawling down into my lungs as we descended and descended.

"You've actually been here?" I asked. I was gasping for breath. We might as well have been alive, I thought, so complete was the sense of bodily function.

"Again and again," Albert said.

"I couldn't do it."

"Someone has to help," he replied. "They can't help themselves. "

They, I thought. A convulsive shudder wracked my body.

What did they look like, the denizens of this forbidding pit? I hoped I didn't have to find out. I prayed that Albert would-with a sudden burst of discovery-know exactly where Ann was and take me there, away from this hideous place. I couldn't stand much-

No. I stopped myself. I mustn't think that way. I could stand anything I had to in order to reach Ann.

The lower realm. Not an adequate description for this region. Not bad enough by half. No light; the blackness of unfathomable night. No vegetation. Nothing but chilled stone. A foul, repugnant, never ceasing odor. An atmosphere to make the strongest man feel sick and helpless.

The blackness was enshrouding now. It took every bit of concentration I possessed to keep alive the weakest glimmer of illumination. I couldn't see my hands any more. Spelunking must be just like this, the thought occurred. The darkness pressed against my flesh as well as we descended down and down. Would we be safer not to carry light at all? I wondered. So as not to be caught sight of by-?

I gasped as, with the thought, abysmal blackness covered me. "Albert!" I whispered.

"Conceive of light," he told me quickly.

I clung to the cold rock wall and strained to do as he had said, my brain laboring to create an image of illumination. In thought, I struck a match that would not ignite. Again and again, I raked its head across the rocky surface but the best I could manage was the vision of a furtive, random spark in the distance.

I tried to imagine a torch in my hand, a lantern, a flashlight, a candle. Nothing worked. The darkness tightened its grip and I began to panic.

Abruptly, I felt Albert's hand clamp down across my shoulder. "Light," he said.

Relief washed over me as illumination came back like a pale corona around my head. I felt a glow of reassurance: at the light but, even more, at Albert's still intact ability to restore, in me, the strength to bring it back.

"Keep it strong in your mind," he said. "There is no darkness in the universe to match that of the lower realm. You do not want to be devoid of light here."

I reached out with my right hand to squeeze his arm in gratitude. At the same moment, something cold and many legged scurried across my left hand and I almost jerked it from the wall, remembering only at the last instant to keep myself from doing so. I clutched back at the wall with my right hand and closed my eyes. After a few moments, I murmured, "Thank you."

"All right," Albert said.

As we continued down, I wondered what would have happened if I'd fallen. I couldn't die. Still, that was little comfort. In Hell, death has to be the least of threats.

The curdled air was getting colder now, clinging to my skin with a crawling dampness that felt alive. Conceive of warmth, I told myself. I struggled to envisage the air of Summerland, to feel its warmth on my skin.

It helped a little. But the smell was getting worse now.

What did it remind me of? At first, I couldn't recall climbing downward, ever downward; would we never reach the bottom?

Then it came to me. A summer afternoon. Marie returning from a ride on Kit. Just before she wiped Kit's lathered coat, I smelled it. I pressed my teeth together 'til they ached. The odor of Hell is the odor of a sweating horse, I thought. Was this the place that Dante had confronted in his awful. visions?

It came to me, at that moment-slowly, far too slowly, every thought an effort now-that, just as I was able to repress the dark and cold, I could, by logic, shut away the odor as well. How? I wondered. My brain turned over like a foundering ship. Think, I ordered myself-and managed to evoke a memory of the fresh aroma in Summerland. Not a perfect memory by any means but enough to ease the smell, to make my downward climb more bearable.

Thinking to tell him what I'd done, I looked around for Albert and a sudden burst of terror struck me as I failed to see him.

I spoke his name aloud. No answer.

"Albert?"

Silence.

"Albert!"

"Here." His voice just reached me and, by peering hard, I presently was able to see the faint glow of this presence moving toward me.

"What happened?" I asked.

"You lost attention," he told me. "And, looking down, I did the same."

Breath shook inside me as I looked down. All I saw was total and immeasurable blackness. How could he see anything there?

I caught my breath then, listening.

From the dark pit, I could hear a collection of nearly inaudible sounds-screams and cries of agony, mad, raucous laughter, howlings of derangement. I tried not to shudder but I didn't have the strength. How could I go down to that? I closed my eyes and pleaded: God, please help me to survive.

Whatever lay below me on the floor of Hell.

Chapter Twenty-Five

Hells Within Hells

I wonder, now, if someone with a psychic birth right, someone who, in supraconsciousness, had traveled to this place-had named the English sanitarium Bedlam.

A noisome pestilence, the phrase occurred as we reached the bottom of the crater.

The air was rent by every horrible sound which man is capable of emitting. Screams and howlings. Shouted curses. Laughter of every demented variety. Snarls and hisses. Bestial growlings. Unimaginable groans of agony. Shrill utterances of pain. Savage roars and lamentations. Screeches, bellows, wails, clamorings and outcries. The jangled tumult of countless souls in throes of derangement.

Albert leaned in close and shouted in my ear. "Hold on to me!"

I needed no encouragement. Like a child terrorized by every known and unknown dread in his mind, I clung to his arm as we started across the crater base, threading our way among forms that sprawled in almost every spot, some moving fitfully, some with spasmed jerks and hitches, some crawling virtually like snakes, some as motionless as corpses.

All of them resembled the dead.

What I could make out, through the feeble light we carried with us, cowed my soul. A cloud of vapor hung above the rock-strewn ground, threatening to suffocate us until, once again-for what innumerable time-we adjusted our systems to survive it.

Below the vapor were the figures. Clothes in filthy rags which showed great gaps of gray and purple flesh. Glowing eyes in lifeless faces, staring at us.

And I heard a buzzing sound.

People sat on boulders, heads together as though they were conspiring. People copulated on the ground and on the rocks, screaming and laughing. People struck at each other, choked each other, battered each other with rocks, tortured each other. All with shouts and snarls and curses. A mass of crawling, twisting, wrenching, jerking, lurching, clashing, convulsive creatures filled the crater's basin.

And I heard this buzzing.

Now, as sight adjusted to the smoky gloom, I saw bands of apelike figures roving close together, talking to each other in guttural voices, moving-I could only guess-in search of some prospective evil, some brutal violence they might commit.

And the buzzing continued, an interminable drone from a source I couldn't spot.

Now I saw that, interspersed throughout the area we crossed, were pools of dark and filthy-looking liquid; I hesitate to call it water. A loathsome stench beyond that which I had ever been exposed to rose from these pools. And I was horrified to see movement in them as though unfortunates had slipped beneath the surface and were unable to rise.

And the buzzing continued, growing louder and louder, a haze of constant sound above the cacophony of human and inhuman noises.

A sudden burst of vicious thoughts struck violently at me! But I thought we couldn't pick up thoughts, the idea came. I felt crushed beneath the weight of the assailing visions and could only assume that such thoughts were so rabid in their focus that telepathy was not required to absorb their vibrations. That such thoughts were actually tangible to the senses, more a wave of physical shock than a conflux of immaterial ideas.

Feeling that wave as it seared and sickened me, I looked around and saw a knot of people standing about ten yards from us, illuminated by a lurid, dirty-looking orange glow. Some had sneering grins on their faces, others expressions of savage hatred. It was a wave of their thoughts-

Suddenly, I cried out, stunned, the sound of it unheard beneath the lunatic din.

The buzzing I heard was that of flies. Millions of them.

Everyone was covered with shifting clumps of flies. Faces moved with them. They were settled in the corners of eyes and crawling blackly in and out of mouths.

A ghastly vision filled my mind. Kit with a barbed wire cut on her face, a solid pack of flies collected on it like a lump of living coal, those on the bottom gorging on her blood, their bellies red and swollen with it. Even when I'd waved my hand at them, crying out in revulsion, those flies hadn't stirred.

The sickened horror I'd felt at that moment was nothing compared to this. My fingers dug into Albert's arm and I closed my eyes, trying to escape the sight.

That was worse.

The instant my eyes were shut, a rush of other sights began to flash across my mind. White faced ghouls devouring rotted flesh. Grinning vampires wallowing in gouts of dark blood from the throats of screaming children. Figures of garbage and excrement embracing in hideous union. Men and women-

I opened my eyes with a jerk. As ghastly as they were, the sights around us were preferable to the ones I'd been compelled to see with my eyes closed.

"Resist their thoughts!" Albert shouted. "Don't let them weaken you!" I looked at him in wordless dread. Had he known?

I tried to resist. Robert, how I tried. Attempting to avoid the grisly sights and sounds those people constantly inflicted on me; the smells and tastes and feels of this place. Ann couldn't be here, I told myself.

I wouldn't allow myself to believe it.

Abruptly, now, as though there were some connection with my thought of Ann, the most elaborate of despairs and anguishes began to flood my consciousness.

I can only say that nothing in my life had come even remotely close. Because the physical brain is incapable of dealing with multiple thoughts at one time whereas the spirit mind can take on mass impressions. Even a mind as lowered as mine had become.

These impressions were like sprays of acid burning at my mind. Utter hopelessness and dolor vied for the very existence of my consciousness. A melancholia so vast it yawned beneath me like a pit without a bottom. Ann isn't here. The thought became my only defense.

Not among these.

I started, crying out in shock, as a man came lurching up to us, wearing what appeared to be the remnants of a toga, now blackened shards hanging from his body. His limbs were so devoid of flesh as to be skeletal. The hands he stretched out toward us were like talons on a bird of prey, the fingernails like black claws. His face was scarcely recognizable as such, distorted and malformed. His glittering eyes were small and red, his open mouth repulsive, filled with teeth like yellow fangs.

Much of his face was decayed, gray bone showing through the rotted flesh. I cried out, horror-stricken, as he clutched my arm, his touch causing an intense nausea to billow up inside me.

"There!" he cried, pointing with one of his claw-like hands.

Involuntarily, I looked where he was pointing and saw a man dragging a woman toward one of the darkly viscid pools. She was shrieking in mindless terror, the sound of it cutting through me like razor slashes.

I cried out again as I recognized her. "Ann!"

"Chris, no," Albert warned.

Too late. I had, already, let go of his arm, already eluded his desperate grab for me. "I'm coming!" I shouted, lunging toward Ann.

All Hell broke loose.

I'd never truly known the meaning of that phrase till then.

In the instant I broke free of Albert, his protection vanished and a mass of figures rushed at me, howling with demonic glee.

As they closed in rapidly, I knew, with a bolt of horror, that I'd been tricked by the man. Had he known that I was searching for my wife? Was his mind that cunning?

Whatever it was, he'd only made me think that it was Ann. Already, I knew it wasn't. The moment I'd pulled away from Albert, the woman's face had altered to the ghastly look of all the others.

Jarring to a halt, I tried, in vain, to turn, twisting around in a frenzied panic.

No use. I'd barely begun to move when they were on me from every side, waves of shrieking figures clutching at me.

I staggered and lost balance, tried to catch myself and started falling. Howls of savage mirth enveloped me. I cried out, horrified, as I went toppling to the rocky ground, their bodies crashing down on top of me, hands clawing at my face and body, tearing at my clothes, my flesh.

Faces blurred across my sight, some charred, some fiery red, all disfigured by scars or burns or ulcerous sores. Some had no faces at all but something made of hair and bone where features should have been.

I screamed out Albert's name, then had the hideous sensation of a swarm of flies flooding into my open mouth, into my ears and eyes. They seemed aroused by my helplessness. I tried to spit them out. I slapped at my eyes and ears with maddened hands.

Again, I tried to scream out Albert's name but the only sound I made now was a choking gurgle as a surge of flies began to clog my throat. I tried to wrench myself onto my stomach so I could vomit them up but the clamoring, screaming people wouldn't let me. They were hauling me across the ground on my back, yanking at my arms and legs, kicking me and screeching with insane delight at my impotence.

The light I'd carried was virtually gone now. All I saw were twisted forms and shadows hovering all around me. All I heard were cries of demented joy as they dragged me over the ground, shredding my clothes and ripping my skin on razor-sharp rocks. That and the buzzing of flies.

Albert! I thought in pleading anguish. Help me please! Total blackness now. The deafening buzz of fly swarms in my ears, the sensation of their crawling, by the hundreds, in my mouth and throat, across my staring eyeballs.

Abruptly, then, I felt myself being plunged into icy liquid, shoved beneath its surface. Instantly, it flooded down my throat and pressed against my face, an indescribable sensation-a combination of every vile taste and smell conceivable.

I felt the claw-like hands forcing me down into the liquid, my horror increasing even more-how was that possible?-as below the surface, other hands began to clutch at me.

I tried to scream but only made a strangled, bubbling noise as hands kept pulling at me, passing me down from unseen grasp to unseen grasp, dragging me deeper and deeper into the noxious depths.

Bodies started clinging to me now, skeletal, with streamers of rotting flesh. My eyes were tightly closed but I could see their faces nonetheless. The faces of the living dead regarding me with gleeful, burning eyes as I went down and down and down.

Ann! I thought. My consciousness began to fade. I've failed you!

* * * *

I sat up with a shocked cry.

Albert held his hand on my shoulder as I stared at him. At last, I looked around.

We were sitting on a barren plain, all gray, its sky the color of muddy slate. A cold wind moaned across its stark, unending flatness.

Yet, I tell you Robert that, compared to where I'd been, that plain was paradise.

"How did you get me?" I asked. That I was with him seemed beyond my comprehension.

"You were only in their grasp a few moments," he told me.

"A few moments?" I knew I was gaping. "But they knocked me down and dragged me to a pool and pushed me underneath the surface where-"

He shook his head, smiling grimly. "You were in my sight the entire time, no more than several feet away. They touched you only with their minds."

"God," I shivered uncontrollably. "That has to be Hell. It has to be."

"One of them," he answered.

"One!" I stared at him, appalled.

"Chris," he told me, "there are Hells within Hells within Hells."

Chapter Twenty-Six

Where Ann Now Stayed

We walked across the wide, gray plain, sandals scuffing at the hard soil. "There's no one place called Hell," Albert was telling me. "What men have called Hell is a vacuum in which undeveloped souls find themselves after death. A level of existence which they cannot rise above because they are unable to think abstractly but can only dwell on temporal matters."

"Why did we have to go there then?" I asked. "Surely Ann-"

"I can only say, Chris, that the signals, if you will, led through there," Albert said. "And, thank God, out of there."

"Are we still following them?" I asked anxiously. He nodded.

"I believe we're getting close now."

I looked in all directions, seeing nothing but the lifeless plain. "How can we be?" I asked.

"Be patient," he told me. "A little while longer."

We walked in silence for a while. Then, thinking of him, I said, "That man who tricked me."

"A tragic figure," Albert said. "He spent the greater part of his life inflicting physical and mental torture on others. His crimes, turned back on him, have kept him prisoner in that place for centuries. The pity is that, in spite of the fact that the memory of each unspeakable act he ever committed is printed indelibly on his mind, he does not, to this moment, repent or regret his actions in the least."

"Why do you call him tragic?" I asked, remembering the man's vicious, feral expression.

"Because," Albert answered, "in ancient Rome, he did not live the life of a criminal but that of an Administrator of Justice."

I could only shake my head.

"Of course the justice he administered was nothing but a travesty," Albert said. "And, now, he suffers the pain of true justice-an eye for an eye."

He stopped abruptly, looking to our right. I turned my gaze in that direction and saw, to my surprise, a range of low hills in the distance.

"She's over there," Albert said.

I looked at him with sudden joy.

His expression did not encourage joy. "Don't feel happiness," he said. "It isn't cause for celebration. Now the hardest part begins."

* * * *

Strange that, after all I had experienced in the crater, I should feel a greater sense of foreboding at the sight before me even though it should have been a reassuringly familiar one-the hill which led to our home.

I looked at Albert in disturbed confusion. Why had we gone so far afield if she'd never left home? "She's here?" I asked.

"Here?" he replied.

"In our home," I said. But, even as I spoke, I knew why he had turned my question back on me.

This was not the home I'd known even though, from where I stood, it looked virtually identical.

"What is it then?" I asked.

"You'll see if you go up there," he answered.

"Up?" I looked at him, astounded.

"I'd rather you left," he said. "Yes, even here, where you're only steps away from her."

I shook my head.

"Chris." He took my arm and held it firmly; how thick and earth-like, I suppose the word would be-my flesh now felt. "What happened to you in the crater only happened in your mind-and only your mind suffered. What happens here could affect your soul."

I knew he spoke the truth. Still, I shook my head again. "I have to see her, Albert," I told him.

He smiled but it was no more than a sad, accepting smile.

"Remember then," he said, "resist, at all times, the despair you'll feel. Your astral body must enshroud itself even more so Ann can see and hear you. In doing so, it makes you vulnerable to everything to which she's vulnerable. You understand that?"

"Yes," I nodded.

"If you feel yourself being-how shall I put it?-drawn in," Albert said, "oppose it with all your strength. I'll try to help you but-"

I broke in. "Help me?"

"I'll do what I can to assist you-"

My expression must have stopped him. He looked at me in alarm. "Chris, no," he said. "You mustn't."

"Yes." I looked up at the house, the roof of which was just visible on the hilltop. "I don't know what's up there or what's going to happen. But I have to help her by myself. I feel it," I said, not letting him speak.

He gazed at me in deep distress.

"I feel it," I repeated. "I can't explain it but I know it's so."

He stared at me in silence for a long while, obviously wondering whether he should try to argue with me.

Finally, without a word, he stepped forward and embraced me slowly. He held me for a long while, then stepped back, hands still on my shoulders, and managed a smile.

"Remember you are loved," he said. "There is a home for you and people who care." He let his hands drop from my shoulders. "Don't let us lose you," he said.

I had no reply. There was no way of my knowing what I'd face on the hill. I could only nod and try to return his smile before he turned away and started walking from me.

I watched until he'd disappeared from sight, then turned and started up the driveway toward the house. A sudden thought occurred. Driveway? Did she have a car? And, if she did, where could she drive it?

I stopped and looked around, the answer readily apparent. There was no neighborhood, no houses in the distance, no Hidden Hills, no nothing. The house was isolated.

I listened to my footsteps on the driveway as I started up again. The paving was cracked and grimy, I noticed, with tufts of yellow weeds growing through.

I thought, again, of what Albert had said before he'd left me.

"She won't believe a word you say; remember that at all times. There is no point in your trying to convince her that she's not alive. She thinks she is. She thinks that only you are dead. For that reason, it will be as well you don't identify yourself immediately but, rather, try, in some way-I don't know what that way is, Chris-to gradually convince her who you are. I leave that to you; you know her better than I. Just remember that she won't recognize you and won't believe you if you tell her, straight out, who you are."

I was halfway up the hill now. How dreary everything appeared. I've described the driveway. In addition, all the trees that lined it were dead and leafless. Passing one, I bent a twig and felt it snap off dryly in my fingers. The ground cover looked parched, the ground itself cracked by jagged fissures. I remembered how I used to complain about the look of our hill in late summer.

It had been glorious compared to this.

I stopped and hitched back suddenly from the driveway just ahead. A snake was slithering from the weeds to cross it. As I watched, it undulated slowly across the cracked paving. I tried to see its head, to make out if it was triangular. When I couldn't, I looked at its tail to see if there was a rattle. We'd had rattlesnakes occasionally. Once, a three-footer had been living underneath a cardboard box behind the garage.

I didn't move until the snake had disappeared into the brown grass to the right of the driveway. Then I started up again, wondering what would have happened if I'd extended my hand to the snake. It couldn't kill me obviously but, at this level, would I have felt the burning poison in my veins?

Looking up now, I could see the roof of the house more clearly. It appeared shadowy and blurred and I realized that I was going to have to lower my vibration again to reach this level.

It happened of its own accord once more, a feeling like the ones I'd had before, that sensation of congealing. My walk became a trudge. A transparent film crossed my eyes and the light grew even dimmer, what little color there was grew duller yet. Through a sombrous haze, I saw the house completely solid now. It looks so depressing, I thought.

I caught myself. Already, I thought. What Albert had warned me of; a sense of despair. It was easy enough to feel, God knew, my body laden, the hillside brown and arid, the sky a dullish gray, far worse than the smoggiest ugliest day I'd ever known in life.

I wouldn't let it touch me though. I'd be with her in moments and, no matter what it entailed or how long it took, I'd do something to help her.

Something.

I reached the top of the hill and turned right toward the house where Ann now stayed.

Chapter Twenty-Seven

To Reach Her Soul

The house looked smaller. Dingier. Rundown. Again, I remembered complaining, in life, about the roof; that it needed re-shingling. I remembered Ann's being disturbed about the outside of the house which needed repainting. The bushes around the house usually needed pruning, the garage straightening up.

Yet, compared to what I saw before me now, that house had been perfection.

These shingles were cracked and dirty, many of them missing. The paint on the outside walls and on the doors and window frames and shutters was faded and smudged, parts of the walls defaced by long, meandering cracks. The bushes, like those on the hill, were brown and dry, the garage a dismal sight, its oil-stained floor covered with blown-in dirt and leaves. All the trash barrels were overflowing, two of them turned over, a gaunt cat eating garbage from one.

Catching sight of me, it jerked around in fright and raced out through the rear doorway of the garage which had no door now. Through the opening, I saw the elm tree standing dead, the cracked fence sagging toward the hill.

Ann's Honda was parked in front of the house. At first, I felt surprised to see only her car and looked around for the others, especially the camper.

It came to me then that this was her particular limbo and could only possess what she expected to see in it.

I walked to her car and examined it. The sight made me queasy. She'd always been so proud of it, kept it so immaculate. Now it looked old, its chrome pitted with rust, its paint faded, windows streaked with dirt, one side dented, one tire flat. Is this what everything is like here? I wondered.

I tried not to think about it but turned toward the front doors.

They looked old too, stained, their knobs corroded. The glass cover on the porch light was broken, shards of glass lying across the porch. A section of the slate floor was missing, the rest chipped and dirty.

Again, that sense of bleak depression. I fought it off. And I haven't even gone inside, I thought, the idea chilling me.

Bracing myself, I knocked on the left door.

It felt grotesque to knock on the door of my own home-well, it looked like my home albeit a distorted form of it-but I knew how abrupt appearances alarmed Ann. Often, coming home at an unexpected time, I'd walked into our bedroom, meeting her as she emerged from the dressing room. She'd gasped in shock and, literally, recoiled, saying, "Oh! I didn't hear you come in!"

So I knocked. It was better than frightening her.

No one answered. I stood on the porch for what seemed, to me, a very long time. Then, giving up, I turned the knob and started to open the door. Its bottom scraped on the floor as I pushed it; the hinges must be loose, I thought. I stepped inside. The slate floor in the hallway looked as bad as the one on the porch.

I shuddered as I closed the door. It actually felt colder in the house than it had outside, a clammy chill hovering in the air. I clenched my teeth and walked into the living room. No matter what I saw, I vowed, I wouldn't let it dissuade me from my reason for being there.

I'd always loved our living room, Robert: the rich, oak paneling, the built-in bookcases, the heavy, earth-tone furniture, the enormous sliding door and window overlooking the back deck and swimming pool.

I couldn't love this room.

Its paneling and bookcases were cracked and lusterless, its furniture worn and faded. The carpeting, which I recalled as being forest green, was, now, some drab shade in between dull green and black. There was a huge, ocherous stain near the coffee table and the table itself was scratched and splintered, its oak tone completely flat.

I'd had that table handmade, always loved it. Walking over to it, I looked down at the chessboard and men Ann had had made for me one Christmas. It had been a stunning piece of craftsmanship, the board made of oak with inlaid silver filigree, the men hand-cast in pewter with bases of turned oak, all impossible to duplicate.

Now the board was cracked and dingy and five of the pieces were missing, two sagging, almost broken. I turned away from the table, telling myself that this was not the chess set i had lived with. It was hard to keep that in mind though because everything looked so familiar. The bookcases were as I remembered them-except that these were only half filled with dusty, aging books. The shutters were as I recalled-except that one of these was broken off and lying on the dirty, sun-bleached cushion of the window seat.

I gazed out toward the deck and saw the fruitless mulberry tree. No, this wasn't the same one, this was dying. The deck was littered with dry leaves and the pool looked stagnant, a slime-like growth on its motionless surface.

Turning back-there was a crack in the sliding door I noticed as I did-I stepped over to the baby grand. Its case once a glossy brown, was now drab. I touched the keys. The sound they evoked was tinny. The piano was completely out of tune.

I averted my eyes from the dreary room and called Ann's name.

There was no answer.

I called repeatedly, then, when the silence was unbroken, walked through the bar room to the family room, remembering the day-it seemed a century ago-I'd walked this same way in our earth house, the day of my funeral, before I'd realized what had happened.

The family room was as bad as the others-frayed and dusty furniture, faded paneling and drapes, tile floor grimy. In its fireplace, a small fire burned. I would never have believed, until that moment, that a fire could be anything but cheerful. This one was, so small and mean looking-a few, pale, licking tongues of flame around some scraps of wood-that it seemed to give no heat at all and certainly no comfort.

No music, I realized then.

Our home had always been filled with music, often a conflux of it from two to three sources at once. This house- this dour, unpleasant version of our house-was weighty with silence, cold with silence.

I didn't look at the photographs on the walls. I knew I couldn't bear to see the children's faces. Instead, I moved into the kitchen.

Dirty dishes, pots and cutlery in the sink, the windows streaked with grime, the floors spotted. The oven door was open and I saw, inside, a baking pan half filled with hard, white grease, a few small scraps of dried-up meat.

I opened the refrigerator door and looked inside.

The sight repelled me. Wilted lettuce, dry, white cheese, stale bread, yellow-edged mayonnaise, an almost empty bottle of dark red wine. A fetid smell of rot came from the barely cool interior and I closed the door. Turning from it, trying not to let the look and feel of the house get past my mental guard, I moved across the family room and down the hallway toward the back of the house.

The children's rooms were empty. I stood in each of them.

They were not as cold and gloomy as the rest of the house but certainly not pleasant either. Only Ian's room looked used, its bed unmade, papers lying on his desk as though he'd just been doing homework.

I wondered why.

* * * *

Ann was sitting on the grass outside our bedroom.

I stood by the glass door, looking at her, tears in my eyes. She wore a heavy, dark blue sweater over her blouse, a pair of wrinkled slacks, old shoes. Her skin, what I could see of it, looked pale and chapped. Her hair was lank as though she hadn't washed it in a long time.

To my distressed surprise, I noticed Ginger lying by her side. I didn't know it then but, after Ann was gone, Ginger had stopped eating and mourned herself to death in a month. Now she was here, so filled with love that she'd chosen this bleak environment rather than leave Ann alone.

Ann was slumped, immobile, holding something in her cupped hands. I'd never seen her in a posture which bespoke such abject misery and, moving to see what she held, I saw that it was a tiny, gray bird stiffened in death.

I remembered, suddenly, that this had happened before. She'd found a bird in the street, struck down, unnoticed, by some motorist. She'd brought it home and sat down on the back lawn with it, cupping its small, pulsing body in the warmth of her palms. I remembered what she'd said, that she knew the bird was dying and wanted it to hear, in its final moments, the sounds it knew in life-wind rustling in the trees and songs of other birds. A burst of sudden fury hit me unexpectedly. This was not a person who deserved to live in such squalor! What kind of stupid justice was that?

I had to struggle with the feeling. I could feel the anger, like a magnet, pulling me toward something I didn't want to reach. If I hadn't sensed, at the same time, that it was, also, pulling me away from Ann, I might have succumbed at the outset.

As it was, I remembered Albert's warning once again and was able to repress the anger. This wasn't judgment, I told myself. Or, if it was, it was self-inflicted. She was here because her actions had put her here. It wasn't punishment but law. My resentment of it was a waste of energy. All I could do was try to help her understand. That was why I was there. And now it was time to start. I'd reached her body.

Now I had to reach her soul.

Chapter Twenty-Eight

A Poor Beginning

The sliding glass door was pushed halfway aside and, stepping to the opening, I spoke her name.

Neither she nor Ginger reacted. I thought it possible that she might not have heard but knew that Ginger would have.

Clearly, I had not "descended" far enough as yet.

I hesitated for a while. It gave me such a grimy feeling, is the only way I can describe it, to lower my vibration and take on further thickness, further weight.

I knew I had to do it though and, bracing myself, allowed it to take place. I shuddered at the feeling. Then, gripping the handle of the sliding screen door, I eased it open.

Instantly, Ginger jerked her head around, ears standing high, and Ann began to turn. Seeing me, Ginger lurched to her feet with a growl and scrabbled around to face me. "Ginger, don't-" I started.

"Ginger. "

The sound of Ann's voice almost made me cry. I stared at her as Ginger faltered back, glancing around. Ann was pushing to her feet and, for a glorious instant, I thought she recognized me. With a beginning sound of joy, I moved toward her.

"Who are you?" she demanded.

I froze in mid-step. Her tone had been so cold, I felt an icy clamp snap shut on my heart. I stared at her, dismayed by her hard, suspicious voice.

Ginger still growled, hair raised on her back; obviously, she didn't know me either. "She'll attack if you come any closer," Ann warned. I sensed that she was more frightened than threatening but, again, the hardness of her tone cowed me.

I had no idea whatever how to proceed. I recognized her, of course. She returned my look and found me totally alien. Was it possible, I wondered, that there was still a vibratory distance separating us?

I was afraid to find out. Did she see me clearly? I wondered. Or was I blurred to her as Albert had been to me the first time I'd seen him after I died?

I cannot say how long we would have stood there mutely if I hadn't spoken. We were all like statues, she and Ginger staring at me, Ginger silent now but still standing taut, ready to defend Ann if she had to. I felt a rush of affection for her. To love Ann so that she accepted this in place of Summerland. What more can be said in praise of her devotion?

My mind seemed like the works of some old clock, its wheels revolving inchingly. There had to be something I could say, I thought. Some way to begin. But what?

I have no idea how long it took for the initial concept to form in my mind. As I've indicated, Robert, time in afterlife is not the same-and, even though this place was closer to Earth than to Summerland, its time scale was, in no way, similar to the clock and calendar continuum Ann and I had known in life. What I mean is that the period of time we spent in gazing at each other may have taken many minutes or a second or two; I believe the former, however.

"I've just moved into the neighborhood," I finally said. My voice seemed to sound on its own. I didn't know what I was getting at. Or, if I did, the knowledge was deeply buried in my mind. At any rate, the words came out unbidden; a start however small.

I cannot convey to you the pain it gave me to see a look of such distrust on her face as she reacted to my words. "Whose house?" she asked.

"Gorman," I told her.

"They haven't sold their house," she said.

I took a calculated risk. "Yes, they have," I told her.

"Some time ago. I moved in yesterday."

She didn't respond and I was forced to wonder if I'd lost my cause already, caught in a palpable lie.

Then, when she didn't challenge me, I guessed that my calculation had been accurate. She had memories of the Gormans but was out of touch with everything beyond this immediate environment and had no way of knowing whether what I said was true or not.

"I didn't know they'd sold their house," she finally said, confirming my assumption.

"Yes. They did." I felt a sense of minor achievement at the point I'd won. But, even as I spoke, I knew I still had a long way to go.

I tried to evolve the next move in my mind. There had to be some definite approach to this; some step by step method of getting through to her.

The realization struck me as I tried. There wasn't any definite approach. I'd have to feel my way along from moment to moment, always on the lookout for some special opportunity.

Ann provided the next step though, I'm sure, unknowingly. "How do you know my name?" she asked.

"From the Hidden Hills directory," I said, gratified to notice that the answer was acceptable to her.

The gratification was nullified immediately as she asked, once more suspicious, "What were you doing in the house?"

I made the mistake of hesitating and Ann tensed, drawing back. Instantly, Ginger growled again, the hair erecting on her back.

"I knocked on the door," I said as casually as possible. "There was no answer so I came inside and called. I kept calling for you as I moved through the house. I guess you didn't hear me."

I could see that the answer dissatisfied her and a sense of hopelessness washed over me. Why doesn't she recognize me? I thought. If she didn't even know my face, what hope was there that I could help her?

I resisted the feeling, once again recalling Albert's warning. How many times would I have to fight against that hopelessness before this ended?

"I just came by say hello," I began without thought; I had to keep things moving. Then, on impulse, I decided on a second calculated risk. "You seemed to recognize me when you saw me," I told her. "Why was that?"

I thought-again, for a glorious instant-that a sudden breakthrough had been made when she answered, "You look a little like my husband."

I felt my heartbeat quicken. "Do I?"

"Yes. A little bit."

"Where is he?" I asked without thinking.

A bad mistake. She drew back noticeably, eyes narrowing.

Had my question sounded menacing to her? The answer to that became apparent as Ginger growled once more.

"His name is Chris?" I asked.

Her eyes grew narrower yet.

"I saw it in the directory," I told her; not too suspiciously fast, I hoped. I felt myself tense as the realization came that, in her mind, my name might not be in the directory anymore. But she only murmured, "Yes. Chris."

Shall I tell you, Robert, of the agony of yearning to take her in my arms and comfort her? Knowing, even as I yearned, that it would be the worst thing I could possibly do?

I forced myself to continue. "The Gormans told me that he's written for television," I said, trying to sound no more than neighborly. "Is that right? What-?"

"He's dead," she cut me off, her voice so bitter that it chilled me.

I knew then, with complete and overwhelming impact, what a task I faced. How could I hope that Ann would ever recognize my face and voice much less my identity? To her I was dead and she didn't believe the dead survived.

"How did he die?" I asked. I didn't know why I spoke; I had no plan. I simply had to labor on, hoping that something useful would occur.

She didn't answer at first. I thought she wasn't going to speak at all. Then, finally, she said, "He had an auto accident."

"I'm sorry," I told her, thinking, with the words, that an air of quiet sympathy might be the best approach. "When did it happen?"

An odd, somewhat disturbing surprise. She didn't seem to know. Confusion flickered on her face. "A ... while ago," she faltered. I thought of using that confusion to my advantage but couldn't figure how.

"I'm sorry," I repeated. It was all I could summon.

Silence again. I tried to come up with something, anything, reduced, at last, to reviving my second risk. "And I look like him?" I asked. Was it possible, I thought, that constant repetition of the idea might, in time, induce her to see that I more than resembled her husband?

"A little," she answered. She shrugged then. "Not too much."

I wondered momentarily if it would help for me to tell her that my name was, also, Chris. But something in me shied away from that. Too much, I decided. I had to move slowly or I might lose it all. I almost said My wife is dead too, then decided it was, also, dangerous and let it go.

It was as though she read my mind although I was sure she couldn't have. "Does your wife like Hidden Hills?" she asked.

The sense of encouragement I felt that she had asked a reasonably social question was muddied by my confusion as to how to answer it. If I told her that I had a wife, would it enable me, eventually, to lead her thinking toward herself? Or would it place an irreparable barrier between us for her to think that there was some other woman in my life?

I decided, on impulse, that the risk was greater than I dared and answered, "My wife and I are separated." That was literally true and should satisfy her.

I hoped that she'd ask me if we were planning on a divorce-in which case I could answer that the separation was of a different nature, thus opening up another area of thought.

She said nothing though.

Silence once more. I almost groaned to find it happening again. Was my attempt to help her to be an endless series of false starts broken by these silences? Desperately, I tried to think of an approach that would result in some immediate perception on her part.

I could think of nothing.

"How did the bird die?" I asked on impulse.

Another mistake. Her expression became more somber yet. "Everything dies here," she answered.

I stared at her, not realizing, until several moments had passed, that she hadn't really answered my question. I was about to repeat it when she spoke.

"I try to take care of things," she said. "But nothing lives." She looked at the bird in her hands. "Nothing," she murmured.

I began to speak then didn't as she went on.

"One of our dogs died too," she said. "She had an epileptic fit."

But Katie's safe, I thought. I almost said it but realized that of course I mustn't. I wondered if there were anything at all I might pursue on that subject.

"My wife and I had two dogs too," I said. "A German Shepherd like yours and a fox terrier named Katie."

"What?" She stared at me.

I didn't say more, hoping that the idea was at work on her mind: a man who looked like her husband who'd been separated from his wife and had had two dogs like hers, one with the same name. Should I add that our German Shepherd had, also, been named Ginger?

I didn't dare.

Nonetheless, I had just begun to feel a flutter of hope when something seemed to film across Ann's eyes-something almost visible-as though she'd just caught sight of something for an instant, then been forcibly removed from it-doubtless by herself. Was that the process which kept her prisoner here?

She turned away from me and looked across the polluted greenness of the pool. I might have vanished from her sight.

It was a poor beginning.

Chapter Twenty-Nine

The Sheltering of Melancholy

When she spoke at last, I couldn't tell whether she was addressing me or herself. "My pine trees died too," she said. "People kept telling me they would but I didn't believe it. I believe it now." She shook her head slowly. "I try to water them but the pressure is off. They must be repairing pipes in the neighborhood or something. "

I don't know why it struck me with such vivid force at that moment. Perhaps the mundane quality of what she said. But I remembered Albert's words. There is no point in your trying to convince her that she's not alive; she thinks she is.

That was the true horror of this situation. If she knew that she'd committed suicide and that this was the end result, some kind of approach might be made. As it was, there could be no possible meaning to this plight for her, no logic whatever to this dismal state in which she found herself.

I really didn't know what to say, yet, once more, heard myself speaking. "I have water in my house," I told her.

She turned as though surprised by my continued presence.

"How can that be?" she asked. She looked confused and irritated. "What about electricity?"

"I have that too," I said, realizing, then, why I'd spoken as I had. I was hoping that she'd discover, by comparison, that what was happening in her house was, logically, unrealistic and, thus, be led to examine her surroundings more closely.

"What about your gas service?" I asked, pursuing the idea.

"That's off too," she said.

"Mine isn't," I replied. "What about your telephone?"

"It's ... out of order," she said. I felt a momentary glimmer of expectancy at her tone-one which asked of itself: How can this be?

"I don't understand," I said, trying to press my advantage. "It doesn't make sense that all your services would be out at the same time."

"Yes, it's ... odd." She stared at me.

"Very odd," I said. "That only your house would have none of them? I wonder why?"

I watched her carefully. Was any degree of awareness reaching her? I waited anxiously to see.

I should have known.

If convincing her was all that simple, in all likelihood someone would have done it already. I knew that as a look of apathy replaced the one of doubt-replaced it instantly. She shrugged. "Because I'm on a hilltop," she said.

"But why-?"

She broke in. "Would you call the phone company for me and tell them my service is out?"

I stared at her, confounded by my own frustration. For a moment, I had a reckless urge to tell her everything directly-who I was and why she was there. Something held me from it though, sensing the peril of attempting to convince her that way.

Another idea occurred.

"Why don't you come to my house and call them yourself?" I asked.

"I can't," she said.

"Why?"

"I ... don't leave," she said. "I just-"

"Why not?" My voice was edged with impatience now, I was so disturbed by my failure to help her in the least.

"I just don't leave," she repeated. She averted her face but, before she did, I saw the beginning of tears in her eyes.

I didn't think but reached out automatically to comfort her. Ginger growled and I drew back my hand. Would I feel it if she attacked, the thought occurred? Could I bleed, suffer pain?

"The pool looks so awful," Ann said.

That sense of cold despair again. How terrible her existence was, spending endless days in this place, unable to do anything to ease its drab appearance. "I used to love it out here," she said, unhappily. "It was my favorite place. Now look at it."

My question was answered. I could suffer pain at that level. I felt it deeply as I looked at her, recalling how she used to come out on the deck each morning with her coffee, sit in the sunshine in her nightgown and robe and gaze across the crystal water of the rock-edged pool, looking at the lush planting we'd put in. She had loved it; very much.

Her tone grew sardonic. "Some exclusive area," she said.

"Yet everything works at my house," I said, trying again.

"How nice for you," she responded coldly; and I knew, in that instant, that no approach could work twice. I was back to square one in this dreadful game, forced to start all over again.

Silence once more. Ann standing motionless, looking across the ugly expanse of the pool, Ginger beside her, eyes fixed on me. What was I to do? I wondered in discouragement. It seemed as though the more time passed, the less aware of possibilities I became.

I forced myself to concentrate. Was that the danger Albert had warned me about? That I would let these dismal surroundings draw me in and make me part of them?

"You have children?" I asked on impulse.

She turned to look at me with distant appraisal. Then she answered. "Four." Looking away again.

I was going to ask about them when I decided to attempt, once more, to set up, in her mind, a series of provoking "coincidences." The area of children hadn't been approached yet.

"I have four children too," I said. "Two daughters and two sons."

"Oh?" she said without turning.

"My two girls are twenty-six and twenty," I told her. "My sons are twenty-three and seventeen." Was I pressing too far? I wondered.

She was looking at me again. Her expression hadn't changed but it seemed to me there was a tightening around her eyes.

I braced myself and said, "My children's names are Louise, Marie, Richard and Ian."

Now she was drawing back again, a distrustful look on her face. The expression of a woman who sensed that she was being baited but didn't know how or why. I felt a pang of fear at that expression. Had I made a dreadful mistake?

Even as I wondered that, I heard myself ask, "What are your children's names?"

She said nothing.

"Mrs. Neilsen?" I said. I'd almost called her Ann. That look of filming across her eyes again-and sudden, gut-wrenched realization on my part.

No matter how close I came, I could never reach her. Whenever I came too close, something built-in would affect her, causing her to cut herself off. Already, she had mentally shrugged off my words, perhaps blanked them out entirely.

Yet still I went on with a kind of blind, unwilling dread.

"My older girl is married and has three children of her own," I said. "My younger girl-"

I broke off as she turned away and started toward the house, the dead bird dropping, unnoticed, from her hands. I started after her but Ginger, at her heels, looked back with a warning growl. I stopped and watched Ann moving off from me.

Had the end already come?

Suddenly, Ann glanced aside and made a sickened noise, then ran inside the house through the family room doorway, sliding the glass door shut with a bang.

I looked at the ground where she'd glanced and saw a huge tarantula crawling over a rock.

I groaned, not out of fear of the tarantula but at the realization that one of Ann's deepest fears was embodied here. She'd always been terrified of tarantulas, made virtually ill by the sight of them. How hideously predictable that her private hell would include these giant spiders.

Walking over to the tarantula, I looked down at it. Bulbous and hairy, it clambered sluggishly across the rock. I looked around and saw Ann at the glass door, looking at it in panicked revulsion.

I looked around again and saw a shovel leaning against the house. Moving to it, I picked it up and returned to the tarantula. I angled the blade in front of it until it had crawled onto the metal. Then, carrying the shovel to the edge of the deck, I flung the spider as far as I could, wondering, as it arced across the pool and into the ivy, whether it was real or not. Did it exist on its own or only because Ann feared it?

I looked toward the family room door as it was opened slightly. And my heart leaped as I saw a look of childlike gratitude on Ann's face. "Thank you," she murmured. Even in Hell there can be gratitude, I thought in wonder.

I moved quickly to strengthen my position. "I noticed that your Sparklett's bottle is empty," I said. "May I put up a new one for you?"

She looked immediately suspicious and I almost groaned at the sight. "What do you want?" she asked.

I forced myself to smile. "Just to say hello," I told her. "Invite you to my house for coffee."

"I told you I don't leave," she said.

"Don't you ever go for walks?" I asked, trying to sound pleasantly casual. She and I had walked a lot in Hidden Hills.

I wanted her to realize her isolation and to question it. She questioned nothing, turning from me as though my words had offended her. I followed her inside the house and shut the glass door. As I did, Ann turned to look at me and Ginger growled again, her neck fur raised. A vision of endlessly futile attempts to reach Ann's mind assailed me. I struggled with despair again.

Then I became aware of the dozens of framed photographs on the walls and another idea occurred. If I could get her to look at one of the photographs of me, the obvious similarity to my present appearance might impress her.

Ignoring Ginger's growl, I moved to the nearest wall and looked for a photograph of myself.

All the photographs were faded and impossible to make out.

Why did that happen? I wondered. Was it part of Ann's self-denying punishment? I was going to mention it, then changed my mind. It could only disturb her.

Another idea. I turned to her and said, "I wasn't really telling you the truth before."

She looked at me, suspiciously uncertain.

"My wife and I are separated," I said, "but not in the way you may think. We're separated by death."

I felt myself wince at the spasmodic shudder my words caused in her; the look on her face as though a knife had just been plunged into her heart.

Still, I had to pursue it, hoping I was finally on the right track. "Her name was Ann too," I said.

"You like it here in Hidden Hills?" she asked as though I hadn't spoken.

"Did you hear me?" I asked.

"Where did you live before?"

"1 said her name was Ann."

The shudder again, the expression of staggered dismay. Then the empty look returning. She moved away from me, headed for the kitchen. Ann, come back, I wanted to say; I almost did. I wanted to shout: It's me, don't you understand?!

I didn't. And, like a cold weight in my chest, depression returned. I tried to resist but, this time, I was less successful. Some of it remained.

"Look at this place," Ann said. She spoke as though she was alone, her voice mechanical. I had the feeling it was part of the process she endured; constant repetition of the details of her plight reinforcing her bondage to them. "Nothing works," she said. "The food is spoiling. I can't open cans because there's no electricity and the hand opener is gone. Without water, I can't do the dishes and they keep piling up. There's no TV; I think it's broken anyway. No radio, no phonograph, no music. No heat except for scraps of wood I burn; the house is chilly all the time. I have to go to bed at dark because there are no lights and all the candles are gone. The rubbish company never picks up anymore. The whole place smells of trash and garbage. And, I can't complain about anything because the phone is out.

She broke off her somber catechism with a laugh that chilled me.

"Put up a Sparklett's bottle?" she said. "They haven't made a delivery in such a long time I can't remember the last one." She laughed again, a dreadful, bitter sound. "The good life," she said. "I swear to God I feel like a character in some Neil Simon play, everything around me falling apart, everything inside me shriveling."

A sob shook her body and I started toward her instinctively. Ginger blocked my way, teeth bared, a fierce growl rumbling in her chest. She looked like a hound of hell, I thought, despair returning again.

I looked at Ann. I knew exactly what she was doing but I had no strength to stop her.

She was fleeing from the truth by immersing herself in the relative safety of afflictive details-the sheltering of melancholy.

Chapter Thirty

Yet Pain and Blood

"What do you drink?" I asked her as another idea came. She looked at me as though I were a fool.

"What do you drink?" I repeated. "If the water's off and you have no Sparklett's."

"I don't know," she muttered, glaring at me. "Juice or-"

"Isn't it spoiled?" I interrupted.

"Canned juice; 1 don't know."

"You said-"

She turned away from me. "What do you eat?" I persisted.

"I can't cook without electricity," she said as if it were an answer rather than an evasion.

"Are you hungry now?" I asked. Again, that baleful look. "Are you ever hungry?"

"Not often," she answered coldly.

Was any of this getting through to her? I was growing weary of tortuous effort.

Rashly, I made my point direct. "Do you ever eat or drink?"

She averted her eyes with a hiss of irritation. "What do you think?" she snapped.

I tried walking closer to her only to stop as Ginger growled again. "Why does she keep doing that?" I asked. I sounded irritated now. "I'm not here to hurt you."

"You couldn't if you wanted to," she said.

I almost answered in kind. God help me, Robert. There to assist her and I almost responded with anger. Closing my eyes, I fought to regain my motivation.

When I opened my eyes again, I noticed her car outside and yet another notion came.

"Is that the only car you have?" I asked.

For the third time, that critical look. "We all have cars," she said.

"Where are they then?"

"Being used, of course."

"By your children?"

"Obviously."

"What about your husband's car?"

"I told you he was in an accident," she said, stiffening.

"Someone said you have a camper."

"We do."

"Where is it?"

She looked at the place where we had always kept it parked and a look of confusion distorted her face. She'd never even thought about it before, the realization came.

"Do you know where it is?" I prodded.

She turned on me in annoyance. "It's being repaired," she said.

"Where?" I asked.

She blinked, looked momentarily disturbed. Then the vacant look was back again. "I don't remember," she said. "I'm sure I have it written down some-"

She broke off as I pointed at her car. "How did it get dented?"

"Someone hit it in a parking lot while I was shopping." Her smile was bitter. "That's the way people are," she said. "Whoever did it just left without telling me."

"You were shopping?" I asked. "I thought you said you never left the house."

I heard a tinge of instability in her voice as she answered, "That was before the battery went dead."

We were back where we started, the convoluted turnings of her mind endlessly thwarting me. No matter what I tried, I couldn't make a point she'd recognize much less react to. This gray world she existed in made sense to her. Horrible, depressing sense but sense nonetheless.

The wheels in my mind were turning more slowly now. I could think of nothing new to try and, so, returned to an earlier approach. Maybe if I pushed it harder.

"You never told me what your children's names are," I said.

"Don't you have to leave?" she asked.

I started, not expecting that. I'd forgotten this was life to her. In life, she would have wondered why a strange man lingered in her house.

"I'll leave soon," I said. "I just want to talk to you a little longer."

"Why?"

I swallowed. "Because I'm new in the neighborhood." It seemed like a feeble answer but, for some reason, she didn't question it. "What did you say your children's names are?" I asked.

She turned from the window, walking toward the living room. It was the first time she'd avoided a question by refusing to answer, I thought. Was this a positive sign? I followed her and Ginger, asking, "Is your younger son named Ian?"

"He's in school," she answered.

"Is his name Ian?"

"He'll be home later."

"Is his name Ian?"

"You'd better leave. He's very strong."

"Is his name Ian?"

"Yes!"

"My son's name is Ian too," I told her.

"Really?" Disinterest. Was it feigned or actual?

"Is your older girl named Louise?" I asked.

She glanced across her shoulder as she moved into the living room. "Why don't you-"

"Louise?"

"Why don't you go home?"

"Louise?"

"What if it is?" she demanded.

"My older daughter's name is Louise too."

"How interesting." Sarcasm as resistance now. She walked to the glass door, Ginger at her heels. Was she retreating from me bodily now? And did she know that she was doing it?

"Is your older son's name Richard?"

"Look at that pool," she murmured.

"Is your older son's name Richard?"

She turned, an expression of resentment on her face. "Look, what do you want?" she asked, her voice rising.

I almost said it all-unvarnished, laid out in a row. Then something stopped me. It was amazing I still had that much awareness. My perceptions were becoming more and more blunted as time passed.

I smiled as nicely as I could. Love, I thought. It has to be done with love. "I'm just interested in the remarkable similarities in our lives," I said.

"What similarities?" she lashed out.

"That I look like your husband for one."

"You don't." She cut me off. "Not at all."

"You said I did."

"No, I didn't."

"Yes, you did."

"Then I was wrong!" she flared. Growling, Ginger showed her teeth once more.

"All right, I'm sorry," I said. I had to be more careful. "I wasn't trying to make trouble. It just seemed remarkable to me."

She gazed out through the glass door again. "I don't see anything remarkable at all," she muttered.

"Well ... my wife was named Ann. My children's names the same as yours."

She turned on me again. "Who said they were the same?" she demanded.

"And my name is Chris," I said.

She twitched sharply, gaping at me. For an instant, something lifted from her eyes instead of settling over them. I felt my heartbeat jolt.

It passed as quickly as it came.

A burst of raging anguish filled me. Damn this filthy place! I thought. I shuddered with the rage. And felt myself grow denser with it.

Stop! I thought. I couldn't though. I had no ability to reverse the process. Instead of helping her, I was descending to her world.

No, I thought. I won't do that. I was here to take her from this place, not join her there.

She'd turned away again by then, staring through the murky glass, once more drawing her oppression around her like a guarding mantle.

"I don't know why I don't just put this place up for sale and leave," she said.

Another sound of embittered humor. "Who'd buy it though?" she continued. "The best real estate agent in the world couldn't sell it." She shook her head in disgust. "The best real estate agent in the world couldn't give it away."

She closed her eyes now, lowering he head.

"I keep polishing the furniture," she said, "but dust keeps settling on it. It's so dry; so dry. We haven't had a drop of rain in such a long time, 1-"

She broke off. That, too, I thought, despondently. Of course that would be part of Ann's particular hell: lack of rain and browning greenery.

"I can't stand filth and confusion," she said, her voice beginning to break. "Yet all I see is filth and confusion."

I started forward once again and Ginger braced herself to leap.

"Damn it, can't you see I only want to help," I said, my voice rising.

Ann jerked around, recoiling from me and I felt a burst of agonized reproach inside myself. I drew back quickly as Ginger started for me, snarling. "All right, all right," I murmured, raising my hands in front of me.

"Ginger," Ann said sharply.

Ginger stopped and looked at her.

My mind felt numb with defeat. Everything I'd tried had failed. Now this blunder. For all I knew, I was farther from helping Ann now than before I'd arrived. How vividly I saw what Albert had meant.

This level was a cruel and cunning trap.

"People borrow books and don't return them," Ann said, continuing as though nothing had occurred. "My best jewelry is gone. I can't find it anywhere. My best clothes are missing."

I stared at her with no idea whatever what to say or do. She was hiding again, holding the details of her plight between herself and any possible understanding of them.

"I don't know who took those chessmen either," she said.

"My wife had a chess set like that made for me," I told her. "One Christmas. A man named Alexander built it."

Ann shuddered. "Why don't you leave me alone?"

I lost control.

"You must know why I'm here," I said. "You must know who I am." That maddening look in her eyes again; the filming away, the blind withdrawal.

"Ann," I said. I reached out, touching her.

She gasped as though my fingers burned and, suddenly, I felt Ginger's teeth clamp hard into my arm. I cried out and tried to pull away but she tightened her grip so that I dragged her across the carpeting by her hind legs. "Ginger!" I shouted.

My voicing of her name came simultaneously with Ann's. Immediately, the bite was released and she was back beside Ann, trembling with reaction.

Raising my arm, I looked at it. Yes, pain was definitely possible there. And blood. I watched it oozing darkly from the punctures.

Afterlife, I thought. It seemed a mockery. No flesh, yet pain and blood.

Chapter Thirty-One

There is Only Death

I looked up from my arm to see Ann start to cry. She was stumbling across the room, tears running down her cheeks. As I watched, she slumped down on the sofa and pressed her left hand over her eyes.

The pain in my arm seemed slight now compared to the new despair I felt. Without thinking, I started toward her again, then jerked to a halt as Ginger made a lurching movement toward me, her growl now mixed with a frantic wheezing sound which told me how disturbed she was. I drew back hastily as Ann looked up, her face a mask of wretched anger.

"Will you go?" she cried.

I backed off slowly, watching Ginger. As she settled down into a nervous crouch, I stopped. Looking behind me, I saw that I was standing near the piano bench and, backing up another few feet, I lowered myself onto it slowly, my gaze still fixed on Ginger.

"I want Chris," Ann murmured, sobbing.

I stared at her, completely helpless.

"I want him back. I need him," she said. "Where is he? Oh, God, where is he?"

I swallowed. My throat was dry; it hurt. My arm ached from the bites. I might as well be alive again. This level was so horribly close to life. And yet so horribly far, only racking sensations present, no compensations of any sort.

"Tell me about him," I heard myself ask. I didn't know why I said it. I was straining now. The effort grew more arduous with every passing moment.

She only wept.

"What did he look like?" I asked. Once again, I knew what I'd begun. What I didn't know was if it would work. Why should it? Nothing else had. Still, I went on. "Was he tall?" I asked.

She drew in shaking breath, fingering tears from her cheeks.

"Was he?"

She nodded jerkily.

"As tall as I am?" I asked.

She didn't reply. A shuddering sob instead. "I'm six foot two. Was he as tall as me?"

"Taller." She pressed her lips together.

I ignored her reaction. "What color hair did he have?" I asked.

She rubbed her eyes.

"What color hair?"

"Go away," she mumbled.

"I'm only trying to help."

"I can't be helped." Through gritted teeth.

"Everybody can be helped," I told her. She looked at me, expressionless. "If they ask," I said.

She lowered her gaze. Had the significance of what I'd said reached her mind in any way at all?

I asked another question. "Was he blond?" She nodded once.

"Like me?"

Her teeth clenched again. "No."

I fought an overwhelming urge to give up, stand, walk out of the house, go back to Summerland and wait. It all seemed so utterly hopeless.

"What did he do?" I asked.

She had her eyes shut. Tears squeezed out from underneath the pressing lids and trickled down her pale cheeks.

"I heard he wrote for television." She mumbled something.

"Did he?"

"Yes." Through gritted teeth again.

"I do too," I said.

It seemed unbelievable to me that she could not see the connection. It was so incredibly obvious. Yet she didn't. Never had the meaning of the phrase been so vivid to me: None so blind as those who will not see.

I wanted to leave. But I couldn't desert her. "Were his eyes green?" I asked, plodding on.

She nodded weakly.

"Mine are too," I said. No response.

I shuddered fitfully. "Ann, can't you see who I am?" I pleaded.

She opened her eyes and, for another of those moments, I had the feeling that she recognized me. I tightened, leaning toward her.

Then she averted her face and I shuddered again. Dear God, was there no way in heaven or hell of reaching her?

She turned back quickly. "Why are you doing this to me?" she demanded.

"I'm trying to convince you who I am."

I waited for her inevitable question: Who are you? It never came. Instead, she slumped back on the sofa, closing her eyes, shaking her head in slow, weary turns from side to side.

"I have nothing," she said. I couldn't tell if she was speaking to herself or me. "My husband's gone. My children are grown. I'm all alone. Deserted. If I had the courage I'd kill myself."

Her words horrified me. To have committed suicide and ended up in a place so dreadful that it made her think of committing suicide. A twisted, unrelenting reflection within a reflection.

"I feel so heavy," she said. "So tired and heavy. I can barely lift my feet. I sleep and sleep but always wake exhausted. I feel empty. Hollow."

Albert's words returned to torment me. "What happens to suicides," he'd said, "is that they have a feeling of being hollowed out. Their physical bodies have been prematurely eliminated, their etheric bodies filling the void. But those etheric bodies feel like empty shells for as long a time as their physical bodies were meant to live."

It came to me, at that moment, why it had been impossible to reach her mind.

By placing herself in this spot, she had removed her mind from all positive memories. Her punishment-albeit self-inflicted-was to recall only the inimical things in her life. To view the world she remembered through a lens of total negativism. To never see light but only shadow.

"What is it like to be here?" I asked impulsively. There was a cold sensation in my stomach. I was starting to feel afraid.

Ann looked at me but seemed to gaze into the darkness of her thoughts as she answered. Speaking at length for the first time.

"I see but not clearly," she said. "I hear but not clearly. Things happen that I can't quite grasp. Understanding always seems a few scant inches from me. I can never reach it though. Everything is just beyond me. I feel angry for not seeing or hearing distinctly, for not understanding. Because I know it isn't me that's missing things. But that everything around me is vague and held those few, scant inches from my understanding. That I'm being fooled somehow. Tricked.

"Things happen right in front of me and I see them happen but I'm not sure I'm getting them even though it seems I am. There's always something more going on that I can't figure out. Something I keep missing even though I don't know how I'm missing it or why.

"I keep trying to understand what's happening but I can't. Even now, as I speak to you, I feel as though I'm missing something. I tell myself that I'm all right, that everything around me is distorted. But, even as I'm thinking it, I get a premonition that it is me. That I'm having another nervous breakdown but can't identify it this time because it's all too subtle and beyond my comprehension.

"Everything eludes me. I can't describe it any better. Just as nothing works in the house, nothing works in my mind either. I'm always confused, off center. I feel like my husband must have, in dreams he used to have."

I found myself leaning toward her, anxious to capture every word she spoke.

"He'd be in New York City, for instance, and be unable to get in touch with me no matter how he tried. He'd talk with people and they'd seem to understand him and he'd seem to understand them. But nothing they'd say would work out. He'd dial telephones and get wrong numbers. He'd be unable to keep track of his belongings. He couldn't remember where he was staying. He'd know he was in New York for a reason but couldn't remember what the reason was. He'd know he didn't have enough money to get back to California and all his credit cards were missing. He'd never be able to figure out what was going on. That's how I feel."

"How do you know this isn't a dream then?" I asked. A glimmer.

"Because I see and hear things," she answered. "I feel things."

"You see and hear ... you feel in dreams too," I replied. My mind was laboring but I sensed that there was something there. A connection.

"This isn't a dream," she said.

"How do you know?"

"It isn't a dream."

"It could be."

"Why do you say that?" She sounded upset again.

"I'm trying to help you," I said.

She answered, "I wish I could believe that."

It seemed as though a faint light touched the shadows in my mind. She hadn't believed me at all before. Now she was wishing she could believe. It was a small step but a step.

A new idea occurred; the first I'd had in a long time, I realized. Was something clearing in my mind? "My son, Richard, has been ... " I paused, the word eluding me. "looking into ESP," I finished.

When I'd spoken his name, her face had tightened. "He's been talking to a psychic," I said.

Again, the tension in her face. Was I harming her or helping? I didn't know. But I had to go on.

"He's come, after much thought, to believe-" I braced myself. "-that there's life after death."

"That's stupid," she said immediately.

"No." I shook my head. "No, he believes it. He feels there's proof that survival exists."

She shook her head but didn't speak.

"He believes that murder is the worst crime anyone can commit," I said. I looked directly into her eyes. "And suicide."

She shuddered violently; tried to stand but didn't have the strength and sank back down again. "I don't see ... " she said.

My mind felt clearer now. "He believes that the taking of life is reserved to God alone," I told her.

"Why are you telling me this?" she asked in a low, shaking voice. She trembled as she spoke, huddling against the sofa. Ginger was looking at her frightenedly, ears back. She knew something was wrong but couldn't fathom what.

Again, I braced myself. "I'm telling you because my wife committed suicide," I said. "She took an overdose of sleeping pills."

That blank look crossing her eyes again. For some reason, it lifted almost instantly as though she couldn't manage to retain it. She shook her head. "I don't believe... " she started. Her voice sounded feeble.

My mind felt clearer yet. "What bothers me is that Richard believes she still exists," I said.

No sound. A shaking of her head.

"That she's in a place not unlike our house," I said. "But a gloomy, negative version of it. Everything depressing and cold. Not functioning. Dirty and disordered."

Her head kept shaking. She mumbled inaudible words.

"I think he's right," I said. "I think that death is a continuation of life. That the person we are persists afterward."

"No." An escape of sound, like a stricken breath.

"Can't you see?" I asked. "Your house was beautiful and warm and bright. Why should it be like this? Why?"

She kept drawing back. I knew she was terrified but had to continue. This was the first approach that had accomplished anything.

"Why should your house look so ugly?" I asked. "Does it make any sense? Why should the gas and electricity and water and telephone all be off? Is there any logic to that?

Why should the lawns and bushes and trees all be dying? Why should the birds all be dying? Why shouldn't it rain? Why should everything in your life go bad at the same time?"

Her voice was faint. I think she said, "Leave me alone."

I kept it up. "Don't you see that this house is only a replica of the home you knew? That you're only here because you believe it's real? Don't you see you're making this existence for yourself?"

She shook her head, looking like a panicked child. "Can't you understand why I'm telling you these things?" I said. "It's not just that my children have the same names as yours. Not just that my wife has the same name as yours. Your children are my children. You are my wife. I'm not just a man who looks like your husband. I am your husband. We've survived-"

I broke off as she lurched to her feet. "Lies!" she shouted.

"No!" I jumped up. "No, Ann!"

"Lies!" she screamed at me. "There is no afterlife! There is only death!"

Chapter Thirty-Two

The Battle Ended

We faced each other, now, like gladiators on the sands of some mysterious arena. A struggle to the death, the strange thought came to me. Yet both of us were already dead. What was our struggle then?

I only knew that, if I failed to win it, both of us were lost. "There's no afterlife," I began.

"None." Glaring at me, almost cowing me with her defiance.

"Then I couldn't know of anything that happened after my death."

A moment's confusion on her face before she muttered, scornfully, "Your death."

"I say I'm Chris," I told her.

"You're-"

"Your husband Chris."

"And I say you're a fool for saying it." Now she seemed to be regaining strength.

"Believe what you will," I persisted. "But, whoever I am, I couldn't know what happened to you after your husband died, could I? I mean details," I added, cutting her off. "Could I?"

She looked at me suspiciously. I knew she wondered what I was getting at. I continued quickly to keep her off balance. "No, I couldn't," I answered myself. "You know I couldn't. Because if I did-"

"What details?" she interrupted fiercely.

"Details like you and the children sitting in the front row of the church. Like someone touching your shoulder, making you start."

I knew, from her reaction, that my opening move was a failure. Obviously, she didn't remember my touch. She gazed at me with open contempt.

"Things like the house filled with people after the funeral," I went on. "Richard serving drinks at the bar-"

"Do you think-?" she started.

"Your brother Bill there, Pat, your brother Phil, his wife and-"

"Is that what you call-?"

"You in the closed bedroom, lying on our bed, Ian sitting beside you, holding your hand."

I knew I'd made a hit for she jerked as though I'd struck her. It was something she'd remember vividly, being a moment of sorrow. I was on safer ground now-unhappy ground but safer. "Ian saying, to you, that he knew it was insane but he felt that I was there with you."

Ann began to shake.

"Your telling him: I know you want to help-" She whispered something.

"What?"

She whispered it again. I still couldn't hear. "What, Ann?"

"Leave me alone," she told me in a rasping voice.

"You know I'm right. You know I was there. Which proves-"

The filming across her eyes again. So fast it appeared almost physical. She turned her head away. "I wish it would rain," she murmured.

"I'm right, aren't I?" I demanded. "These things really happened. Didn't they?"

She labored to her feet, looking groggy.

"Are you afraid to hear the truth?"

She sank back down. "What truth?" Her body jerked spasmodically. "What are you talking about?"

"There's no afterlife?"

"No!" Her face gone rigid with fear and fury.

"Then why did you agree to a seance with Perry?" She jerked again as though struck.

"He told you I was sitting by you in the cemetery," I said.

"I'll tell you what he said, word for word. 'I know how you feel, Mrs. Neilsen, but take my word for it. I see him right beside you. He's wearing a dark blue shirt with short sleeves, blue checked slacks-' "

"You're lying. Lying." Her voice was guttural, her teeth clenched tightly, her expression one of malignant wrath.

"Shall I tell you what you said to Perry at the house?" She tried to stand again but couldn't. The filming of her gaze came and went.

"Not interested," she mumbled.

"You said 'I don't believe in survival after death. I believe that when we die we die and that's the end of it.' "

"That's right!" she cried.

A leap of futile hope. "That is what you said?"

"Death is the end of it!"

I fought off momentary loss. "Then how do I know these things?" I asked.

"You made them up!"

"You know that isn't true! You know that everything I've described is exactly the way it happened!"

She managed to stay on her feet this time. "I don't know who you are," she said, "but you'd better get out of here before it's too late."

"Too late for whom?" I asked. "You or me?"

"You!"

"No, Ann," I said. "I know what's happened. You're the one who doesn't understand."

"And you're my husband?" she asked.

"I am."

"Mister," she said; she almost spat the word at me. "I'm looking right at you and you're not my husband."

I felt a sudden, wrenching coldness in my chest.

She saw the depth of my reaction and took immediate advantage of it. "If you were my husband," she said, "you wouldn't say such things to me. Chris was kind. He loved me."

"I love you too." I felt depression rising. "I'm here because I love you."

Her laugh was a cynical, chilling sound. "Love," she said. "You don't even know me."

The ground was slipping out from under me. "I do!" I cried. "I'm Chris! Can't you see that?! Chris!"

My loss was complete as she smiled in cold victory. "How can you be here then?"

she asked. "He's dead."

It had all been in vain. There was no way of convincing her because she, literally, could not conceive of afterlife. No one can conceive of the impossible. And, to Ann, survival after death was an impossibility.

She turned and walked from the living room, followed by Ginger.

At first, the shock of it failed to register. I sat watching her go as if it had no importance to me. Then it struck and I stood in dumfounded shock. I'd done everything I could to convince her, thought I'd had her on the razor edge of belief only to discover I'd accomplished nothing.

Nothing.

I moved after her but, now, without hope. Each step seemed to bring another condensation to my mind and body-a curdling of thought, a clogging of flesh which grew increasingly worse.

For a ghastly moment, I thought I was home again, that this was where I belonged.

Stopping, I resisted the hideous process. I couldn't bear to stay in that place. It was too horrible.

Ann's cry of terror from our bedroom made me break into a run. I say a run but it was more a hobble, my legs coated with lead. It was then that I knew what Ann had described. Like her, I could barely lift my feet. And it was worse for her.

I stopped in the bedroom doorway, Ginger whirling to face me. Ann was pressed against the wall, staring at our bed.

Across its dingy, faded spread, a tarantula the size of a man's fist was crawling.

The moment was frozen. Ann against the wall. Ginger staring at me. Me in the doorway.

The only thing that moved, with bloated sluggishness, was the enormous, furry spider.

As it started up the pillow on Ann's side, she made a gagging noise.

I wondered, for a dreadful moment, if she'd done this to herself; an unconscious punishment for not believing what I'd told her. Created an image of the most repugnant thing she could imagine-a huge tarantula walking on the place where she lay her head in sleep.

I don't know why Ginger made no move as I entered the room. Was it because she, now, sensed that I was really there to help Ann? I have no answer. I only know that she let me walk by Ann and reach the bed.

Picking up the pillow gingerly, I started to turn and flung it from me as the spider made a sudden, hitching movement toward my right hand. Ann cried out, sickened as the tarantula thudded on the bedspread.

Hastily, I snatched up the pillow and dropped it on top of the spider. Then, as quickly as I could, I grabbed the spread at each corner and pulled it over the pillow. Picking up the bundle, I carried it to the door and slide it open. Tossing the spread outside, I shut the door again and locked it.

As I turned back, Ann was stumbling to the bed and falling on it, stone-like.

Motionless, I stared at her.

There were no movements left to make. I'd exhausted all possibilities.

The encounter was over, the battle ended.

Hell Be Our Heaven

Ann lay immobile on her left side, legs drawn up, hands clasped tightly underneath her chin. Her eyes stared sightlessly, still glistening with tears that no longer fell. She hadn't even stirred when I'd sat down on the other side of the bed and, if she sensed my gaze on her mask-like face, she gave no indication of it.

Ginger slept, exhausted, at the foot of the bed. I turned to look at her and felt a rush of pitying love. She was so unquestioning in her devotion. If only there was some way she could understand what was happening.

I looked back at Ann. My body felt cold and aching and I knew that, as I sat there, that dark, terrible magnetism was waiting to draw me to the void where she existed. I had only to allow it and the atmosphere would totally absorb me, making me as she was, a prisoner forgetting everything that had gone before.

I knew, with dreadful clarity, how foolish and misplaced my hopes had been. Albert had tried to warn me but I hadn't listened. Now I understood at last.

There was no way to reach Ann.

Still, words came. Words I wanted her to hear, now when I could speak them to her, face to face. Words which I knew could not affect her but words that filled my mind and heart.

"You remember how you used to write thank-you notes to people all the time?" I asked. "For dinners, presents, favors? I used to tease you because you wrote so many of them. But they were lovely gestures, Ann. I always knew that."

No sound from her. Completely inanimate on the bed. I reached out and took her right hand. It was cold and limp. I held it in both of mine and continued speaking.

"I want to give you thanks in words now," I told her. "I don't know what will happen to us. I pray we'll be together somewhere, sometime, but, at the moment, I have no idea if that's possible.

"That's why I'm going to thank you now for everything you've done for me, everything you've meant to me. Someone you never met told me that thoughts are real and eternal. So, even if you don't understand my words now, I know the time will come when what I say will reach you."

I pressed her hand between my palms to warm it and I told her what I felt.

"Thank you, Ann, for all the things you did for me in life, from the smallest to the largest. Everything you did had meaning and I want you to know my gratitude for them.

"Thank you for keeping my clothes clean, our homes clean, yourself clean. For always being fresh and sweet smelling, always being well groomed.

"Thank you for feeding me. For the preparation of so many lovely meals. For baking for me at a time when so few women bother anymore.

"Thank you for worrying about me when I was having difficulties of any kind. For sympathizing with me when I was depressed.

"Thank you for your sense of humor. For making me laugh when I needed it. For making me laugh when I neither needed nor expected it but enjoyed the extra savor of it in my life. Thank you for your wry perception of our life together and the world we lived in.

"Thank you for caring for me when I was ill. For seeing to it, always. that bed and pajamas were clean, that I was well fed and had fresh juice or water to drink. That I had something to read or that the television set or radio was on or that the house was kept quiet so I could sleep. All this in addition to your other work.

"Thank you for sharing my love of music and for sharing your love of music with me. For the sharing of each other's love of beauty and nature.

"Thank you for helping us to find the lovely way of life we had. For the furnishing and decorating and enjoying of our different homes, the opening of them to the people we knew.

"Thank you for being affectionate with my friends and loving to my family. Thank you for helping us to build so many mutual friendships.

"Thank you for being someone I was proud to be with no matter where I was or who I saw.

"Thank you for our physical relationship. For sharing your female being with me. For making the bodily part of our life so satisfying and exciting. For keeping my sexual ego intact. For enjoying my body as much as I enjoyed yours. For the warmth of your flesh on cold nights and the warmth of your love always.

"Thank you for having faith in my work and in my ultimate success. I know it wasn't easy when there were children and bills and pressures of every kind. But you never wavered in your trust that I'd succeed and I thank you for that.

"Thank you for the memories of things we did together and with the children. Thank you for suggesting that we buy a camper for the family, for helping to bring the joys of outdoor living to me and the children. I know it will be part of their lives now as it was a part of ours. Thank you for all the lovely national parks we saw together. For Sequoia and Yosemite, Lassen and Shasta, Olympic and Mount Ranier, Glacier and Yellowstone, Grand Canyon and Bryce. For Canada and all the states we camped through from coast to coast.

"Thank you for helping us to find, and for sharing with us, the pleasures of traveling to Hawaii and the South Seas, to Europe and throughout the United States.

"Do you remember all our Christmases together, Ann? How we used to go out, all of us, in the camper, drive to the Y.M.C.A. lot in Reseda and pick out a tree? How we walked through aisles of bushy, pungent-smelling pine and spruce trees and chose one, laughing, voting and contending until we found one everybody liked? How we took it home and set it up and put the lights on, then the decorations and the tinsel? How we sat together, looking at it, the only sound our Christmas records playing? How we always said, each year, that that tree was the best we ever got and it was always true for us? I remember all those lovely moments and I thank you for them.

"Thank you for the memories of you and me alone together. Taking weekend trips or drives to interesting places. Shopping together. Walking. Sitting on the bench and looking at the hills at sunset. I'd put my arm around your shoulders and you'd lean against me and we'd watch the sun go down. That was contentment, Ann.

"Do you remember the sheep that used to graze on those hills? How we watched them, smiling at their constant baaing and the delicate clank of the bells around their necks? Do you remember the herds of cattle that were out there sometimes? Sweet recollections, Ann. I thank you for them.

"Thank you for the memories of watching you with birds. Watching you take care of them and heal them, give them your loving attention, year after year. Those birds are waiting for you, Ann. They love you.

"Thank you for giving me the example of your courage and tenacity in recovering from your nervous breakdown. It was a dreadful time in your life, in both our lives. The sleepless nights, the fears and uncertainties, the painful reliving of your past. The years of trying, struggling, hoping.

"Thank you for never letting those years make you surrender. For never letting the scars of your childhood make you give up your efforts to grow and strengthen yourself. And, even though I never wanted you to, thank you for doing all you could to keep me from being exposed to what you suffered during that time.

"Thank you for valuing your marriage and family so highly yet still expanding as an individual. For your desire to grow and your success at doing it.

"Do you remember going back to school? First, taking an isolated course or two, then, later, going at it more intensely until you'd earned your Associate of Arts degree, then your Bachelor's, then started working toward a profession as ,an adult counselor? I was so proud of you, Ann. I wish you were still doing it. You would have made a wonderful counselor-full of empathy and love.

"Thank you for our children. Thank you for providing the clean and lovely vessel of your body for the creation of their physical lives. Do you know I still remember the exact moment each of them was born? Louise at 3:07 p.m. on January 22, 1951, Richard at 7:02 a.m. on October 14, 1953, Marie at 9:04 p.m. on July 5, 1956 and Ian at 8:07 a.m. on February 25, 1959. Thank you for the joy I felt at seeing each of them for the first time-and for the joys that each has brought to my life. Thank you for teaching me to be considerate of them and respect their separate identities. Thank you for being such a fine example to our daughters and sons, showing them what's possible in a wife and mother.

"Thank you for letting me be myself. For dealing with me as I was, not as you imagined me to be or wanted me to be. Thank you for being so compatible with my mind and my emotions. For helping me to keep my airy thoughts on earth, for being neither dominant nor passive but each as the occasion demanded. For being female and accepting what I had to offer as a male. For making me feel, always, like a man.

"Thank you for being tolerant of my failings. For neither crushing my ego nor allowing it to grow beyond the bounds of sense. For keeping, in my mind, the realization that I was a human being with responsibilities. Thank you for remaking me without ever doing it deliberately. For helping me to understand myself better. For helping me accomplish more with you than I could ever have accomplished alone.

"Thank you for encouraging me to talk about our problems, especially as the years went by. Our increasing ability to talk to each other made our marriage better and better. Thank you for helping me combine my ideas and feelings and communicate with you as a total being. Thank you for liking me as well as loving me, for being not only my wife and lover but my friend.

"Thank you for your imagination in our life. For helping me to grow in appreciation of new activities and new ideas. For making my tastes more adventuresome in all things from the least to the greatest.

"Thank you for reminding me in acts, not words, of the right things to do where others were concerned. For teaching me by example, that sacrifice can be a positive and loving gesture. Thank you for the opportunity to mature.

"Thank you for your dependability. For always being there when I needed you. Thank you for your honesty, your values, your morality and compassion. Thank you even for the bad times between us because, in those as well, I learned to grow.

"I apologize for every time I failed you, every time I lacked the understanding you deserved. I apologize for not being patient and kind when I should have been. I apologize for all the times I was selfish and failed to see your needs. I always loved you, Ann, but, often, let you down. I apologize for all those times and thank you for making me feel stronger than I was, wiser than I was, more capable than I was. Thank you, Ann, for gracing my life with your lovely presence, for adding the sweet measure of your soul to my existence.

"I thank you, love, for everything."

* * * *

She was looking at me now, with such a suffering expression that, for an instant, I regretted having spoken as I had.

Immediately, that vanished. There was something in her eyes. Vague and formless, struggling for existence. Like a candle flame in wind.

But definitely there.

How she tried. God in heaven, Robert, how she tried. I saw each moment of it on her face. Something in my words had ignited a tiny flame in her mind and now she strained to keep it burning. Not even knowing what had sparked it into life. Not even knowing it was lit but only sensing that it was. Aware of something. Something different. Something other than the wretchedness she'd been existing with.

I didn't know what to do.

Should I speak, attempting to nourish the flame? Or remain silent, giving her the time to nurture it herself? I didn't know. In that most urgent moment in our entire relationship, I was mentally adrift.

So I did nothing. Staring at her face. Her face so like a child's, striving to understand some vast, remote mystery.

Try, I thought.

It was the only word my mind could summon. Try. I think I nodded in encouragement. Try. I think I smiled. Try. I held her hand so tightly. Try. I felt us both begin to tremble. Try, Ann. Try. Every second of our long affinity from the moment we'd met to this incredible instant-was in climax now. Try, Ann try. Try. Please try.

The flame went out.

I saw it die. One second it was there, barely alive. Then it was gone, the faint illumination of it vanished from her mind. And the falling off of her expression-anxious hope to dull oblivion-was, to me, the most hideous sight I'd seen since my death.

"Ann!" I cried.

No response. In word or facial recognition. The cause was lost.

I stared at her in silence, moments passing. Until the one remaining answer came to me. I couldn't leave her there alone.

Strange how the most horrific decision I had ever made in my existence should impart a sense of peace to me.

Instantly, I let the waiting magnetism start to envelop me. There was no stopping it now. I felt an icy curdling in my flesh, a horrible, clotting, chilling condensation of my entire body.

I almost tried to fight it off as mindless terror swept across my mind.

I stopped that.

This was the one thing I could do for her.

I'd lose the knowledge of it soon; not even have the solace of recognizing my own gesture. But, now, for these limited moments, I knew exactly what I was doing. The only thing left to do.

Forswear heaven to be with her.

Show my love by choosing to remain beside her for the twenty-four years she had to remain there.

I prayed that my companionship-whatever it might prove to be when I had lost awareness-might ease, in some small way, her pain at living in this awful place. But stay I would, no matter what. I started, looking around.

Ginger was licking my other hand.

As I stared at her, incredulous, I heard what was, to me, the most beautiful sound in the universe.

Ann's voice speaking my name.

I turned to her in wonder. There were tears in her eyes. "Is it really you?" she murmured.

"Yes, Ann. Really." I saw her through a shimmering haze of tears.

"You did this ... for me?"

I nodded. "Yes, Ann, yes. Yes." Already, I could feel awareness fading. How soon would it be gone? How soon would desolation triumph?

It didn't matter.

For those few seconds, we were reunited.

I drew her up and put my arms around her, felt her arms around me. We wept in each other's embrace.

Suddenly, she pulled back, her expression one of dread.

"Now you can't leave," she said.

"It doesn't matter." I laughed and cried at once. "It doesn't matter, Ann. Heaven would never be heaven without you."

And, just before the darkness crept across my consciousness, I spoke, for the last time. To my wife, my life, my precious Ann. My last words, whispered to her.

"Let this hell be our heaven."

Chapter Thirty-Four

India

The sensation of awakening was peculiar; as though I were emerging from a thick, heavy chrysalis. I opened my eyes and stared up at a ceiling. It was pale blue, softly tinted. I heard nothing but the most profound of silence.

Attempting to turn my head, I found, to my surprise, that I was too weak to move it. For several moments, I felt with a sense of dread that I was paralyzed.

Then I realized it was exhaustion and closed my eyes again.

How long I slept, I cannot say. The next thing I recall was opening my eyes again. The same blue ceiling, pale, irradiant. I looked down at my body. I was lying on a couch, wearing a white robe.

Was I back in Summerland?

Using my right elbow, I raised myself slowly and looked around.

I was in an immense hall which was ceilinged but not walled, tall Ionic columns serving as side supports. There were hundreds of couches in the room, almost all with people on them. Men and women, dressed in robes the color of the ceiling, moved among the couches, leaning over now and then to speak to reclining figures, stroking their heads. I was back in Summerland.

But where was Ann?

"Are you all right?"

I looked around at the sound of the woman's voice. She was standing behind me.

"Am I in Summerland?" I asked.

"Yes." She leaned over and stroked my hair. "You're safe: rest."

"My wife ... "

Something flowed from her fingertips into my mind; something soothing. I lay down again.

"Don't worry about anything now," she said. "Just rest." I felt sleep drifting over me again; warm, soft, silken sleep.

I closed my eyes and heard the woman say, "That's right: close your eyes and sleep.

You're perfectly safe."

I thought about Ann.

Then was asleep once more.

Again, I cannot tell how long I slept. I only know I woke again to see the blue, effulgent ceiling overhead.

This time I thought of Albert, speaking his name in my mind. When he failed to appear, I felt alarmed and pushed up on my elbow.

The hall was still the same-peacefully still. The floor was thickly carpeted, I saw, and, here and there, handsome tapestries hung down from above. All the floor space, as I've said, was spaced with couches. I looked to my right and saw one six or seven feet away, a woman sleeping on it. To my left, another couch, an old man on it, also asleep.

I forced myself to sit up. I had to find out where Ann was.

Again, I thought of Albert but to no avail. What was wrong? He'd always come to me before. Hadn't he returned to Summerland? Was he still in that terrible place? I struggled to my feet. I felt incredibly heavy, Robert. As though, despite the shedding of that chrysalis, my flesh was still encased in stone. I could hardly move across the hall, past endless ranks of sleeping people, male and female, old and young.

I stopped in the entrance to an adjoining hall.

Here, there was no scene of rest. People thrashed in frantic sleep or, partially conscious, tried to sit up, had no strength to do so and fell back heavily or struggled to rise, restrained by men and women in blue.

Nor was it silent like the hall I'd left. This one was discordant with sobs and cries, embittered and dissentient voices.

Nearby, I saw a man in blue talking to a woman on a couch. She looked confused and angry and kept trying to sit up but couldn't. The man patted her on the shoulder and spoke to her reassuringly.

I looked across the hall in startlement as a man began to shout. "I'm a Christian and a follower of my Saviour! I demand to be taken to my Lord! You have no right to keep me here! No right!"

I saw a man in blue gesture to several of his associates and they gathered around the furious man to touch him. In seconds, he was heavily asleep.

"You should be resting," said a voice.

I looked around and saw a young man in a blue robe smiling at me. I tried to answer but my tongue felt thick and weighted. All I could do was stare at him.

"Come," he said. I felt his hand on my arm and, with the touch, that sense of silken comfort once again. Everything began to blur around me. I knew that he was walking me but couldn't see. What was this subtle narcotic in their touch? I wondered as I felt the soft couch under me once more and sank into a deep sleep.

* * * *

When I woke up, Albert was sitting on the edge of the couch, smiling at me.

"You're better now," he said.

"What is this place?" I asked.

"The Hall of Rest."

"How long have I been here?"

"Quite a while," he told me.

"Those people in the next-" I pointed.

"Those who've died suddenly and violently, waking for the first time," he said. "Refusing to believe that their bodies are gone but they still exist."

"That man ... "

"One of many who expect to sit at the right hand of God and believe that those who fail to share their ideas are doomed to eternal torment. In many ways, these are the most backward souls of all."

"You didn't come before," I said.

"I couldn't until you were adequately rested," he replied. "I received your calls but wasn't permitted to answer them."

"I thought you were still-" I broke off, reaching out to grip his arm. "Albert, where is she?" I asked.

He didn't answer.

"She's not still in that awful place."

He shook his head. "No," he told me. "You spared her that."

"Thank God!" I felt a burst of joy.

"By going there and staying with her of your own free will, you gave her just enough awareness to escape."

"Then she's here," I said.

"You were with her for some time," he told me. "That's why you've been here, regaining your strength." He put a hand on my arm and squeezed it. "I really didn't think it could be done, Chris," he said. "I never foresaw what you were able to do for her. I thought in terms of logic. I should have realized that only love could reach her."

"She is safe," I said.

"Safe from where she was."

I felt a tremor of uneasiness. "She's here?" I asked. "In Summerland?"

He seemed reluctant to answer.

"Albert." I looked at him anxiously. "Can I see her?"

He sighed. "I'm afraid not, Chris."

I stared at him in blank dismay.

"You see," he said, "although the love of someone close can, on occasion, elevate a soul to Summerland-though I've never seen it done with a suicide-that soul is, rarely, if ever, able to remain here."

"Why?" I asked. That I was back in Summerland seemed, suddenly, a hollow victory.

"There are a hundred different answers to that question," he said. "A thousand. The simplest of which is that Ann just isn't ready for it yet."

"Where is she then?" I was sitting up now, gazing at him apprehensively.

He seemed to brace himself. Was that a smile? "Well," he started, "the answer to that brings up a subject so immense I don't know where to begin. You haven't been in Summerland long enough to have been exposed to it."

"What subject?" I asked.

"Rebirth," he said.

I felt dazed and lost. The more I learned of afterlife, the more confusing it became. "Rebirth?"

"You've actually survived death many times," he said.

"You remember the identity of the life you just departed but you've had-we've all had-a multitude of past lives."

A memory surfaced from the darkness in my mind. A cottage and an old man lying on a bed, two people nearby, a white-haired woman and a middle-aged man, their dress foreign, the woman's accent unfamiliar as she said, "I think he's gone."

That old man had been me?

"Are you telling me that Ann is back on earth again?" I asked.

He nodded and I couldn't restrain a groan of despair. "Chris, would you rather she was still where you found her?"

"No, but-"

"Because you helped her understand what she'd done," he said, "she was able to replace her self-imprisonment with immediate rebirth. Surely, you can see the vast improvement in that."

"Yes, but-" Again, I couldn't finish. Of course, I was grateful that she was free of that dreadful place. Still, now, we were separated again. "Where?" I asked.

He answered quietly. "India."

Chapter Thirty-Five

The Path Begins on Earth

At last, I spoke. One word. "India?"

"It was immediately available," he said, "as well as offering a challenge to her soul; a handicap to overcome which can counterbalance the negative effect of her suicide."

"Handicap?" I asked uneasily.

"The body she's chosen will, in later years, contract an illness which will cause severe sleep deprivation."

Ann had taken her life with sleeping pills. To balance the scales, she'd acquire a condition which would not permit her to sleep normally.

"And she chose this?" I asked, wanting to be sure of that.

"Absolutely," Albert said. "Rebirth is always a matter of choice."

I nodded slowly, staring at him. "What about-the rest?" I asked.

"The rest is good," he said. "In compensation for the pain she endured and the progress she achieved in her last life. Her new parents are intelligent, attractive people, the father in local government, the mother a successful artist. And she'll have another name, of course-will be given much love and opportunity for creative and intellectual growth."

I thought about it for a while before I spoke. Then I said, "I want to go back too."

Albert looked distressed.

"Chris," he said, "unless one has to, one should never choose rebirth until one has studied and improved the mind so that the next life is an improvement over the last."

"I'm sure that's true," I conceded. "But I have to be with her and help her if I can. I feel guilty for not having helped her enough in our past life together. I want to try again."

"Chris, think," he said. "Do you really want to return so soon to a world where masses are robbed and cheated by a few? Where food is destroyed while millions starve? Where service to state is a brute hypocrisy? Where killing is a simpler solution than loving?"

His words were harsh but I knew he spoke them for my benefit, hoping to convince me to remain in Summerland and grow.

"I know you're right," I said. "And I know you have my best interests at heart. But I love Ann and I have to be with her, helping her as best I can."

His smile was sad but accepting. "I understand." He nodded. "Well, I'm not surprised," he said. "I've seen you both together."

I started. "When?"

"When both of you were taken from that etheric prison."

His smile was tender now. "Your auras blend. You have the same vibration, as I told you. That's why you can't bear being separated from her. She's your soul mate and I understand completely why you want to be with her. I'm sure Ann chose rebirth in hope of bringing both of you together somehow. Still-"

"What?"

"I wish you could understand the implications of returning."

"It can be done, can't it?" I asked with concern.

"It may not be simple," he answered. "And there could be risks."

"What sort of risks?"

He hesitated, then replied. "We'd best have an expert tell you."

* * * *

I thought I could return immediately. I should have known that such a complex process was not so easily effected; that, like everything in afterlife, it required study.

First came the lecture.

Near the center of the city I was in is a giant, circular temple seating thousands. A shaft of white light shines down on it, clearly visible in spite of the abundant illumination.

When Albert and I entered the temple, we moved unhesitatingly to a pair of seats halfway to the speaker's platform. I cannot tell you why. They weren't marked or different, in any way, from all the other seats. Still, I knew those seats were ours before we reached them.

The massive audience was talking quietly; by which, of course, I mean without an audible sound. Many smiled at us as we took our places.

"Are all these people planning to be reborn?" I asked in surprise.

"I doubt it," Albert said. "Most of them are probably here to learn."

I nodded, trying not to acknowledge my mounting unrest. It was similar to the feeling I'd had when I first arrived in Summerland; when something in me had, unconsciously, been aware of Ann's impending suicide.

Similar, I say. It couldn't be the same. I knew that she would live now, not die. Still, our separation was equally distressing to me. I couldn't tell you, Robert, what the higher ramifications are of being soul mates. I can tell you this however. As long as you are separated from your own that long are you troubled. No matter what the circumstances, no matter how exquisite the environment in which you find yourself. To be half of one can only be a torment when the other half is gone.

* * * *

A lovely woman walked up to the platform now and smiled at us, began to speak. "Shakespeare put it this way in referring to death," she said. "The undiscovered country from whose bourn no traveler returns."

She smiled again. "Beautifully expressed," she said, "if totally inaccurate. We have all discovered this country following our 'deaths.' What is more, it is a bourn from which all travelers must, eventually, return.

"We are triune," she continued. "Spirit, soul and body; this last third-in earthly life-composed of physical, etheric and astral bodies. I will not discuss our spirit at this time. Our soul contains the essence of God within us. This essence directs our course of life, guiding the soul through many life experiences. Each time a portion of the soul descends into flesh, it absorbs that experience and evolves, becoming enriched by it. Or-" She paused. "-detracting from it."

Which was essentially what Albert had said, I recalled. Ann's suicide had detracted from her soul and, now, she had chosen to absorb enough positive experience to rebuild it.

How is this larger self added to or subtracted from? By memory. Each of us has an external and an internal memory, the external belonging to our visible body, the internal to our invisible-or spiritual-body. Every single thing anyone of us has ever thought, willed, spoken, done heard or seen is inscribed on this internal memory. This comprehensive recollection always remains in its "Father's house," growing or diminishing with the results of each new physical life. The astral-or spirit-body returns to earth but remains the same. Only the body of flesh and its etheric double is altered.

There is a line of communication between the higher self and whatever physical form the soul has, currently, chosen. For instance, if the physical self receives an inspiration, it comes from the soul. The so-called "still, small voice" is knowledge from former lessons, which warn an individual not to commit some act which would do injury to its soul.

However, by and large, except in cases of those born receptive to its existence or who, by looking inward meditating-become aware of it, the penetration of this true self into matter is rarely perceived.

"The process, then, is this," the woman told us. "Life after life of effort, interspersed with periods of rest and study on this plane, gradually shapes the soul to that which it aspires to be. Sometimes, what it has failed to achieve in life can be achieved in afterlife so that the next rebirth is attended by more awareness, more ability to effect the ultimate aspiration toward God.

"Thus, the triunity which we are experiences a triad of incarnation, disincarnation and reincarnation. Man should be well aware of how to die for he has done it many times. Yet, every time he returns to flesh-with rare exceptions-he forgets again."

* * * *

A question occurred to me. Amazingly, the woman answered it as though she'd picked it from my mind.

"You appear now as you did in your last incarnation," she said. "You have, of course, had many different appearances, some of the opposite sex. You retain the look of your previous life, however, because it is most vivid in your memory.

"When that life terminated, your consciousness receded in stages, toward its source, dissociating itself from its involvement in matter. This process of relinquishment took place in the etheric world where your desires and feelings were refined, all nonregenerated forces from your life focused and transmuted. At length, your consciousness receded to this mental or 'heaven' stage where it is, now, completely, free of matter."

I didn't know whether she'd receive my thanks for the answer but I nodded once. It may have been imagined but it seemed as though she smiled and nodded back.

"The length of the stay in afterlife varies," she continued. "Sometimes a thousand years may pass between incarnations. When awareness comes after death, the initial impulse' of the personality is to reincarnate. Newcomers invariably begin to practice the method by which vibrations are controlled so they can be reborn.

"The real discipline is for a soul to decide to remain in Summerland and study to improve so that the next incarnation will be a larger forward step in the soul-growth process."

Another question occurred to me; immediately answered again. I wondered if I was the only one thinking it.

"Not everyone is reborn," the woman said. "Some souls are so advanced they no longer reincarnate but pass on to a level of existence beyond anything that earth can offer, achieving a final reunion with God.

"These souls, having found no remaining lack in their attempts to atone for misdeeds or acquire knowledge, elect to join the Creator and are drawn into a state of perfect. oneness with Him, becoming, as it were, integral with the universal pattern."

She did not go into the details of this so-called "third" death since it is too complex and all of us had much experience to face. Yet, much to learn and many limitations to overcome. Limitations which can only be dealt with on earth because it is the only place where they can be externalized. Summerland is far too malleable, far too easy to control. Only in the density of matter can any personality face the most severe of trials. It is man's primary testing ground, the place for action and experiment.

All of us have a path to follow and the path begins on earth.

Chapter Thirty-Six

Through All Eternity

"How, specifically, is it done?" the woman continued. "For those concerned, in this manner."

I found myself leaning forward. What she'd said, to that point, had been interesting. Now, however, she was going to tell us-tell me how I could go about rejoining Ann once more.

Here is what she told us, Robert.

When a soul who seeks reentry into flesh selects his preference of parents, he-or she-clears it with what might be termed a computer. Then, if there is competition, so to speak, for a particular placement, the computer will decide which soul is most appropriate to the task-or, more likely, most in need of it.

I call it a computer but, of course, it is more complex than that, being capable of blending the thought patterns of all those who have applied for a similar type of heredity and environment. As this mass of thought material is synchronized into an overall pattern, the soul most qualified comes to recognize that he or she is the one to be selected and the rest, unquestioning, search further.

She warned us that it is tempting, In the state of freedom enjoyed in Summerland, to plan a life ahead as being one of great ambition.

"Let me caution any of you who plan rebirth," she said, "to be aware of the restrictions you will face in physical life. Demand less in order to accomplish more is the preferable method."

The details will fascinate you, Robert: In the Far East, souls desiring to reenter matter remain in the abodes of men and women and, when the time is propitious, visualize themselves as cells and enter the wombs of their mothers to be. It is simple and uncomplicated.

It is, also, dangerous. Should the child be born dead, the soul becomes locked in a coma on the etheric level, no longer a viable entity but one which cannot free its consciousness. This is because the soul mind is in deep sleep when rebirth takes place.

No mental action is possible until a child's faculties are ready to be utilized.

Another danger of this method is that the soul may, inadvertently, select a vehicle which is mentally or physically deformed. In that event, the mistake must be borne for life. At times, of course, this way is chosen deliberately as a means of "paying off" Karmic debts, Karma being the doctrine of inevitable consequence for our deeds. A soul entering a sick or damaged body, who meets and overcomes these handicaps with good cheer, grows faster spiritually than one who, by earthly standards, has everything to live for. As, God willing, in Ann's case.

While, in any area of the world, the soul has the option of entering its new vehicle of life at any stage from conception to post-birth, the Occidental method is usually, to wait until the child is born. That way, no soul can ever be locked into the coma I mentioned.

The actual process of rebirth depends on the ability of the soul to contract its spiritual bodies-astral, then etheric- until they can be coordinated with the body of the child. This coordination usually takes place immediately after birth and is not easy to accomplish. For this reason, the process usually requires the assistance of a spirit physician who can see, in his or her mind's eye, the spinal cords of both child and spirit bodies and merge them.

As I indicated, another method of reincarnation occurs as follows: The soul does not enter the body until the child has developed for five to eight weeks. That way, the certainty of a proper physical vessel becomes completely defined.

"Upon incarnating," the woman continued, "all memories of the previous life and the interval in afterlife are obliterated and a fresh set of mental impressions begun. Occasionally, if the reincarnation is precipitate, the memory lasts-which explains the high incidence of such cases in· India, for instance.

"For several months, the soul sleeps in the baby which utilizes animal instincts to learn the operations of its body- feeding, sleeping and performing organic functions. Only when the soul begins to awaken does the child begin to demonstrate active intelligence.

"The soul does not wake all at once but progressively throughout the childhood and youth of the new individual. Infrequently, a soul wakes prematurely and recalls, if not its past life, its past skills; thus the occasional appearance of child prodigies.

"The soul gradually merges with the body so that, at approximately the age of twenty-one, it has incarnated fully. Sometimes, a soul will not 'wake up' until its vehicle is nearly middle-aged. In that case, the personality shows no signs of full intellectual activity until then.

"And following its new life span, the immortal soul, which has gone forth into incarnation to struggle for the mastery of its nature, returns, once more, to home for refreshment and new study before returning again to earth in its cyclic search for perfection-and reunion with God."

* * * *

I will say no more about the lecture. Further information on reincarnation is not essential to my story; there are books you can read if you are interested.

My next step was to reopen the closed book of my memory and examine it once more.

By utilization of my individual wave length, I was shown my past lives. It was a dizzying spectacle, Robert, in which nothing was withheld. I scarcely had time to react as the details flooded before me, a vivid burst of events, each moment reproduced in total detail.

I have had many lifetimes but I will mention only the last two in which Ann and I were together.

I was in contact with her in the 1300's when both our souls expressed themselves in what may be termed "the feminine framework." We were sisters, eleven years apart-myself the older-but so close in our relationships that friends and family remarked on it with wonderment. All our lives we were, psychologically, inseparable.

We came together again in the 1700's, in Russia, me in the masculine valence, she in the feminine. We grew up, knowing each other, lost contact for a while, then met again in our teen years, fell in love and married. I was a writer in that lifetime too; novels and short stories. Ann (her name was different then, of course) believed in me loyally though my success was minimal.

It was the end of that life that I'd witnessed at my second death.

Now I saw not only its conclusion but all of it, given a perspective which allowed me to observe what plan and purpose not only that former life had possessed but all my other lives as well.

I will not go into details here; again, it is irrelevant to what I have to say. Suffice to mention that I decided that the one factor needed more than any other to enhance the growth of my soul is the helping of others. Which tied in perfectly with my desire to be with Ann again. Albert had told me that, in time, she will need much medical care.

I will become a doctor. At first, I considered being born in India as well. The difficulties of doing so and ending up a doctor, however, are close to insuperable and I have had to alter the idea. Being born in India is not the objective anyway. Ultimately reaching India to help Ann is.

Which is why I've chosen who I have as parents: Dr. and Mrs. Arthur Braningwell of Philadelphia. They are young and well-to-do and I will be their only child. I will have a comfortable upbringing, attend medical school and believe I am to follow in my father's footsteps.

At the age of thirty, that resolve will change entirely, for reasons I will not go into, and I will leave the path of comfort to practice medicine in the deprived areas of the world.

Eventually, I will arrive in India, take care of, fall in love with and, finally, marry a young woman whose soul will be Ann's. Whether we will ever know or even sense what is really happening is not important. We will be together again.

Nothing else matters.

* * * *

The infant body chosen by me is four and a half weeks old now. It will not be strong enough for the entry of my etheric bodies until it is seven weeks old. I have been lingering near the body constantly, experimenting with the process of reducing those bodies to the size of the child. When I am ready for transition, a doctor, skilled in the procedure, will set up a radioactive current, which will make it possible to connect the bodies through a gland at the base of the child's brain. Then I will enter.

In the final moments before incarnation, I will try to evolve a clear image of the type of body I need. In this way, I can help to generate the health and strength required to do the life work I have planned. If I fail to do this, the child's body could, conceivably, be carried off by an early illness or I might, like Ann, be weak and sickly.

I confess to you, Robert, that I feel a strong revulsion toward rebirth. Enough time has elapsed so that the idea of returning to flesh is no longer inviting to me. At the moment, only the knowledge that Ann has gone back makes me want to return. For, in truth, it is not courageous to die. True courage is involved in being born voluntarily, leaving the manifold beauties of Summerland to plunge back into the depths of dark, imprisoning matter. Trauma isn't caused by death but by life. One can die without knowing it.

Birth invariably entails a shock of recognition.

I will reassure myself by thinking of my dream. That, one day, we will be together here in Summerland. That we will share our love in this exquisite clime, our oneness an abiding comfort to each other.

Perhaps, as Albert has suggested, we will be remarried someday in one of heaven's great cathedrals, the ceremony performed by a Master from a higher level a chorus singing a hymn of joy to our united love. I will give her gifts of my own creation-flowers, clothing, jewels and ornaments, furnishings for the home we will make together. A home which will blend our tastes and desires, located in a lovely, natural setting we will cherish always.

There we will, I pray, remain and learn and grow until the time when we will rise together to the ultimate heights, changing in appearance but never in devotion, sharing the transcendent glory of our love through all eternity.

Chapter Thirty-Seven

Return to My Love

There was one thing more I had to do before departure. Dictate this book and have it brought to you.

Again, I will not detail how I was put in contact with the woman who brought you this manuscript. Originally, I'd planned to have it given to my children. But when it turned out that the only sensitive available was on the east coast, I decided to have the book brought to you instead.

I hope it is published and read by many. I hope that, at the very least, a few people are prepared for the inevitable transition which will take place at the end of their lives.

* * * *

My account draws to a close.

Remember this: What I have told you is partial. It could be no other way. I could only tell you what I, personally, saw and heard. It is my recollection of what happened, nothing more. Recall what Albert told me.

The mind is all.

I emphasize that strongly. The experience was my experience and no one else's. While it is all completely true, it is not, by any means, definitive regarding afterlife experience, Another person would tell a different story.

Remember this as well: Things I have not told you would fill a hundred volumes. Accept my word that the variety in afterlife is boundless. There is so much more that my account is as a grain of sand to all the beaches and the deserts in the world.

I must mention, too, that all I have described has taken place on a relatively low level of spiritual existence. There are planes which I have never known and may not know for eons.

In brief, there is no standard afterlife reality. I told you my experience. Yours will be different. You can be sure of only one thing.

It will happen.

I feel it vital to enlarge upon my point. Nothing is as simple as I have stated it.

In actuality, the conditions of survival cannot be explained in terms of time, space and form. I have described people, locations and events but these were subject to my ability-or lack of it-to see things as they really are.

In point of fact, the entire experience may have been precisely what I told myself it was following my death.

A dream.

When you sleep, your dream world is as real to you as life, isn't it?

So it may be here as well.

By that token, it is only natural that what I have referred to as Summerland would appear as it does. Since the phenomena of this level are essentially thought pictures carried over by the consciousness of those newly arrived from earth, what else could Summerland be but an idealized version of earth?

Albert told me, at the very outset, that heaven was a state of mind, It is.

Consider though. Isn't earth a state of mind as well?

Matter is no more than energy which, to the human intellect, appears static. Life is the state of consciousness which perceives this energy as matter. Death is the state of consciousness which no longer perceives it as such.

Life on earth is only a panorama of vivid observations which seem real to you.

Why should afterlife seem less real? Let me not confuse you though.

It will seem real enough to you.

And, please, my brother, do not fear it. Death is not the king of terrors. Death is a friend.

Consider it this way. Do you fear to sleep at night? Of course not. Because you know that you will wake again.

Think of death the same way. As a sleep from which, inevitably, you will awaken.

True life is a process of becoming. Death is a stage in this progression. Life is not followed by un-life.

There is only a single continuity of being.

We are part of a plan, never doubt that. A plan to bring each one of us to the highest level of which we are capable. The way will be dark at times but it leads, assuredly, to light.

Never forget, however, that we pay for every act and thought and feeling we commit.

One statement from the Bible says it all. Whatsoever a man soweth, that shall he also reap.

People are not punished for their deeds but by them,

If only everyone believed that.

If only every man and woman in the world knew-beyond a shadow of a doubt-that they would have to face the consequences of their lives.

The world could change overnight. God bless you.

I return to my love.

Epilogue

I have just returned from Philadelphia. Maybe it was foolish of me. It's entirely possible that the woman who brought me the manuscript was aware of the existence of Dr. Braningwell and his wife. There is no way of knowing for certain. I can only wonder again. If this is so, why should she go to all that trouble to deceive me?

At first, I thought of knocking on the Braningwells' door and telling them my story. Rationality soon dispensed with that.

What I did was wait until their maid took the baby for a carriage ride, I walked behind her to a small neighborhood park, and, there, while she was sitting on a bench, I stopped and chatted with her briefly, glancing at the child. Feeling a perfect fool for doing so. But feeling something else as well as I stared into the eyes of that child.

Awe.

Why does that baby boy possess the soul of my brother Chris? Did he really go to India when he has passed his thirtieth year, meet a young woman possessing the soul of my brother's wife Ann and marry her?

I wish to God I knew.

I'm sixty-three years old, however. It's obvious I'll never live to verify it. I could tell my children to check it out but I'm sure they'd find it difficult to retain interest in a vague improbable event which may or may not occur decades hence in a country thousands of miles away.

So there it will, doubtless, end.

All I can do is repeat: If the manuscript is true, all of us had better examine our lives.

Carefully.

THE END

Bibliography

Appleman, John Alan. *Your Psychic Powers and Immortality*, New York: Frederick Fell, Inc., 1968.

Atkinson, W. W. *Reincarnation and The Law of Karma*. Chicago: Yogi Publication Society, 1936.

Bayless, Raymond. *The Other Side of Death*. New Hyde Park, NY: University Books, Inc., 1971.

--. *Apparitions and Survival of Death*. New Hyde Park, NY: University Books, Inc., 1973.

Borgia, Anthony. *Life in The World Unseen*. London: Odhams Press, Ltd., 1954.

--. *More About Life in The World Unseen*. London: Odhams Press, Ltd., 1956.

--. *Here And Hereafter*. New York: The Citadel Press, 1959.

Boss, Judy. *In Silence They Return*. St. Paul, MN: Llewellyn Publications, 1972.

Brandon W. *Incarnation*, New York: C & R Anthony, Inc., 1936.

--. *Love in The Afterlife*. New York: C & R Anthony, Inc., 1956.

--. *We Knew These Men*. New York: C & R Anthony, Inc., 1957.

--. *Open The Door!* New York: C. & R Anthony, Inc., 1958.

Brennan, J. H. *Five Keys to Past Lives*. New York: Samuel Weiser, Inc., 1371.

Brown, R. *Unfinished Symphonies*. New York: William Morrow & Co., 1971.

Cayce, Hugh Lynn. *Life After Death* (cassette) Hollywood,' CA: Dak Enterprises, 1975.

Colton, Ann Ree. *Men in White Apparel*. CA: Arc Publishing Co., 1961.

Conan Doyle, Arthur. *The New Revelation*. New York: George H. Doran Co., 1918.

Crookall, Robert. *Intimations of Immortality*. Greenwood, SC: The Attic Press, Inc., 1965.

--. *The Next World-and the Next*. London: Theosophical Publishing House, 1966.

Daniels, Dr. John C. *Incarnation and Reincarnation*. New York: Pillar Books, 1975.

Delacour, J. B. *Glimpses of the Beyond*. New York: Delacorte Press, 1974.

Desmond, Shaw. *You Can Speak With Your Dead*. London: Methuen & Co., 1941.

Dresser, C. *Spirit World and Spirit Life*. San Jose, CA: Cosmos Publishing Co., 1927.

Ebon, Martin. *They Knew The Unknown*. New York: The World Publishing Co., 1971.

Evans-Wentz, W. Y. *The Tibetan Book of the Dead*. New York: Oxford University Press, 1960.

Farthing, Geoffrey. *When We Die*. London: Theosophical Publishing House, 1968.

Findlay, Arthur. *On The Edge Of The Etheric*. Great Britain: Psychic Press, 1931.

--. *The Way of Life: A Guide to the Etheric World*. London: Psychic Press, Ltd., 1956.

Ford Arthur. *The Life Beyond Death*. New York: Berkley Medallion Books, 1971.

--.*Unknown but Known*. New York: Harper & Row, 1968.

Fortune, Dion. *Through The Gates of Death*. London: The Aquarian Press, 1968.

Francis, J. R. *The Encyclopedia of Death*, Amherst, WI: Amherst Press, 1896.

Garrett, Eileen. *Does Man Survive Death*, ed. with Introduction and Notes. New York: Helix Press, 1957.

--. *Great Mystery of Life Hereafter*, The. London: Hodder & Stoughton, 1957.

Hampton, Charles. *The Transition Called Death*. Illinois: Theosophical Publishing House, 1943.

Heindel, Max. *The Passing-and Life Afterward*. Oceanside, CA: The Rosicrucian Fellowship, 1971.

Heywood, Rosalind. *Beyond The Reach of Sense*. New York: E. p, Dutton & Co., 1961.

Hodson, Geoffrey. *Through The Gateway of Death*. India: Theosophical Publishing House, 1967.

--. *Reincarnation: Fact Or Fallacy?* Wheaton, Ill.: Theosophical Publishing House, 1967.

Jacobson, Nils 0., M.D. *Life Without Death*. New York: Dell Publishing Co., 1973.

Keith, M. R. *What Everybody Ought to Know About Heaven*. Palmer Publications,

1968.

--. *So You're Going to Heaven.* Palmer Publications, 1969.

Kennedy, David. *A Venture In Immortality.* Gerrards Cross, England: Colin Smythe,1973.

Langley, Noel. *Edgar Cayce on Reincarnation.* New York: Paperback Library, 1967.

Ledbeater, C. W. *The Life After Death.* India: Theosophical Publishing House, 1952.

Leek, Sybil. *Reincarnation: The Second Chance.* New York: Stein & Day, 1974.

LeShan, Lawrence. *The Medium, the Mystic and the Physicist.* New York: The Viking Press, 1974.

Lodge, Sir Oliver. Raymond. New York: George H. Doran Co., 1916.

Loehr, Franklin. *Diary After Death.* Los Angeles: Religious Research Frontier Books, 1976.

Matson, Archie. *Afterlife.* New York: Harper & Row, 1977.

Medhurst, R. G. *Crooks and the Spirit World.* New York: Taplinger Publishing Co., 1972.

Michael, Russ. *There Is No Death.* Lakemont, GA: CSA Press, 1971.

Montgomery, Ruth. *A World Beyond*, New York: Fawcett Crest, 1971.

Moody, Raymond, M.D. *Life After Life.* New York: Bantam Books, 1977.

Moore-Douglas. *Reincarnation.* York Cliffs, ME: Arcane Publications, 1968.

Moss, Thelma. *The Probability of The Impossible.* Los Angeles: J. P. Tarcher, Inc., 1974.

Osis, Karlis & Nester, Marian L. "Deathbed Observations by Doctors and Nurses," International Journal of Parapsychology, Vol. 14, No.2.

Owen, the Rev. G. Vale. *The Life Beyond the Veil* in five volumes: *The Lowlands of Heaven; The Highlands of Heaven; The Ministry of Heaven; The Battalions of Heaven; The Outlands of Heaven.* London: The Greater World Association, 1964.

Panchadasi, Swami. *The Astral World.* No publisher or publication date given.

Pauchard, A. *The Other World.* London: Rider & Co., 1952.

Perkins, James S. *Through Death to Rebirth.* Wheaton, IL: Theosophical

Publishing House, 1961.

Ramacharaka, Yogi. *The Life Beyond Death*. Chicago: Yogi Publication Society, 1937

Randall, Edw. C. *Frontiers of the After-Life*. New York: Alfred Knopf, 1922.

Roberts, Jane. *Seth Speaks*. New York: Prentice-Hall, 1972.

--. *The Seth Material*. New York: Prentice-Hall, 1975.

Rogo, D. Scott. NAD, *A Study of Some Unusual "Other World" Experiences*. New York: University Books, 1970.

--. *Spiritual Unfoldment: One*. Hampshire, England: The White Eagle Publishing Trust, 1972.

Sculthorp, F. C. *Excursions to the Spirit World*. London: A1moris Press, Ltd., 1962.

Sherman, Harold. *You Live After Death*. New York: C. & R. Anthony, Inc., 1949.

--. *You Can Communicate With the Unseen World*. New York: Fawcett Gold Medal, 1974.

Sherwood, Jane. *The Country Beyond*. London: Neville Spearman, 1969.

Smith, Suzy. *The Book of James*. New York: G. P. Putnam's Sons, 1974.

--. *Spiritual Unfoldment: One*. Hampshire, England: The White Eagle Publishing Trust, 1972.

Spragget, Allen. *The Case For Immortality*. New York: New American Library, 1974.

St. Clair, Mae Gimbert. *On Life and Death: The Edgar Cayce Readings*. Compiled by Virginia Beach, VA: Association for Research and Enlightenment, 1973.

Stearn, Jess. *The Search For a Soul*. New York: Doubleday and Company, Inc., 1972.

Sullivan, Eileen. *Arthur Ford Speaks From Beyond*. New York: Fawcett Crest, 1975.

Thomas, The Rev. C. Drayton. *Beyond Life's Sunset*. London: Psychic Press, Ltd., 1940.

Van Dusen, Wilson. *The Presence of Other Worlds*. New York: Harper & Row 1974.

Vivian, Margaret, *The Doorway*. London: Psychic Press, Ltd., 1941.

Watson, Lyall. *The Romeo Error*. New York: Doubleday, 1975.

Weiss, JE, *The Vestibule*, ed., / written. New York: Pocket Books, 1974.

Welch, William Addams. *Talks With the Dead*. New York: Pinnacle Books, Inc., 1975.

White, S. E. & H. Across The Unknown. New York: E. P. Dutton & Co., 1939.

White, Steward Edward. The Stars Are Still There. New York: E. P. Dutton & Co., 1946.

--. *The Betty Book*. New York: Berkley Medallion Books, 1969.

Willink, A. *The World of The Unseen*. New York: MacMillan & Co., 1893.

Wright, L. L. *After Death- What?* San Diego, CA: Point Loma Publications, 1974.

We hope you enjoyed this book.
If you'd like additional information, please contact:

Transformational Book Circle
12711 Ventura Blvd., Suite 330
Studio City, CA 91604
866-288-4469 (customer service)
866-300-4386 (orders)
www.transformationalbookcircle.com
info@transformationalbookcircle.com